Praise for the novels of Christie Ridgway

"Christie Ridgway writes with the perfect combination of humor and heart. This funny, sexy story is as fresh and breezy as its Southern California setting."

—Susan Wiggs, *New York Times* bestselling author

"Delightful."

—Rachel Gibson, *New York Times* bestselling author

"Tender, funny, and wonderfully emotional."

—Barbara Freethy, *USA Today* bestselling author

"Pure romance, delightfully warm, and funny."

—Jennifer Crusie, *New York Times* bestselling author

"Smart, peppy." —*Publishers Weekly*

"Funny, supersexy, and fast paced . . . Ridgway is noted for her humorous, spicy, and upbeat stories."

—*Library Journal*

"Christie Ridgway is a first-class author."

—*Midwest Book Review*

"Christie Ridgway's books are crammed with smart girls, manly men, great sex, and fast, funny dialogue. Her latest novel . . . is a delightful example, a romance as purely sparkling as California champagne." —*BookPage*

"Ridgway delights yet again with this charming, witty tale of holiday romance. Not only are the characters sympathetic, intelligent, and engaging, but the sexual tension between the main characters is played out with tremendous skill." —*Romantic Times*

Titles by Christie Ridgway

HOW TO KNIT A WILD BIKINI
UNRAVEL ME
DIRTY SEXY KNITTING

CRUSH ON YOU
THEN HE KISSED ME
CAN'T HURRY LOVE

Can't Hurry Love

CHRISTIE RIDGWAY

BERKLEY SENSATION, NEW YORK

THE BERKLEY PUBLISHING GROUP
Published by the Penguin Group
Penguin Group (USA) Inc.
375 Hudson Street, New York, New York 10014, USA
Penguin Group (Canada), 90 Eglinton Avenue East, Suite 700, Toronto, Ontario M4P 2Y3, Canada
(a division of Pearson Penguin Canada Inc.)
Penguin Books Ltd., 80 Strand, London WC2R 0RL, England
Penguin Group Ireland, 25 St. Stephen's Green, Dublin 2, Ireland (a division of Penguin Books Ltd.)
Penguin Group (Australia), 250 Camberwell Road, Camberwell, Victoria 3124, Australia
(a division of Pearson Australia Group Pty. Ltd.)
Penguin Books India Pvt. Ltd., 11 Community Centre, Panchsheel Park, New Delhi—110 017, India
Penguin Group (NZ), 67 Apollo Drive, Rosedale, Auckland 0632, New Zealand
(a division of Pearson New Zealand Ltd.)
Penguin Books (South Africa) (Pty.) Ltd., 24 Sturdee Avenue, Rosebank, Johannesburg 2196, South Africa

Penguin Books Ltd., Registered Offices: 80 Strand, London WC2R 0RL, England

CAN'T HURRY LOVE

A Berkley Sensation Book / published by arrangement with the author

PRINTING HISTORY
Berkley Sensation mass market edition / July 2011

Cover art by GlowImages/Punch Stock.
Cover design by Lesley Worrell.
Interior text design by Laura K. Corless.

For information, address: The Berkley Publishing Group,
a division of Penguin Group (USA) Inc.,
375 Hudson Street, New York, New York 10014.

ISBN: 978-0-425-24210-0

BERKLEY® SENSATION
Berkley Sensation Books are published by The Berkley Publishing Group,
a division of Penguin Group (USA) Inc.,
375 Hudson Street, New York, New York 10014.
BERKLEY® SENSATION and the "B" design are trademarks of Penguin Group (USA) Inc.

PRINTED IN THE UNITED STATES OF AMERICA

10 9 8 7 6 5 4 3 2 1

For Barbara Samuel, aka Barbara O'Neal.
Your support, friendship, and unending willingness
to talk story and craft make my days richer
and my work better. Love you!

In vino veritas. (In wine is truth.)

—PLINY THE ELDER

1

Giuliana Baci shivered in the June night air, though flames were crackling and roaring just fifty feet away. She clutched the old leather-bound diary to her chest and stared at the spectacle across the street, trying to take it in. A muscle car passed, possibly attracted by the strobing emergency lights, because it slowed to a lookie-loo pace. It veered toward the opposite curb, and she could see the driver's neck crane, his eyes obviously not on the parked obstacle just ahead. "Watch out," she warned, stepping forward.

But it was too late. Two and a half tons of heavy metal had already taken out a headlight and crumpled the hood of a small, innocent sedan. Giuliana's sedan.

Somehow she wasn't surprised to see the over-cylindered other vehicle lurch into reverse, shift forward again, then race away from her latest personal disaster.

The screech of tires against pavement was swallowed by the sound of the fire burning up the rest of her belongings in the now-engulfed four-unit apartment building where she'd been living.

"To hell with threes," she said, her voice as defeated as her mood. Her legs folded and she sank to the curb, the cement cold through her thin robe. One set of bare toes crossed over the other. "If you ask me, bad luck comes in batches."

"I'm sorry," the young woman beside her replied. She was perched on the same old-fashioned suitcase she'd lugged into Giuliana's small apartment when she'd offered her temporary lodging just last week. "I'm so very sorry."

"That should be my line," Giuliana answered, though it looked as if Grace had at least saved her possessions. She'd been living out of that very suitcase and sleeping on the—now likely incinerated—living room couch.

"You'll get through this," Grace said, her freckled face earnest beneath her rumpled strawberry blonde hair. "No doubt about it."

Those should have been her lines, too, Giuliana thought. For the last year she'd been repeating them often enough—ever since her father's death and the Baci sisters' takeover of the family's failing one-hundred-year-old winery.

Only a month to go, she consoled herself now. *And then—*

Another car sped onto the scene. Giuliana's nerves went on instant alert, standing on end as she jumped to her feet, still clutching the old diary. Liam Bennett exited the Mercedes even as it rocked to a halt.

Despite her quaking belly, her jellied knees went rock solid. *The girl still has some fight in her*, she thought, relieved. *Now don't let him sense any weakness in your guard.*

Then he was in front of her, the flickering fire and the flashing emergency lights casting reds and yellows over his lean face. Her stomach cramped again and it was as if the heat of the flames set a torch to her skin. *What is wrong with me?* she wondered for the thousandth time. On a daily basis, people encountered their childhood sweethearts and didn't suffer such an intense physical reaction. But although she'd hidden herself away for a decade, she'd returned only to discover she was still not immune to him.

"What are you doing here?" she croaked out. It sounded more froggy than unfriendly.

Damn it.

He cocked an eyebrow. "This is Edenville."

Yeah, yeah, yeah. Small town of six thousand nosy souls in the northern end of the Napa Valley. Word of what happened had likely run faster through the gossip grapevine than the fire through the clothes in her closet. The mental image made her shiver.

Liam saw it, and he reached for her.

No! every instinct inside her shouted. She swayed back and he froze. Then he stripped off the sports jacket he wore and dropped it over her shoulders, careful that his hands didn't touch her body.

She wanted to grasp the lapels and hug it against her. She didn't. She didn't thank him, either.

The wind shifted, sending smoke across their faces, and she blinked against the sting in her eyes. But it was Liam's scent that was in her nose—spicy, male—and she had to tighten her grip on the diary to remind herself to stay steady. Strong.

When all she wanted was to collapse against him and bury her face at his throat.

"Jules," he said. For a second she thought she heard an ache in his voice that mirrored the one in her chest, but that couldn't be true. Liam's expression appeared as unreadable as it always did.

Only emphasizing the fact that she had to stand on her own two feet. She'd proven she could, all that long time ago, and she wouldn't stumble now. People depended upon *her*, not the other way around, and she was afraid of how she might ultimately be hurt if she forgot that.

Clearing her throat, Giuliana waved away another waft

of smoke. "Look, thanks for checking on us. But we'll be fine."

"Us?" he echoed, looking around, then his gaze found Grace, who offered him a tentative smile.

Giuliana moved closer to her. "You remember Grace? I hired her to pour in the Tanti Baci tasting room two weeks ago."

"Hatch . . . ?"

"Yes," Giuliana confirmed. "The dowser's daughter." Old Peter Hatch had owned some rocky acreage in the backcountry and eked out a living divining for water and doing handyman chores. Known as a mean drunk and even meaner dad, those who knew shy and quiet Grace had been actually happy for her when she'd dropped out of high school to marry a boy in the next county just home from the army. Except he'd been cut from the same cloth as her father, and when Grace had shown up at the winery with final divorce papers and a black eye, what could Giuliana do?

"She's been staying with me," Giuliana explained to Liam.

He glanced over his shoulder at the apartment building that appeared soon to be ashes. "Then you'll both need somewhere to stay. You'll come to my place—"

"No." She shook her head. "Of course not. We're headed for the farmhouse. I've already left a message for Stevie."

He crossed his arms over his chest. He wore a cotton polo shirt tucked into dark jeans. His shoulders had been broad and strong as a teenager, his hips lean, his butt nearly nonexistent. As a man, he'd filled out everywhere in all the best ways. Not that she hadn't tried not to notice.

"That should be fun for you," he said. "Moving in with two sets of honeymooners."

Oh, why bother disguising her grimace? Her youngest sister, Allie, had married Liam's half brother, Penn Bennett, nearly a year before. Though they spent some of their time in Southern California, when they were in Edenville, they took over the first floor of the small frame house the Baci girls had grown up in. The second story was the domain of her other sister, Stevie, who was camping there with her husband of five months, Jack Parini, while they were remodeling the winery on their two-acre vineyard into a home.

She sighed. "It'll be just like old times."

"Except for the addition of your ardent brothers-in-law. Good luck trying to ignore all the squeals and heavy breathing."

"Surely it won't—"

"They're horn-dogs, Jules."

Well, duh. It didn't take more than five seconds in a room with her sisters and the men they'd married to realize their relationships weren't lacking in the physical-desire department. "I'm sure Allie and Stevie will keep the lid on when guests are around."

"Yeah. You Baci girls are always so good at keeping things on simmer."

The way he said it set her blood to boiling. She moved up, toe-to-toe with him. "What's that supposed to mean?"

He looked down his aristocratic nose at her, all golden boy to barefoot peasant girl. The story of their lives. "We could finish this thing, Giuliana. One damn way or another, if you'd just give over. Move in, and we could—"

"We shouldn't! We won't!" Giving over was exactly what she wouldn't do. Rehashing their past had no place in her future.

"Fine. Your choice." His face was composed, his voice steady. "But then it'll bubble and spit and make us both miserable for the *next* ten years."

"No! No, it won't." She had a plan, already set in motion, that would bring it, everything for all of them, finally to an end. No more emotional distress, no more poignant pulls from the past.

He quirked that brow again. "How so?"

His calm made her want to murder him. While her heart pounded and her mouth went dry when she shared even the largest of spaces with him, he appeared as unmoved as ice forgotten in a freezer. He might talk about being miserable, but he didn't fathom a damn thing about that emotion or any other.

"Jules?"

His doubting tone had her inches closer and on tiptoe. "Because—" she started. Then she halted, her brain clicking in before her temper got the better of her—hey, she'd matured, too. Telling too soon could ruin everything she'd planned. "Just because," she said, falling back to her heels.

He didn't twitch a muscle, but she could sense his inner mental eye roll.

The temperature of her blood spiked again. "Don't give me that look."

His gaze narrowed. "I'll tell you what I want to give you—" He broke off as a taxi pulled in beside his vehicle. "Oh, hell."

She ignored Liam's disgust as she turned to the figure exiting the cab. At the sight of Kohl Friday's dark hair and rock-solid form, she let her spine sag. The Tanti Baci vineyard manager didn't hesitate to move in and bolster her with an arm around her shoulders. "Okay?"

"Okay." She leaned against him, his presence diminishing a little of the threat she felt in Liam's company. Kohl smelled of cinnamon gum and tequila—which explained why he hadn't driven himself. "Phone lines been working overtime?" she asked.

"I'm here to give you a lift," he said. Then he half turned, his gaze finding the young woman still seated on her suitcase. "Grace."

Her eyes were wide and focused on Kohl's face. Giuliana saw her gulp. "Hi," she said, her voice nearly a whisper.

Kohl turned back quickly, as if aware he was spooking her. "Ready, ladies?"

Giuliana slid a look in Liam's direction. He'd moved away a few paces to lean against the side of his car, arms and ankles crossed. His expression proclaimed he was bored by the proceedings.

"Ready," she replied, tacking on a smile for him. Then she walked away from her would-be rescuer with perfect composure—just as Liam, her very first lover, had walked away from her a decade before.

~

Giuliana peeked through the holes in the crocheted afghan she'd thrown over her head last night as she'd tried getting comfortable on the love seat in her office. Sleep had apparently arrived at some point, since early-morning sunshine was now in the room, along with something that was rummaging around in the large storage closet located across the tattered Oriental carpet. Drawing the blanket below her chin, she blinked against the light.

"Has the European grapevine moth moved on to paper goods now?" she called out.

A petite brunette peered around the door. "Oh, sorry." Alessandra Baci Bennett, Giuliana's little sister, formerly known as the "Nun of Napa," stepped from the closet, her pretty face contrite. "You're awake?"

Giuliana scooted over to allow the other woman to perch a hip on the sofa cushions and considered the question. "It was all a dream? My apartment didn't really burn last night, my car wasn't bashed in, and I'm not actually relegated to using my office as a bedroom?"

"Not the last, certainly," Allie said, frowning. "You should have bunked down at the farmhouse."

Liam's warnings about squeals and heavy breathing had been hard to forget. "I was perfectly comfortable here," she lied, sitting up. She could smell smoke on her hair and realized she'd have to buy or borrow toiletries along with underwear and clothes and shoes and . . . just about everything. Daunted by the idea, she slid back to prone and closed her eyes. "On second thought, I *am* asleep." If she could manage another hour or two of snooze time, maybe all that lay ahead wouldn't feel so overwhelming.

Pulling the afghan higher on her shoulders, she murmured to her sister, "You don't need me for anything right this minute, do you?"

There was a telltale hesitation. "Of course not."

Even before their mom died when the sisters were sixteen, fourteen, and twelve, Giuliana had been like a second mother to Allie. So there was no way she could ignore the younger woman now. Opening her eyes once again, she rose up on her elbows. "Is there a problem?"

Her sister bounced on the cushions, the dimple at the side of her mouth flickering. "Jules, I've had the most brilliant idea!"

"Does this involve blindsiding Penn with another wedding proposal?"

Allie grinned, unrepentant. "But look how well that turned out." Her arms flew wide. "I'm obnoxiously happy."

It was hard not to smile in the face of all that unrelenting good humor. And it was hard not to feel that Allie deserved every mote of it after the sad outcome of her first wedding attempt. Love and marriage could work if the couple was the right mix of personality and heart. Allie and Penn and Stevie and Jack proved that.

Some pairings, however, clashed, and a woman who worked in the wine business understood that, too.

Allie's eyes narrowed. "Uh-oh. What's wrong?"

Giuliana tried shaking off her lowering mood. "Tell me about your brilliant idea."

Her sister seemed to sparkle. "It's about the Vow-Over Weekend."

Of course it was about the Vow-Over Weekend scheduled for the last days in June. "That's what we've all been working toward," Giuliana said. Not only was it the fiftieth anniversary of the sparkling *blanc de blancs* that they bottled exclusively for weddings, but it also signaled the end of the year they'd agreed to give Tanti Baci to get back on its financial feet.

Allie bit her lip. "You know reservations have been a little slow coming in . . ."

Despite the fact they'd been busting their behinds to get the word out that the winery was hosting a series of events to celebrate their wedding wine and the couples who'd toasted each other with it at their nuptials for the past fifty years. An on-site justice of the peace would even be on hand for those happy couples who would like to renew their vows. "You've done the best you can, Allie," she assured her younger sister.

"Yes, yes, but you won't believe what I've found out. What we can really use to create excitement. The legend—"

Giuliana groaned, her hand lifting to cover her eyes. "Not the legend. I'm begging you. Please don't talk about the legend."

"What legend?" It was a new voice. Grace's.

Giuliana dropped her hand to inspect her fellow refugee. The night before, their taxi had dropped the other woman at the small bungalow of Kohl's sister, Mari. "You didn't have to come in today."

Grace shrugged, looking fresh and wide awake in a pair of jeans and a simple button-down shirt embroidered with the Tanti Baci logo—a delicate ivy garland with heart-shaped leaves. "Mari lent me some things. So why not work?"

Allie beamed at her. "And as a member of the tasting room staff, you should learn all the Tanti Baci legends."

"If you're going to tell bedtime stories, I'm going back to sleep," Giuliana declared. Suiting action to words, she snuggled into her blanket and closed her eyes. She could use the twenty, forty, or sixty winks that it would take for her sister to impart the family's tall tales. But she couldn't tune out her sister's voice.

"There are actually three," Allie was saying. "I'm sure you know a little of the winery history. Alonzo Baci—my great-great-grandfather—along with the great-great-grandfather of the Bennett brothers, the original Liam Bennett, were partners in a silver mine north of here. When the ore ran out, they bought this property and decided to grow grapes. They also both courted the same girl—"

"Anne," interjected Grace. "I know that much. And that Alonzo won her. Their original cottage is the one you renovated last year in order to use it as a wedding venue."

"Exactly," Allie said, sounding pleased with her pupil. "That romance caused a big feud between the Bennetts and Bacis that has waxed and waned over the years, because our business dealings are still tangled. To this day, the Bennetts hold some interest in Tanti Baci."

"In the winery," Giuliana felt compelled to point out, though her eyes were still closed. "Not the land."

Allie let the comment pass. "Anyhow, legend number one is that there was some sort of valuable silver or silver and gold treasure that's been lost since those early days."

"We found a diary hidden in the rockwork surrounding the fireplace in the cottage," Giuliana put in again. "If there's a clue about this supposed treasure in the pages, we haven't found it."

Allie sighed. "Perhaps we're looking for the wrong kind of clue."

"So what's the second legend?" Grace asked. The eager note in her voice made Giuliana grimace. She was surrounded by romantic fools.

"Our papa told us that if you take your true love into the wedding cottage," Allie said, "you'll see the ghosts of those great lovers, Anne and Alonzo."

Under the blanket, Giuliana crossed her arms over her chest. "So I'm sure you and Penn have given them a great big howdy, is that right, Allie?"

With her eyes closed, she could still hear her little sister's delicate sniff. "Maybe."

Point scored. Giuliana wiggled deeper into the cushions and let drowsiness envelop her. "Onto load of baloney number three," she murmured.

Her sister sniffed again. "Jules may scoff, Grace, but maybe she shouldn't. You know that we've been retailing our *blanc de blancs* sparkling wine, to be served exclusively at weddings, for fifty years this month."

"On the website it says you keep a record of the name of each and every bridal couple who have toasted with it."

"Exactly," Allie confirmed. "And you know what else the website says . . ."

The women finished the thought together. "Not one of those couples has ever divorced!"

A cute marketing ploy, Giuliana admitted to herself, feeling sleep beginning to overtake her again. She supposed some slick ad man from San Francisco had been paid well for the idea in the days when the winery had money for such things.

"I haven't played that up enough," Allie admitted. "When I've been publicizing the Vow-Over Weekend and drumming up interest from the papers and other local press, I haven't been spotlighting that—and it's a winner angle if you ask me."

Grace's voice sounded as if it came from far away. "I love that story."

Yeah, but it *was* a story, Giuliana thought. And when she woke up next, she'd have to make clear to her little sister that it was a lousy idea to push something so blatantly false. It didn't pack any punch when it could be proved so patently untrue.

"Thank God for the Internet . . . not to mention the meticulous records of some of my predecessors in the winery's PR office."

Giuliana drew her hand under her cheek and hoped she

wouldn't drool. She was *so* tired. Surely Allie would abandon this silly idea without her big sister's input.

"I've been checking . . . and my husband Penn has been checking, and Stevie and Jack got in on the hunt, too." Something about the thrill in Allie's voice roused Giuliana just as she slipped into sleep.

Her eyelashes fluttered. "What? What are you talking about?"

"I think it's not just a legend. I think no couple that ever toasted each other with Tanti Baci *blanc de blancs* has ever divorced."

Head muzzy, Giuliana struggled into a sitting position again. She worked her fingers through the tangles in her dark hair and tried straightening the thin cotton lapels of the summer robe she was still wearing over her nightshirt. "That can't be true."

"It *is* true," Allie insisted. "At the twenty-fifth anniversary, a lot of follow-up work was done. It hasn't been that hard to check on those older marriages. The more recent ones have been even easier to track down."

"That can't be right," Giuliana declared again. "You can't know all of them are still, um, happy unions."

Allie waved her hand. "I'm not playing marriage counselor here. But I'm telling you, according to the four of us—Stevie and me, Jack and Penn—we've confirmed that all the Tanti Baci marriages are still legal and binding."

Voices outside the office door had her little sister on her feet. She cast a look at Giuliana's likely dumbfounded expression and said, "You need confirmation?"

In seconds, the room was crowded with both her sisters and their spouses. Giuliana's gaze roamed from face to face. "People. No divorces? This can't be . . ."

But they were already nodding.

Giuliana swallowed. "You can't know."

Allie frowned. "We know, okay?" She glanced around

to give her husband a little smile. "And all romance shmomance aside, it is a *great* publicity angle."

Maybe she was still asleep, Giuliana thought. That had to be it. She was dreaming all this. The crowd in the room shifted as another body made his way into her office. Liam. It didn't startle her to see him—he'd been disturbing her sleep for years—nor was she amazed that even while slumbering she'd go dry-mouthed at the sight of him.

"What's a great publicity angle?" her dream man asked her youngest sister.

"You know our books? The ones that list all the Tanti Baci brides and grooms? We've gone through them line by line. None of those marriages ever ended in divorce." Allie sent him a winning smile. "Isn't that fab?"

You'd have to be a keen observer of the man to notice the slight stiffening of his always-cool expression. "You can't know that."

Allie looked disgruntled. "You and Jules. What's going on with you two?"

Giuliana stifled her hysterical urge to laugh. Her gaze met Liam's, and though she thought she should shift it away, it stayed on him as she tried to explain. "We're just, um, uh, surprised, I guess. I mean . . . you've been through *all* those record books?"

"Almost. We're missing one—which is why I was in the closet. But as soon as I find it, I'm going to expose the truth to the world!"

Expose the truth to the world. Giuliana's stomach plunged. She was wide awake now. As a matter of fact, she wondered if she'd ever sleep again.

2

The first item on Liam Bennett's day's agenda was one simple, easy-to-dispatch task. With it in mind, he strode between his home and the Tanti Baci winery, along a shortcut that had been worn years before by foot and bike traffic. His parents hadn't been aware of it—though he'd been aware they would disapprove if they'd known. Calvin and Jeanette Bennett had kept themselves aloof from the working-class family next door. An act fueled by snobbery, he'd always supposed, as well as the decades-long feud between the Bacis and the Bennetts that had never died off.

Once, he'd thought he and Giuliana would be the ones to eradicate all that remained of the old fight.

Now he just hoped that imparting this piece of news to her—that the damn book was still safely hidden—would eradicate the uneasiness that had been tickling the back of his neck and churning his gut since he'd heard about the apartment fire the night before last.

The soles of his work boots encountered the gravel drive that serviced the Baci farmhouse, the winery's caves, its administrative offices, and the wedding cottage. He picked up his speed. It was early enough to hope he'd find his nemesis alone, so he could simply take forty seconds to tell her what he must, then get back to his own ordered world.

A voice sounded from behind him. "Hey!"

He couldn't ignore the hail from his half brother, Penn. Holding back his grimace, he checked his pace and let the other man catch up with him. "Hey."

"Nice to see you," Penn said, in obvious good spirits.

"Yeah," Liam replied, sliding a look at the man who was so much like him in appearance. They both were tall and rangy, with the same straight dark blond hair and blue eyes. They were just a few months apart in age—the SOB who'd fathered them both had been busy thirty-plus years before—and though they'd known each other for over a year, their similarity could still disconcert Liam. It was weird—like looking in a mirror and seeing a happy reflection.

As if to prove that point, Penn grinned at him. "Great day in the neighborhood, huh?"

It made Liam sigh. "Do you always have to be so annoyingly cheerful, Mr. Rogers?" he asked without rancor.

"Oh, come on." Penn gestured to the bucolic scene surrounding them. "The wine country's a place made for good moods. When I first saw it, I thought I'd been levitated to a little slice of heaven."

Brilliant blue sky, rolling hills covered with healthy green vines, the rugged mountains in the distance. Liam could appreciate the comparison with heaven if there weren't so many human dilemmas operating on the very same plane. And if he didn't feel so hellishly tense because of them.

Penn gave him another wide smile, the one that had all the female viewers of his top-rated home-remodeling TV show, *Penn Bennett's Build Me Up*, swooning. "You know, being your and Seth's half brother is the best thing that ever happened to me."

Liam shook his head. Only this charming near-twin of his would claim finding out he was the illegitimate offspring of a wealthy businessman who hadn't acknowledged paternity until after his death was something to crow about. He figured he knew the real source of the other man's sunny morning disposition. "It's rude to rub in the fact that you got laid before your first cup of coffee."

Penn laughed. "Have you seen my beautiful wife? You should be glad I'm not pounding my chest like Tarzan."

"I'm going to pound your head," Liam said. "Really, Penn, we'll kick both you and Jack out of Man Club if you don't tone down these I-love-marriage moods of yours."

"Jack is way more obnoxious than me."

"How do you figure?"

"It's the language thing. He croons to Stevie in French. Even my Alessandra goes a little woozy when he says something to her in Italian."

Italian. In an instant Liam was in Tuscany again, during that last, fateful summer. Wrapped in tangled sheets with Giuliana. He'd been fascinated by the naked curve of her shoulder as she frowned over the phrasebook and complained that her parents hadn't taught her the language they had learned at their own parents' knees.

"You know the most important word," he'd murmured to her, taking the phrasebook from her hands. "*Baciami*, Giuliana. *Baciami.*" *Kiss me.*

She had. They had kissed so many, many times, enough to become intoxicated on them, on wine, on sunshine.

Drunk on love.

He rubbed his hand over the back of his neck. The hangover had lasted for the next ten years.

"Let's pick up the pace," he said, his voice short, his strides lengthening. "I've got things to do."

But he should have known it wouldn't be as uncomplicated as finding Giuliana alone and passing on his assurances. Instead of being holed up in her office, they were told she was somewhere on the vineyard property. He ignored the little spurt of anger he felt at seeing the blanket folded neatly on the love seat perpendicular to her desk. "Damn woman didn't sleep at the farmhouse last night, either?" he asked, glancing at Penn.

The other man shrugged. "We tried to convince her. She muttered something about lusty honeymooners."

Liam was angry at himself now, but he worked to calm his expression and smooth his jerky strides as he set off in search of her. Penn trailed behind, apparently on his own hunt for his bride. "I always start at the cottage," he offered helpfully.

Why it made him even more annoyed that his half brother was right only confirmed that Liam wasn't his usual composed self. They found Allie and her oldest sister outside the cottage that Alonzo Baci had built for his wife, Anne. The summer before, what had been a ramshackle adobe had been completely renovated. Now it stood like a place enchanted under the outstretched arms of a mature oak. The surrounding lawn was bisected by a path that led up shallow steps to carved double doors.

The sisters weren't inside, though. They both stood at one corner of the building, half obscured by a rosebush covered with white buds. Allie gripped a shovel. Giuliana was half bent, examining something along the lower wall.

"Ah, the beautiful Baci sisters," Penn called out. "And to think you used to terrify me."

Giuliana straightened, and when her gaze touched on Liam, she went taut as a bow. Penn hissed in a breath and lowered his voice. "Okay. That one still terrifies me."

Apparently they overheard his remark, though, because the women cast each other long-suffering looks. "As if anything in skirts is immune to your magic," Allie said.

Penn perked up. "I like the sound of that. How about a midmorning break in our bedroom to discuss—"

"We have less than four weeks until the Vow-Over

Weekend," Allie reminded him. "No time for midmorning breaks."

Under the cover of their conjugal flirtation, Liam moved forward to get within personal conversation distance with Giuliana. At five-foot-three, she had a curvy, compact little body that was completely obscured by a T-shirt that almost reached her knees. He noted she was wearing a pair of jeans that were too short. Clearly she was dressed in her sisters' clothes, but she wasn't sleeping at their house. "Why the hell are you spending the night in your office?"

She tucked one wing of her shiny hair behind her ear. The dark stuff curved nearly to her shoulders, and with her chocolate brown eyes and golden skin, it completed the perfect trifecta of Mediterranean beauty. "Hello to you, too." Her voice was sweet, her smile acidic.

Liam stared down at her, struggling against the sudden urge to shake her. How could she do this to him? He was a responsible, upright citizen. Respected. But even after all these years, just one glance at her plum-sweet mouth and her big eyes with their curly dark lashes made him ache to throw off all that comfortable respectability and throw her over his shoulder.

He'd take her into the wine caves, lock the doors behind them, and make love to her until . . .

That was the problem. He wasn't convinced there was some future date when she wouldn't stir this up inside of him. But damn it, he had to get her out of his head. A man like Liam Bennett wasn't a willing victim to his emotions . . .

. . . Especially emotions that Giuliana Baci wouldn't welcome ever again. Outsized emotions that he should have outgrown long ago.

"Jules . . ." But whatever he was going to say next—his mouth was operating separate from his head so he had no idea—was interrupted by her youngest sister.

"What do you guys think?" she asked. With the shovel,

she held back the rosebush to reveal a metal plaque embedded in the two-foot-high stone foundation of the cottage. Embossed in bronze was the year the building was constructed and Anne and Alonzo's names. "We're considering transplanting the roses to expose the cornerstone. I can see people gathering around for photos, can't you?"

Expose. Yesterday morning she'd said she was going to expose the Tanti Baci wedding records—once she located the missing book. He stepped closer to Giuliana, close enough to smell the fresh scent of her shampoo. As he watched, a flush crept up her neck and turned her cheeks pink. She slid him a glance from her dark eyes.

"Jules," he murmured. "I checked. It's safe. There's nothing to worry about."

Her tongue slid along her bottom lip. He felt his own skin go hot and his muscles tense. Her mouth had taken him to paradise—and torn a hole in his soul. These last months, with her back in Edenville, just looking at it had tortured him.

He swallowed his groan and breathed in, searching for a little inner peace. "Jules," he said again, and was pleased at how sensible he sounded. "We have to face facts, though. We can't go on like this indefinitely."

She hesitated, her palms rubbing against her denim-covered thighs. "Four weeks," she finally whispered, her gaze averted from his. "It's all going to be over in four weeks."

"How—" But he broke off when Kohl Friday appeared and grasped Giuliana's elbow. Liam stared at the man's hand on the woman who cringed from his own touch. Then he glared at Kohl. "Where did you come from?"

The ex-soldier and current vineyard manager was as solid as the tanks he'd driven in the Iraq War. And about as verbal. "From the vines," he said, then he directed his attention to the woman between them. "Have a few minutes, honey?"

Honey. It took every ounce of restraint Liam could dredge up to keep himself from tearing into the other man. He'd known Kohl all his life and his reputation as a barroom brawler was legendary, but the battle between them had been stewing for months and he suspected that Kohl was anticipating it as greedily as Liam. Which was exactly why he wasn't going to satisfy the other man today. There was more than one way to fight.

He looked at Giuliana, then slid his eyes to Kohl's hand, still on her skin. Clearly noticing his regard, she flushed again and sidled away from the other man. As Kohl's arm dropped, Liam made sure no triumph showed on his face.

Her pretty mouth turned down in a frown. "I—" she started, then her cell phone trilled.

As she dug it from her pocket, Liam wanted to smack the heel of his hand against his forehead. Jesus! Why hadn't he done that this morning? He could have just called her with his reassurance. But instead, like some besotted kid, he'd made an excuse to visit.

Stepping away, he took a few more deep breaths and focused on the vineyard acres in the distance. He felt the view of the lush lines relax him. Structured order was how he liked his inner life composed as well. Organized, harmonious, stable. All those years ago with Giuliana he'd been driven by high emotion, and it was an experience he didn't relish replaying. It was much better to hold back, to command the world around him instead of letting the world command him.

It wasn't just his own past that informed that preference. Being ruled by his appetites was what had caused the heart ailment that had killed his father—and caused Calvin Bennett to so deeply damage his family. Liam was determined not to make similar mistakes—which meant putting a cap on the craziness that Giuliana could stir up in him.

"Jules?" Allie's voice was sharp. "Jules, what's wrong?"

Liam spun. Giuliana was staring down at her phone, the

sunlight setting off sparks in her brunette hair. Her head lifted, and there was a puzzled expression on her face. "Nothing's wrong," she said. "It's just weird. That was the police."

The uneasiness that had been plaguing him for two nights and a day started tap-dancing up and down Liam's spine with icy feet. He was beside her in the next instant. "Police?"

Her eyes turned up to his and his chest tightened. All his hard-won control unraveled with just that look. Though she couldn't know it, and he hoped like hell he wasn't showing it, calm felt far beyond him now.

"They think the fire at my apartment might be arson."

~

Sitting at one of the tables in the winery's picnic area, Giuliana checked her watch, watching the hands creep closer to that critical hour. Then she looked up again, absorbing the fact that the seats beneath the dozen umbrellas were nearly full with visitors enjoying the seventy-five-degree sunshine. Her gaze moved beyond the happy people to the land surrounding them, the vines appearing robust and the winery buildings freshly painted. Even the gravel in the nearby parking lot had been recently raked.

I'm doing my best, Papa, she thought. On his deathbed, he'd made the three sisters promise to try to bring Tanti Baci back on its feet. *I think I'm making the best decision for us all.*

She spun on her bench to tuck her knees beneath the table as Allie and Stevie threaded through the other picnickers, their hands full of sandwiches, sodas, and fruit from the deli case inside the tasting room in the wine caves. "I don't have a lot of time," she said as they arranged the goods between them and took their own seats on the bench across the table from her.

When they didn't acknowledge her warning, she

squelched a little blip of panic but didn't dare check her watch again. "And remember, you guys have that appointment in town with the caterer for the Vow-Over Weekend."

Stevie unwrapped a huge sandwich, hesitated, then reached for an oversized chocolate cookie. She took a huge bite. "That still leaves us time enough for you to tell me about the arson thing. I missed the excitement this morning."

"If you weren't such a slowpoke," Allie said, frowning, "you would have been there. You used to be an early bird and these days we need dynamite to get you out of bed."

Stevie finished off the cookie. "I wasn't feeling so great this morning."

"Well, you must feel fine now," Giuliana replied. "Dessert first?"

Stevie shrugged. "Sweets for the sweet."

Allie groaned. "I don't think it's right that you're tall *and* you get to eat more than I do. I'd like to see you get fat. It's only fair."

With her turkey and avocado sandwich halfway to her mouth, Stevie hesitated as if about to say something. Then she shrugged again and bit into the stack of bread and meat.

Giuliana plucked a cherry from their cardboard container and wiggled it by the stem. Her appetite had fled the morning before.

"Well?" Stevie prompted. "What did the cops say?"

"They want me to go down to the station for an interview. I had to explain I was car-less at the moment, thanks to another one of their open cases—the hit-and-run that took out my vehicle."

"We can drive you," Allie offered. "Drop you off on our way to the caterers, pick you up afterward."

"No! No." She cleared her throat. "I have a, um, a . . ." *Don't say meeting*, she reminded herself. That would make it too easy for her sisters to ask what kind and with whom. "I think they're sending someone over to question me."

"So what's the motive?" Stevie asked. "For the arson, I mean. Bad blood between drug dealers? A cover-up for a robbery? I know, the corrupt landlord wants to cash in on the insurance money."

"You've been watching too many crime shows on TV," Giuliana said, shaking her head.

"I don't know how she could be," Allie put in. "You wouldn't believe how early she goes to sleep and how much trouble she still has getting up in the morning."

Alarm goosed Giuliana and she leaned forward to inspect her sister more closely. Her skin was clear, her eyes alert, her mood apparently untroubled. Still . . . "Are you sure you're okay? You could have mono or something."

"Yeah," Allie agreed. "Remember? When we were in high school they called it the 'kissing disease' and from the way you and Jack carry on—"

"I do *not* have mono." Stevie made a face. "And as for a kissing disease, Al, I saw that hickey you have on your—"

The youngest sister threw a balled paper napkin, silencing the middle one. They both started laughing. "Okay, okay," Allie said. "I guess all the Baci girls have been infected with a kissing affliction."

"All?" a new voice inquired. Liam Bennett slipped onto the bench on Giuliana's side of the table. He stole one of the cherries she had been playing with and popped it into his mouth. "Does that include Big Girl?"

If she could breathe, she would have moved to another table. If her mouth wasn't so dry, at the very least she would have objected to being referred to as "Big Girl." It only served to emphasize their past history—that went back to forever. She'd been no more than seven when another of the valley kids, too little to say their long Italian names, had dubbed the Baci sisters by their relative size. When she'd topped out at all of five-foot-three, Liam still liked to tease her with the nickname.

Come over here, Big Girl, I have a surprise for you, a

teenaged Liam would say. And cupped in the hands behind his back would be a flower, or her favorite flavor of ice cream cone, or a black and yellow butterfly. Those little gestures had just as firmly trapped her heart.

But that grinning teenager of the past looked nothing like the self-assured, über-confident male beside her now. Even in Tuscany, at twenty, there'd been shadows inside him she couldn't pierce.

Now, she watched his long fingers steal toward her pile of cherries again. "What have you been up to, Stevie?" he asked.

"I've been trying to get to the bottom of Jules's mystery."

The jerk of his hand scattered the red fruit. "*What?*" He cast Giuliana a quick glance. "What, uh, mystery?"

She cleared her throat. "She means about the arson. Her latest theory is that the building's owner torched the place for the insurance money."

"Ah." Liam appeared to relax. "However, given that Giuliana's landlords are Ed and Jed, I doubt it."

She stared at him. The elderly twins owned and ran the old-fashioned hardware store in town, but it surprised her that Liam knew they also held the deed to the property where she'd—formerly—lived. As if he sensed her regard, he turned his head. Their eyes met.

She avoided that as often as she could—their eyes meeting. But it was too late to look off now, with her heart already halfway to her throat, leaving her insides jittering. Her breath was stuck in her lungs and it was as if he'd stripped her of clothes while he was fully dressed. The surface of her skin prickled and she felt her pulse thrum in panic. *Don't look at me,* she was ready to beg. *Please, don't look at me.*

"Oooh," Stevie's voice sounded in soft wonder. "Check it out, Allie."

The connection between her and Liam snapped. She sucked in a needed breath and turned her head to see what had caught her sisters' attention. They were both half turned on their bench, in the process of engaging with the group on the table behind them. Giuliana already had a polite half smile tugging up the corners of her mouth. She wasn't the PR type like her sister Allie, but winery owners learned early to be good with the public.

The object of their attention right now was a tiny infant, wrapped in tiny infant-wear and cocooned in the arms of a woman whose fond face screamed *mother*.

Allie glanced back at Giuliana. "Look how sweet, Jules."

She nodded. "Sweet." Then she glanced at her watch. "Allie—"

But her sister had already turned back to the child, going through the obligatory sheaf of questions. Name. Age. Place of birth.

"For God's sake, we can't ask that much when we're interviewing someone for a job," Giuliana muttered as Stevie started carrying on in a similar fashion. She took another urgent glance at her watch. "Allie, look, I've got to go."

Her sister sighed, her attention still focused on the bundle. "Us, too." She didn't move.

Giuliana felt more anxious by the second. She was expecting the people she was meeting with at any moment, and with the picnic area adjacent to the parking lot, there was too much chance of an untimely encounter.

She rose to her feet. "You guys can't be late," she said, raising her voice to hurry her sisters along. "We all should be going."

They continued to ignore her. Giuliana glanced around, trying to think. Her gaze lit on Liam, who was studying her in a way that made her pulse jolt again. She closed her eyes a moment, peeked at her watch again, and then made a quick decision. Desperate times, and all that.

Raising her eyebrows at him, she extended her hands in his direction. Then she put her right fist on her left palm and brought them toward herself. American Sign Language. They'd played around with it years ago. *Will you help me?*

Liam immediately rose to his feet. "Steve? Allie? Hey, can I get your guys' help before you head out?"

Where it was easy to ignore a sister, apparently it wasn't so easy to disregard Liam's polite but authoritative tone. Almost immediately her sisters were on their feet and following the oldest Bennett brother in the direction of the wedding cottage.

That left her with the lunch leftovers.

As well as the short-lived relief that she was going to make her meeting undetected.

Short-lived, because of the memory of the little hand gesture Liam had given her in return, behind the backs of her sisters as he ushered them away. His left palm outstretched in her direction. The index finger of his right moving as if he was flicking a coin on his hand toward himself. It was a "pay" gesture.

What he meant was clear: *You owe me.*

3

The next morning, Liam found Giuliana in the vineyard. When she spotted him strolling toward her, she ducked her head and hurried forward, as if trying to catch up with a small group of visitors being led about by an intern. "Don't run on my account," he called out.

As he expected, she responded to the challenge by letting the guests go ahead and swinging around to face him. "I'm sorry, I didn't realize that was you."

He resisted snorting. "It's me."

She wore a skimpy T-shirt and a knee-length cotton skirt that left bare the rest of her tan legs. A pair of dime-store rubber thongs were on her feet. She crossed her arms over her chest. "Four visits in four days, Mr. Bennett? That may be a record."

In their teenhood, he'd found reasons to see her four times before noon. Those days were over now, though, and she was right about the record. The fact was, for the last year that she'd been back in Edenville, he'd worked very hard at avoiding her as often as possible.

But that hadn't done a thing to ease the tension between them. They couldn't even speak without snapping at each other. Today, he hoped that by taking a different tack—by actually talking and engaging in some civil discourse—they could start to forge a new kind of relationship. Some casual visits, some casual conversation, and maybe they could become friends. Then finally they might address their underlying issues without stirring up animosity—or feelings even more dangerous.

So he worked on his most pleasant expression and glanced around, taking in the healthy look of the Tanti Baci vines. Two weeks before, as in his own vineyards, the buds had flowered and formed clusters that looked like small green beads. Though laborers might do some shoot, leaf, or crop thinning as the season wore on, at this time of year Mother Nature did most of the work.

What started out as hard and acidic softened and sweetened under the summer sunshine.

He hoped to do the same with Giuliana's attitude toward him. "Good fruit set this year," he ventured.

From the corner of his eye, he saw her shoulders relax a little. *Score.*

She reached out to trace the edge of a cabernet sauvignon leaf, her fingertip following the defined lobes. Gold beads in a delicate bracelet she wore around her wrist glinted in the sunlight. "We're optimistic," she said.

He nodded, then made a gesture, indicating the spring green brightness surrounding them and tried keeping the conversation going. "You must have missed this over the years."

"I was in the wine business."

In Southern California. Working for a wine distributor. After that summer in Tuscany, she'd not matriculated at nearby UC Davis as she'd planned, but instead ended up at a college in the central part of the state. "No offense, but what you were doing in LA compared to winemaking here in the valley is the difference between selling ice cream bars and milking dairy cows."

Her laugh was a tad dry. "Okay, I won't take offense. But not everyone wants to get their hands dirty."

"You loved getting your hands dirty."

Her shrug frustrated him. "You mix me up with Stevie. She was the tomboy."

"I could never mix you up with anyone." He leaned down to scoop up a fistful of powdery red dirt, then held his palm under her nose. "Come on, admit this is in your blood."

Shaking her head, she turned away. "I was gone for a decade, Liam. I lived without all this just fine."

He allowed the dirt to sift through his fingers as he looked out over the vineyard and tried imagining it—a world lacking the summer's eager anticipation, the mad frenzy of sweat and toil during harvest, the dormancy of the vines after the first frost that was followed by bud break in early spring. It was the ruler of life in the valley—both in the sense that grape growing was king and that it was the measure of their days in the beautiful wine country.

And ten growing seasons had passed since he'd held Giuliana in his arms.

"Anyway," she continued. "What do you have against the ice cream man? Dairy farmers love the guy."

His head snapped toward her, all thoughts of being pleasant and friendly flying—just like that—from his mind. "Is that it? You found some slick 'farmer' who said he loved you and that kept you away from . . . from your family?"

She bristled. "I saw my family."

Now he did snort. "At Disneyland. You didn't come back to the real world to face your real problems."

"I wasn't aware of what was happening at Tanti Baci. You know that Papa kept the financial crisis from all of us until he knew he was dying."

"I'm not talking about the problems at Tanti Baci."

"Is this about you?" Her eyes narrowed. "Liam, if you've found someone—"

"Damn it!" That was the problem. He hadn't found anyone—not in the way she meant.

She stiffened. "Don't talk to me like that."

"I'm not." He closed his eyes instead of tearing out his hair like he wanted to. His voice lowered and he evened out his breathing. "I'm talking to myself like that. I didn't come over here to have this kind of conversation."

"What kind of conversation did you want?"

He inhaled another calming breath. "Cordial. Neighborly."

"Really?" She blinked.

"Really. Perhaps we could even find some area of mutual interest."

She looked suspicious. "What kind of mutual interest?"

"I don't know." He shrugged. "But we have things in common. Winemaking. Our family connections. Two of the guys I hang out with the most are newly married. Your two sisters as well."

"Do you have a mutual interest in wanting to smack them silly sometimes?"

His lips twitched. "What gets you the most? The smug smiles when they're with their spouse or the unseemly haste to get back to him or her when they're apart?"

"I've been half blinded by the rings my sisters are always flashing in my face."

"My ego's permanently bruised by how many baseball games Penn and Jack are just too 'busy' to attend with me."

Giuliana was smiling at him now. A genuine smile. "Speaking of family . . . how's your mom?"

He appreciated the interest, especially since Jeanette had never gone out of her way to be friendly with the Bacis. "Okay. Seth and I visited her in New York last Christmas. She has her bridge and tennis cronies and I think is happy to be far away from the crap that came down on her after dad died."

"Calvin Bennett." Giuliana shook her head. "He—"

"Was a black-hearted son of a bitch."

She frowned. "I know he hurt your mother—"

"You don't know the half of what he did." Liam felt his fingers curl into fists and forced them to relax. "But let's not ruin all our newfound geniality with talk of him. I saw your cousin Gil and his wife, Clare, in the deli."

Giuliana rolled her eyes, but she was half smiling again. "Just more newlyweds flying high on cloud nine." Then she hesitated and cocked her head. "Would you like to check out the chardonnay grapes? I wouldn't mind your opinion."

And that she didn't mind his company for five more minutes was a positive step, he figured. As they walked, she glanced up at him through the veil of her lashes. "I think we were right about here that night we went treasure hunting with the metal detector. Remember, the one you borrowed from Ed and Jed?"

"I remember."

"I was fifteen, and half convinced we'd find the legendary Bennett-Baci silver."

"Not much hope of that."

"I know it *now*, but then—"

"Not then, either." He checked out the pure lines of her profile. "In the spirit of goodwill, I feel compelled to confess that the detector was broken that night. Ed and Jed had a replacement on order but were happy to let us play around with the defective one."

Her feet halted. "What? Why did you want to do that? We spent hours out here, until it was way past dark!"

"Truth? I needed all the time I could get. I was working up my nerve to kiss you."

Her jaw dropped.

"Alessandra was always tagging around after us, so I

dreamed up the treasure-hunt idea, hoping she'd get tired of it sooner than later . . . which she did."

Giuliana just stared at him. "You . . . you . . ."

"I apologize."

Her face flushed. "For the deception? Or the kiss?"

"You remember it then." They'd finally given up the hunt and were heading back to the farmhouse. Out by Anne and Alonzo's cottage, they'd gotten into one of those adolescent horseplay matches—any excuse to touch—and he'd taken her down, frontier-wrestling style, onto the grass. Lying half across her, he'd brought his mouth to hers. "I won't ever apologize for that."

Her head ducked. "You'd kissed other girls before me."

"I don't remember them." God's truth.

"Oh, Liam." She looked up, her smile wry. "Penn's charm must be rubbing off on you."

"Maybe." He almost smiled back. *I should have done this before. I should have tried to be her friend.*

A cloud of dust heralded the return of the vineyard tour group. He and Giuliana scooted close to the trellised vines to let the visitors pass. There were three middle-aged couples, an elderly pair of women who carried walking sticks, and bringing up the rear was a family. The father had a small kid on his shoulders. The mother led a toddler by the hand who stumbled over Liam's boots. Automatically he lifted the child to its feet, noticing the pronounced baby bump on the mom as he ushered the child into her arms.

His gaze followed them as they hurried to catch up with the rest of the tour. Then he felt Giuliana's eyes on him. He turned to her.

"Nice," she said. But the animation was gone from her face.

"Jules . . ."

"I don't know how my mother did it. Three girls, one right after the other. Imagine how busy that woman will be when her new baby comes in—what? Two months or so?"

"I have no idea."

Her nose wrinkled. "I don't either, really." Then she raised her brows. "Ready for the chardonnay, buddy?"

Buddy. Jesus. Could he really make that work? "We should talk."

"Sure. About grapes. About our mutually annoying friends and relatives. About friendship."

"About before, Jules. About the future. Hell, about *now.* We have a problem."

She was already shaking her head as she turned away. "I can't. We'll have to wait. Four weeks."

He was responsible. A rational, logical person. And he'd already let too much time pass. "Giuliana," he started. He'd been doing so well with this new neighborliness that he thought he had a hope to get through this as well. "Let's be sensible. Grown-up."

She whipped around. "Don't patronize me."

"I'm not." But frustration was bubbling again.

"Then just leave it alone. Leave *me* alone."

He couldn't. "I won't." He stepped toward her.

She scuttled back, then pivoted to walk past him. "See you later."

He grabbed her arm to hold her still.

He hadn't touched her in ten years.

They both froze. The sensation of her skin under his hand jolted through his system. It electrified his skin, turned his veins to paths of fire, melted his brain.

Intention tumbled one hundred eighty degrees. All his unsettling settled. He figured he was still as screwed as he'd been before touching her, but his mind was finally clear. The friend idea was fucked.

Before he could do anything about that certainty, she wrenched free. He let her go—for now. It was time to find a Plan B.

~

Giuliana squeezed out her sponge, ready to plunge her rubber-gloved arm back into the depths of the display refrigerator in the tasting room. The cold drinks she'd cleared from the racks were in an oversized cooler until she finished her cleaning.

With her free left hand, she lifted her coffee and took another sip. It burned upon landing in her stomach, a signal that she needed to take in some solid food as well, but nothing had appealed to her appetite in days.

"Are you okay?" Grace asked. The other woman was nearby, dusting the shelves that held glass decanters of local olive oil and fancy jars of special mustards.

"I'm fine! Fine." She modulated her voice. "Why wouldn't I be fine?"

"You just looked a little . . . stressed after that break you took earlier."

That break when she'd been confronted by Liam and his offer of friendship. God, for a moment she'd been seduced by the possibility. There he was, tan, golden-haired, and gorgeous, and she'd imagined confessing to him all that had been whirling around in her head—her dilemma, her conflicts, her choices. For a second she'd actually believed it could be as it was before Tuscany. That it could be like it was when they were kids. After her mother had died, he'd been her rock.

But then he'd touched her. Just a simple graze of fingertips to flesh and she'd experienced a yearning that pierced both bone and heart. Getting close to him again, she'd realized, would only shatter her.

She glanced over, noting that Grace was still studying her with concern. Panic added kindling to that burn in her belly. She couldn't afford to have people speculating on her moods, not when she just had to get through the next few weeks. "I'm in a perfectly great place," she assured the young woman. "What about you? Is Mari treating you all right?"

"You didn't look well even before you went into the vineyard," Grace said. "You can't be comfortable sleeping on that love seat in your office. *You* should stay at Mari's, and I—"

"No!" Giuliana said again. Kohl's sister could ferret secrets from a stump. "I just have to remember to turn off the ringer on the winery phone. Someone kept calling last night and hanging up."

Grace shook her head. "Really, Giuliana. You should stay with Allie and Stevie. I'm surprised they don't insist."

"I'm the big sister." Giuliana smiled. "What I say goes."

"Really?"

"Really." Giuliana remembered Grace hadn't grown up with anyone besides her odd and often bad-tempered father. "It seems like I was always looking after my little sisters. After my mother died, I considered myself in charge of them." *And I did okay, Mom, didn't I? I know I stayed away from Edenville, but we did more than Disneyland together over the years when I lived in Southern California.* "And now they're happily married to two good men."

Grace ducked her head, her dust cloth running busily over a selection of different wineglasses.

After her own bruising marriage, Grace was likely as leery of any male animal as Giuliana was of Liam. How bad had her husband been? "Grace—"

A crash from outside the tasting room had them both whirling around. At the sound of Kohl's cursing voice, Grace jumped. Her eyes went wide as he clomped into the room.

"Who left the—" He broke off, his gaze focused on Giuliana's face. "Are you okay?"

She frowned at him. "Why are you asking me that? You should direct your question to Grace. Your stomping and swearing had her jumping out of her skin."

He glanced at the helper, looking a little ashamed. But though he quieted his voice, he stalked toward Giuliana. "You look like hell."

Another swig of coffee went down like battery acid. "I need to take a run into town and pick up some more makeup," she said. "Allie lent me her stuff but clearly I need additional help."

Kohl grabbed the mug from her hand. "What you don't need is more caffeine," he said, heading for the sink behind the bar.

Grace shrank against the shelves as he passed by. Her eyes didn't leave his massive form. "He wouldn't hurt you," Giuliana whispered in assurance.

"I know." Grace didn't take her eyes off him as she whispered back. "He wouldn't hurt anybody."

Hmm, Giuliana thought. Most people kept their distance from Kohl because of his brawler reputation and his big size. *I wonder*—but the idea was lost as Kohl returned to her side.

With a hand under her chin, he lifted her face. "You need new scenery. A good meal. Go out with me tonight."

She hesitated. Off the top of her head, she could think of half a dozen reasons to nip Kohl's interest in the bud. Since she'd returned to Edenville, though, he'd been the one to nurse her New Year's Eve hangover, the one to play buffer between herself and Liam, the one who could make her smile when she was swamped by distressing financial news. "Kohl . . ."

"Go with me," he insisted.

"Go with you where?" Liam asked, as he strolled into the tasting room.

Giuliana nearly groaned aloud. The three of them had been playing out this scene over and over for months. She'd be minding her own business only to discover herself once again the muddle in the middle of the rough-cut rogue and the sleek and sophisticated society guy. Alonzo, Anne, and the original Liam had worked through this same script themselves a hundred years before, and sometimes she wondered if the Baci land really *was* haunted. Maybe their modern-day struggle was being forced on them by specters bent upon reliving that old romantic triangle.

"This is none of your business, Bennett," Kohl ground out.

Liam slid his hands in his pockets as his mouth curved in a smile that held no warmth. "You'd be surprised."

"Not now," she warned them both. She turned back to her bucket and sponge. "We open in a couple of hours and I need to finish up here."

"Just say you'll let me take you to dinner later and I'll get out of your way," Kohl said, moving close again.

Giuliana felt Liam's gaze on the back of her neck. "I'm cleaning out the files in my office tonight."

"You hear that, Friday?" Liam drawled. "Surely you know what it means when a woman says she has to stay home to clean her files. She might as well say she needs the night off to wash her hair."

Giuliana shot him a glare over her shoulder. "I'm really cleaning out the files in my office tonight." Piece by piece, she was putting the business end of the winery to rights. By the end of the Vow-Over Weekend, she'd have everything in order.

Liam's gaze suddenly narrowed. "Are you okay?"

With a frustrated grunt, she threw the sponge into the bucket. "What do I have to do? Take out an ad?" Then she stopped herself, wary of protesting too much. "What are you doing back here anyway, Liam?" Surely he didn't want to start up with the friendship thing again. The fire in her stomach flared.

He shrugged. "Jack called and said to meet him in the tasting room."

"Well, he isn't here—"

Well, he still wasn't, but Allie and Penn entered. "I'm telling you," her youngest sister was saying to her husband. "I've looked everywhere and can't find my watch. The one that was my mother's."

"I haven't seen it," Penn said. As he so often did, he had his fingers tangled in Allie's long hair, as if he couldn't help but keep her close.

The memory of Liam's hand on her rose again, but Giuliana pushed it back down. "I haven't seen your watch, either. Why are you here?" she said to her sister. "You could have just called and asked."

Allie glanced over, then stared. "Are you okay?"

"I'm strangling the next person who asks me that."

"It's just that—"

"On top of the medicine cabinet," Grace piped up. "In the washroom adjacent to the winery's reception area. Have you looked for it there?"

Giuliana sent Grace a grateful look as Allie's attention shifted. "You're right. I remember I took it off when I washed my hands." As she turned, she called over her shoulder, "Don't let Stevie say anything until I get back."

"Stevie?"

"She told Penn and I to meet her here," her younger sister said.

"But . . . why?"

Nobody had the answer, it seemed, and there was no time for speculation. In a few short minutes, Allie was back, standing beside Penn, happy to be reunited with her heirloom. Then Stevie walked into the room with Jack, their hands entwined.

If you asked Giuliana, it was the middle Baci sister that everyone should be worried about. Her usually sun-kissed complexion was pale and she was casting nervous looks around the room. "You're all here," she said.

Grace put down her dust cloth. "This looks like a private—"

"No." Stevie waved off the concern. "Stay. It's time I told everyone." Then her gaze found Giuliana's. "It's time I told you."

It's time I told you. Giuliana froze, those words sinking like stones into her consciousness. Her mind moved back in time. Instead of the winery's tasting room, she was in her parents' bedroom, sitting on her parents' bed, her mother's hand thin and cold in hers. Elena Baci had been propped up by pillows and covered by a quilted cotton throw stained by the strawberry jam that Stevie had spilled that morning when she'd delivered a breakfast tray. As Elena traced it, Giuliana saw that it was shaped like a ragged heart. *You'll have to take good care of your sisters for me,* she'd said to her oldest daughter. *Don't worry, you'll be a wonderful mother.*

It was a chilly sixty degrees in the wine caves, but she hadn't noticed the cold while scrubbing the refrigerator. Now it seeped into the pores of her skin and slowed the flow of the blood through her veins. Only her belly burned as she pulled away from the past and stared at her middle sister. *Oh, God,* she thought, her mouth soundlessly repeating the words. *I can't lose anyone else.*

Stevie cleared her throat. "I have some news."

Jack slipped his arm around his wife. Giuliana didn't look at him, afraid what she might see on his face. She averted her gaze from everyone, her eyes on the rubber of her thongs and the dusting of reddish Baci dirt that stuck to them, just like the old pain and sadness had adhered to the surface of her heart.

"Jules," Stevie said. "Look at me."

She obeyed her sister, even as she remembered. *Jules,* her mother had said. *I'm dying.*

Her sister smiled. "I'm going to have a baby."

Giuliana's cold skin flooded with heat. Her head spun. Black dots swam into her vision.

She saw Stevie start forward. "Are you okay?"

That question! "Of course . . ." She wasn't, she realized, as arms closed around her and the room went dark.

4

Frustration rose within Kohl Friday, enough that he would have thrown a punch if there was a convenient target. But he was standing in the Tanti Baci tasting room, with its bottles of wine, rows of glassware, and decanters of olive oil. As much as he wanted to vent, he wouldn't take pleasure in the mess he'd make.

And then there was Grace Hatch. He wouldn't take pleasure in scaring her, either.

He strode over to pick up the sponge that Giuliana had been using to clean the refrigerator before she'd gone into a near-faint and been carried off by her family. And Liam.

Yeah. Liam. Warm water dribbled down Kohl's wrist as he squeezed the sodden material in his hand—his action a pitiful substitute for the strangling his temper called for. He glared at the fridge's white interior walls as if they were the cause of his piss-poor mood.

"I can finish that up," Grace said.

He switched his stare to her. She was gazing at him out of big, wary eyes. Their blue was almost startling, a bright contrast to the soft reddish blond of her short wavy hair that matched the color of the freckles sprinkled over her creamy skin. When she'd first started working at Tanti Baci, there'd been bruises on her—fresh purple ones, fading green ones, the sick yellow that spoke volumes. The five distinct finger marks ringing her upper arm had been nearly black.

The color of the rage that too often bubbled inside Kohl.

Fuck.

Ignoring the little rabbit in the room, he started scrubbing. He hadn't intended to finish the task, but what the hell. It was too early to hit a bar and start drinking.

Grace began dusting the shelves again. "She's going to be all right," she ventured after a silent moment. "It's just that she hasn't been sleeping well. Or eating."

Kohl grunted. As if he didn't know! He should have dragged Giuliana away for a meal before her sister had a chance to tell her about the baby. Instead of celebrating with Stevie, she'd slumped right into the arms of that rich, overprivileged asshole, Liam Bennett.

"Do you have any cigarettes?" Kohl barked out.

Grace's eyes widened. "I don't smoke."

He hadn't, either, not for a long time, but he thought he might have taken it up again. The morning after the fire, he'd woken to find matches in his pocket, though he didn't actually remember lighting up. He didn't actually remember hours of that night—the time between his first few drinks at one bar until the news of the apartment burning had roused him from a stupor on his stool at another. He'd slapped himself two-thirds sober, then called for cab, downing Dentyne to alleviate the stink of booze clinging to him.

When he'd first left the army and returned to Edenville, he'd spent a lot of lost evenings with his best bud, José Cuervo. It didn't happen nearly as often now, but he still couldn't claim saint status.

He'd been trying, though, for Jules.

Fuck.

Angry all over again, he heaved the sponge. It landed on the fridge's back wall with a loud *splat*.

A bleat reminded him of the little rabbit. Guilt pinched and he swung toward her, ready to apologize for scaring the bejeezus out of her. But she was focused on her work, deftly arranging the items displayed for sale. His gaze narrowed on her hands. They weren't trembling, he was glad to note, but still he didn't look away. How pretty they were, he thought, covered with those same freckles that stood out like cinnamon-sugar snowflakes on her face.

He wondered if they tasted sweet.

She bleated again and he started, embarrassed he might have said that thought aloud. But she was staring down at her forefinger. A drop of blood welled there.

His feet rushed forward. He halted as he reached her, aware that his mere size spooked some women—not to mention his temperament. "Are you all right?"

"It's nothing." She darted him a nervous glance. "I caught it on the edge of this tin of tea."

He eased back a step. "Are you up to date on your tetanus shots?"

Her face flushed. "Yes."

They would have made sure of that at the hospital. He'd known she'd gone there after her ex's last beating. Another spurt of wrath shot through him, and it felt as if a strap was tightening around his chest. It only cinched harder as she brought that slim, cinnamon-dusted hand up to insert the injured digit in her mouth. Sucked.

Lust shot through him, heat arrowing toward his cock. It immediately thickened. "You shouldn't do that," he told the girl, fascinated by the sight. His voice was gruff. *Christ!* This poor little thing was likely terrified of men and he was stuck on Jules, yet still he reacted just like an animal. Only a beast would let his temper and his hungers get the best of him like this . . .

In those hours he couldn't account for, he only hoped they hadn't.

Grace wound a paper towel around her injured finger. "Your sister is very nice," she said, making him suppose she couldn't hear his heavy breathing. "I appreciate her letting me stay."

"Her place is small, but I don't think she's ever there."

"She dates a lot?"

A short laugh escaped him. "A lot doesn't cover—" A thought shut him up. "She wouldn't bring anyone home when you're there," he assured her.

"Anyone?"

"A man," he clarified.

Her face colored again. "I don't think all males are villains."

No, only the ones who should have taken care of her, starting with her father. "No one could—"

"You saved Chester," she suddenly said.

He blinked. "Chester?"

"Our dog. My dad had him tied up to a tree in the yard. He would get himself all tangled, no matter how many times I tried to unknot the rope. Then he'd be stuck in the dirt, unable to reach his bowl of water."

"Jerry," Kohl said, the memory rushing to him. He'd been a loner by choice, but it had killed him to see that scruffy, dirty animal on its own, day after day. "We called him Jerry Garcia—you know, after the guitarist in the Grateful Dead."

At her puzzled expression, he laughed. "You'll have to meet my father and mother someday."

Pink rushed over her face again.

Heat burned on his, too. That had probably sounded like some kind of come-on, and despite her protestations, a woman like Grace Hatch had to feel extra wary. He swallowed and backed up a little more. "It's just that my dad loved that dog from the day I stole him from your house and brought him to our place."

She smiled a little. "My father thought I'd allowed him to run off. I was so happy when I spotted him with your parents a couple weeks later. I asked Mari at school and she told me what you'd done."

A chill cruised along Kohl's spine. "Your father—"

"It didn't matter." She spun back toward the shelves and restarted her cleaning and rearranging. "It doesn't."

Oh, God. It mattered. "He hit you."

She shrugged.

Cold and heat collided inside of Kohl as rage mingled with something tender, a volatile cocktail. His hands fisted and it took everything he had to force his voice to gentleness. "He hit you for what I'd done."

"Sometimes he hit me for making him dinner," she said. "At least that time there was a reason for it."

Kohl found himself facing the refrigerator again. Maybe those white walls would wipe clean his now cluttered conscience. That SOB, Peter Hatch, had hit his little girl for something Kohl had done—a prank on his part, really, though getting that dog into a bath hadn't been a bit of fun. But while he'd been struggling with sixty pounds of stinky fur and shampoo, a man had laid a hand on Grace's sugared skin.

He remembered her as a kid now, too, as scruffy and unkempt as the canine he'd rescued. But he'd left her behind . . . "If he wasn't already dead, I'd kill him," he muttered.

"What's that?"

A promise of more violence wasn't something she needed in her life. "Nothing. Not a thing." Asserting his will over his straining muscles—now he knew what the Hulk felt like—he reached for the sponge and started working once more on the refrigerator.

He cleared his throat, deciding he could take a stab at being civilized. Like that damn Liam Bennett, he thought. "Do you like working at Tanti Baci?"

"I do. I like the people that come into the tasting room. The time passes so quickly! And the Baci sisters . . ."

He glanced at her, catching the smile on her gold-dusted face. "You think they're nice?"

"Stevie and Alessandra want to save the winery so very badly."

He nodded. "Jules, too."

Her blue eyes cut to him. They shook him again, their startling blue, the way they seemed to see him . . . differently than most women did. The females he'd been hanging with in bars the past couple of years looked at him and saw burly muscles and his barely restrained belligerence. Both attracted them, he knew. Then there was Giuliana . . .

"You've been such a good friend to her," Grace said.

"She's needed one." As he'd gained more control of his moods, she'd given over to him more responsibility at Tanti Baci. He'd appreciated that and then come to see that through her trust she was bringing out the better man in him. His time in combat had been hell, and he'd been still partly there upon his return. Jules had seemed the beacon that beckoned the rest of him toward home. "And I owe her a lot."

It made him think of her in Liam's arms again, and he battled the urge to knock something over. But *damn it*—

"I owe you a lot, too," Grace said quietly.

He glanced over his shoulder, his mind still on that smug son of a bitch who had been making him nuts for months. "What? Why? Because I took your dog and you took a hit for it?"

At the harsh tone of his voice, she twitched.

Shit. There he went, scaring her again. "Look. I'm sorry. I'm a lousy kind of man for you to be around . . ."

"Don't say that."

Her big blue eyes were making him want to twitch again. "Honey—"

"You called me that," she said, her gaze glued to his face. She put down her dust cloth and came closer.

For some reason, Kohl backed up, a man who hadn't retreated from anything or anyone in all his life. One shoulder blade caught the edge of the refrigerator. There was nowhere to run.

"A group of boys was chasing me," she said. "Down by the auto upholstery place."

He frowned. The auto upholstery place was in a Quonset-styled, corrugated metal building on the edge of downtown. Just a few blocks from Edenville's center square, but there wasn't always a lot of traffic in that area. "What were you doing there?"

"Just wandering." She shrugged. "Staying away from home. Staying out of the way."

"And the boys?" He had a sick feeling. How come he didn't remember?

"It's not like that. I was seven," she said. "They weren't much older. But I fell and skinned my knee on the asphalt. You picked me up."

He must have been, what? Fourteen? "I had two younger sisters."

" 'Honey,' you said. And you wiped my wet face with the hem of your shirt."

He had no memory of it at all. Still, he pressed tighter to the uncomfortable edge of the refrigerator because the look on her face was unmistakable. She wasn't afraid of him. She probably never would be afraid of him, he thought, feeling sort of awed by the realization.

He'd dried her tears.

He'd saved her dog.

But the light in her eyes scared the hell out of *him*. There was a kind of worship there, and everybody in Edenville knew Kohl Friday was no freakin' hero.

~

Liam prodded one of Giuliana's listless hands with a breadstick he plucked from the pile in the basket on the table between them. "Start with this."

She ignored the poke to gaze around the room. "Are the murals new? I don't remember them."

He looked over. The walls of Vincenzo's were painted in the umber, blues, and greens of Italy. Vine-covered hills, brilliant sapphire skies, a golden-skinned girl with waist-length black hair covered by a white kerchief walked barefooted on a narrow path.

Tuscany. He smelled it in the herb and rose aroma of the Chianti in their glasses and from the basil and garlic in the pasta dish steaming on a neighboring table. His eyes cut to Giuliana and he saw her as she'd been that summer. Wavy hair to her hips, tip-tilted dark eyes bright with happiness, full lips turned up in a smile that could light all but those darkest corners of his heart.

They'd signed up to intern at a vineyard from June until September and had left two days after she graduated from high school. Flying in a seat beside her, he'd thought it was the happiest he'd been in his life. Finally away from the tension in his house and finally free to be with the girl he loved—they'd kept the knowledge that she was his partner in the Italian adventure as much a secret from his parents as their two-year relationship.

There had been so many secrets that summer.

On the flight overseas, she'd slept with her head on his shoulder. He'd pressed his mouth to her shining hair and committed himself to a lifetime of keeping her safe and happy. He'd succeeded for a few weeks. The air-conditioned restaurant wasn't the shaded streets of the tiny town where they'd lived, but he could feel the rough cobblestones under his feet anyway. He remembered a particular day, turning a corner only to spy Giuliana walking in his direction. She'd spotted him too and approached him on a run, flinging herself against his chest in loving abandon. Her body warm, her smile brilliant. *Liam!*

"Liam!"

He blinked, coming back to the present. The woman he remembered was a tabletop away. And scowling. There were shadows under her deep brown eyes, not brightness in their depths.

"You didn't hear me," she said.

"No." But he had. Ten years before he'd heard every word, felt every break in her voice like a lash to his skin, and every sob like a punch to his gut. Yet guilt and remorse and self-disgust had clogged his throat and iced his heart so that he couldn't respond in the way she'd needed.

"I asked you to take me home."

He blinked again, now fully back to the present. "We've already ordered food," he said. "For God's sake, Jules, you fainted in the tasting room. Scared the hell out of everybody."

Her sisters. Her brothers-in-law. Him. As she'd slumped, he'd caught her in his arms, only to discover how very fragile she was, no bigger than a bird much too young to leave the nest. It had stabbed at him. "You've lost weight—"

"I want to go home."

He glared at her. "And apparently you've lost your mind, too. It was either a doctor or food and I'm holding you to your promise to eat a full meal."

"I'll get something back at Tanti Baci," she said, waving a slender hand. "I don't have the time for this."

"I should have known you'd break this vow, too."

Her mouth snapped shut and the look she shot him was black. Bitter. But he ignored it. After a year with Giuliana back in Edenville but without a resolution to their situation, he was prepared to play hardball. That's what this interlude was really about. His Plan B after the friendship fail. Yeah, he wanted to feed her, but he was also planning on using this time to get her agreement that they go forward, immediately, with what needed to be done.

Dropping her gaze, she fiddled with her utensils, lining them up like good soldiers. "I want to see Stevie," she finally said, her voice a little hoarse. "I don't even remember what I said. I want her to know how happy I am for her and Jack."

The blade that had been stuck in his belly twisted. "Once you stopped seeing stars, you expressed yourself just fine."

Liam had been the one without the right words, as usual. His friend and father-to-be, Jack, who could be surprisingly emotional at times, hadn't been content with a congratulatory handshake. He'd yanked Liam into a Super Bowl–win of a man-hug, thumping him on the back. Stevie's embrace had been the one to slay him, though. She'd bussed him on the cheek, coming close enough for him to imagine he could see the swell of new life beneath her navel.

So many memories.

So many secrets.

"Giuliana . . ." He'd survived her once before, but he'd been younger then. "Listen to me. We've got to—"

"It's just like old times!" a new voice commented.

Swallowing his groan, Liam glanced up. Charles Conrad was beaming down on them, his brush cut just turning silver. Beside him was his wiry wife—her tan testament to her passion for golf. They'd lived in Edenville since Charles had been one of the first to sell his Silicon Valley software firm and retire to the Napa Valley, about two decades before. The couple had been part of his parents' wider social set.

Politeness necessitated he stand to greet the older pair. He shook hands with Charles and brushed his lips against

Mary's cheek. Though the town was a mere six thousand, he thought he might need to introduce Jules anyway. "Do you two know Giuliana—"

"Of course." Charles patted the young woman's shoulder. "Why, we've been watching over the Baci girls for years."

Giuliana gave a good-natured grimace. "We've discovered that to be a civic hobby of sorts. Of course, when Allie lost Tommy . . ."

"Tragic," Mary agreed, "but it was *you* who first caught our eye, Giuliana."

"Me?"

"And you," the older woman answered, nodding at Liam. "The whole town held their breath as the two of you fell in love."

His gaze jumped to Giuliana's. A blush was creeping up her cheeks. He felt a little hot himself. "Kid stuff."

"But here you are all over again," Charles pointed out.

"Business stuff," Giuliana said.

"If you say so." Mary sighed, then leaned in. "But I just want it known that we did our part to keep your big romance under wraps all those years ago. Everybody did, you know."

Shit. He'd thought it was because they'd been discreet. But teenagers . . . discreet?

"Well, uh, thank you," Giuliana said. "But my father wasn't so strict—"

"Not your father. What a pleasant fellow he was."

Oh, *shit.* Liam saw where this was going. "Pleasant, yes. And it's been pleasant seeing you again." He shuffled his feet, hoping it would get the older couple moving along.

No such luck.

"Of course, it was because of Liam's mother and father that we all kept it undercover," Charles said, shaking his head. "They . . ." He let the sentence trail off, as if suddenly realizing just where this was going himself. His laugh was too hearty. "I think Mary and I had a little too much wine with lunch."

"Go ahead," Giuliana urged, her face now at full flush. "What about Liam's mother and father?"

Charles turned to Liam, in clear appeal. Oh, hell. He steeled himself to answer her, knowing it would erode any goodwill she felt toward him and make her that much more uncooperative. But otherwise he left Charles in the hot seat. "My parents wouldn't have approved," Liam admitted.

The woman he'd loved stared at him for a long moment. "Oh, I get it," she finally said. "They expected someone better for you."

The food arrived and Charles and Mary departed before he could respond to the charge. As Liam dropped back into his seat, he felt his face settle into the cool mask that camouflaged the roiling of his inner emotions. Jules had to know he'd never thought the same as his parents . . . didn't she?

Her expression was as stoic as his, however, and gave nothing away. His hand tightened on his fork as he watched her move her ravioli around her plate without taking a bite. Damn it! It always went wrong between them, ever since he'd returned to California two weeks early, leaving Giuliana in Tuscany alone. Their transatlantic phone calls had been both frustrating and heart wrenching. After a ten-year hiatus, they'd come together again, but their exchange of verbal slaps and charged silences proved to be no kind of real communication now, either.

Hell, yes, it was as much his fault as hers, but he couldn't work a conciliatory syllable up his tight throat. He watched her play some more with her food, his irritation growing.

"To hell with it," he said, and reached across to spear one of the pillow-shaped pastas, then put it to her lips. "Take a bite. You need to fucking eat."

Her mouth set for a stubborn moment, then her gaze lifted to his and she pulled the piece into her mouth. *Satisfied?* her glare said.

"No," he answered, watching her chew. She was tying him in knots and there was only one way out. "We have to take care of it, Jules." Poking his fork into another ravioli, he presented that to her as well, slightly mollified when she allowed him to feed her again. "It's got to end, sweetheart."

The endearment stilled them both. "No," she said. To the lover's term? To his ultimatum?

"Jules—"

"Four weeks. In four weeks I'll have the time to do what's necessary."

Four more *days* and he'd be a basket case! He couldn't see how another month would change one damn thing and he worried that in four weeks she'd be asking for another four and then another four and pretty soon he'd be begging his brothers to put him out of his misery. Under the current circumstances, Edenville was just not big enough for him and Giuliana both.

He quaffed a gulp from his glass of wine, taking it down like medicine.

"I can get to it after the end of the month. It's just paperwork," Giuliana said, finally attacking the ravioli on her own. "No big deal. Not like real unfinished business."

Did she want to make him furious? He was trying to save his sanity here, but now she was throwing *paperwork* in his face. Pushing his own untouched meal aside, he caught her gaze with his. Her eyes widened. Her fork clattered to her plate.

Maybe she guessed his intention, because he saw her start to scoot away just as he caught one of her hands in his. Just as he trapped one of her bare legs between his denim-covered calves. The shudder that ran through her body matched the bolt of fire that sprinted through his. Touching her only made him want to touch more. Having just this much of her against him had every impulse clamoring to have him under her, over him, every and any way he could.

"See?" he said, his voice hard. "This isn't paperwork. And it's *real unfinished business.*" His pride wouldn't let her deny or reject what they'd once been to each other or pretend that the physical attraction had dissipated in the years they'd been apart.

He rasped a thumb across the back of her knuckles and watched her breath hitch. His own lungs burned, but both made him damn happy. Mutual was always better than singular. "Admit there's still something." God knew why, but it was paramount.

"I can't," she whispered. "Not now, please. Because—"

A shadow fell over their table. Liam ignored the intrusion. Neighbors, waiter, it didn't matter. He didn't want any interruption when he felt this close to finally reaching Giuliana.

"Hello, ma'am," a man's voice said.

Liam's head jerked toward it. A stranger stood beside their table, big, with military bearing, and military-short hair. He glanced at Giuliana. She seemed equally unfamiliar with the other man. Yet she smiled—a winemaker's instinct for hospitality.

Something icy spider-walked up Liam's spine. "What do you want?" he asked, aware he sounded hostile, because Giuliana's fingers tightened on his hand.

"To see her," the stranger said, his gaze resting on Liam's . . . Liam's . . .

Shit. He found himself on his feet. "We're not looking for company." The frozen-footed spider was dancing tarantellas down his back.

The man shoved his hand toward Giuliana. Before Liam could intervene, her winemaker manners kicked in again and a half smile tilted her lips as her palm slid against the other man's.

That was it. Everything clarified for Liam in that moment when the spiders were dancing, Giuliana appeared so vulnerable, and the imprint of her skin against his was still a brand on his flesh. For a man who was so much about common sense, practicality, and rationality, he tossed all that away as he looked upon his first love, her hand touching another man's.

This wasn't the petty, juvenile jealousy that he'd felt toward Kohl. God, that was puerile compared to this.

This was a new kind of understanding. And even as he realized it, Liam leapt forward to grasp the man's shoulder and break Giuliana free of his hold.

The stranger didn't seem to notice. "I'm Grace's husband."

Giuliana's brows pinched. "Grace—"

"I just wanted us to meet. For now."

"I don't think so," Liam said, all his instincts definite about that.

The stranger's gaze shifted to him. And then, like a snake, he slithered free of Liam's grasp and was gone.

"That was weird," Giuliana said.

He couldn't speak, as every thought in his head realigned or receded for the new plan taking shape. In a deliberate set of movements, he returned to his chair across from Giuliana.

Her gaze flicked to his, flicked away. "Okay. Where were we?"

He'd been completely wrong altogether. Since she'd returned to Edenville, he'd been all about getting her back out of his life. What an idiot.

"So in four weeks . . ." Giuliana started.

She was serious. She believed she could make this all go away when she wanted it to—a month from now.

He almost laughed. Waiting until some specious four-weeks' promise came to pass was no longer acceptable—not when she could heat his blood with just a flick of her eyelashes and make him burn with just a brush of her fingertips. If he was going to get back to his normal, civilized self, their "situation" must be ended quickly—and his new strategy was designed for just that. It was clear, now.

He was going to force her hand.

5

On Thursdays, regional wineries, restaurants, farms, and other businesses set up booths in and around Edenville's town square. Tourists were a dependable staple in the summer, but Edenvillians were on hand, too, eager to see and be seen as well as sample wares, buy fresh produce, and catch up on the local gossip.

The weekly Market Day event morphed into Market Night as the afternoon's heat waned. Giuliana relieved the last of the interns in the Tanti Baci booth at five P.M. Her sisters were already on hand. When word had leaked a year ago about their winery's financial difficulties, the sisters had made it a point to spend time pouring the tastes of chardonnay and cabernet sauvignon themselves. "We need to project to the public financial stability and family unity," Allie always said.

At least they had the second going for them, Giuliana thought, as she wrapped an apron around her middle that matched the ones her sisters wore. For now, anyway. At month's end . . . she wasn't sure.

There was a lull in the booth's visitors, a brief respite, because if past experience held true, there'd be a rush around five thirty that wouldn't let up until full dark. She took a moment to breathe a lungful of fresh oxygen, a pleasure after being stuck in her office all day—and all night. During the hours between ten P.M. and six A.M. she was still trying to sleep on her lumpy and getting-shorter-by-the-day love seat.

She sucked in a second long breath. The temperature was in the pleasant seventies, but there was a second element to the wine country air that even her tired eyes could appreciate. Beneath the canopy of the spreading oaks and towering date palms that shaded the town square, the daylight had a golden quality. She swore she could taste it on her tongue, an almost buttery flavor that could be found in a glass of chardonnay.

Better get your fill of it now, she told herself.

Allie nudged her with an elbow. "Did somebody flush your goldfish?"

"What?" She made a face. "You know I don't have one."

"Well something's making you sad."

Giuliana had to smile at her little sister. The youngest Baci's irrepressible spirit made you forget sometimes she had alert eyes, too. "Just thinking that nothing lasts forever, does it? Not even . . . summer."

Stevie sauntered forward. "I thought maybe your mind was on a man."

"Kohl? He's back at the—"

"Not Kohl." Stevie rolled her eyes. "I never believed that could really work. I'm talking about Liam."

"Good God." Giuliana turned to the stack of glassware on the counter and picked one up by the stem to polish the bowl with a towel. "Has marriage riddled your brain with holes like Swiss cheese?"

"No. Though they say that forgetfulness is a symptom of pregnancy."

Pregnancy. Giuliana ignored a little twinge. "That's what's wrong with you then. You've forgotten how Liam and I don't get along."

"Nope. I'm remembering something," Stevie said, her expression smug.

Giuliana sighed. "Yeah? What's that?"

"How many people have stopped by the booth this afternoon asking about the intimate lunch they heard you and he had yesterday afternoon."

"There was no intimacy about it!" Except she could feel herself flushing as she remembered the stroke of his thumb across the top of her hand, the delicious squeeze of his legs around her naked calf. "It was two people eating lunch."

He'd fed her from his own fork. There *had* been an intimacy to that. She should have slapped his hand away or excused herself for the ladies' room or . . . But her strength had been sapped by his nearness. Her will had been mesmerized by his familiar blue eyes. Fine lines fanned from their corners now, reminding her they were no longer those impetuous kids. She wasn't an eighteen-year-old under the influence of hormones and passion; he'd matured, too, though she sensed those unreachable places that had so frustrated her then were even darker and more hidden now.

Stevie shrugged. "The way I heard it—from Eileen Brown, Scott McDougall, and Ed and Jed from the hardware store—is that you two looked like a romance rekindled."

"Oh, please." She returned her attention to the wineglasses. "I didn't see any of those people during lunch. They're all just repeating rumors."

"Natch," Allie said, bending to pick up a cardboard carton. "But they really started flying once Liam didn't refute them."

"*What?*" Her enjoyment of the summer afternoon was flying, too. Flying away.

Her youngest sister pulled open the flaps of the box and

stood on tiptoe to peer inside. “Yep. He was standing right there and didn’t say a word. If you ask me, he looked more than a little . . .” Her voice trailed off as she frowned and stuck her hand inside the box.

“Looked a little what?” Giuliana stomped closer as her sister didn’t answer. “A little what?”

Allie was still frowning.

“What have you got there?” Giuliana asked, distracted for the moment.

“I brought a few of the wedding wine ledgers to display,” she said. “I thought I grabbed four, but there’s five in the box. Oh, well, all the better to flog the legend.”

Those damn ledgers. That damn fable. “Allie . . . I thought we talked about this.”

Her sister didn’t even try to look guilty as she pulled a leather-bound volume from the box. “I’m a PR girl. It’s in my blood, okay?”

Giuliana watched as Allie drew out the books one by one. They were identical and legal-sized. As she knew, inside were ivory-colored lined pages that listed the bride and groom’s names, the location, and the date of their wedding. They’d bought them from the same source for the last fifty years and there were always a few on hand in case the latest one was filled . . . or lost.

Some sixth sense drew her attention from her sister and toward the crowded square. In the near distance she glimpsed a tall man, the lowering sun glinting off his dark gold hair. Her heart hiccupped, and she swore at the stupid thing as her skin seemed to tighten on her bones. He’d been right about one thing: there was still that attraction between them.

But not a romance! Why hadn’t he denied it? Surely he knew that his silence would only swell the fruit on the Edenville gossip vines, like the summer sunshine worked on the grapes in the local vineyards.

"What was his look?" she demanded from her little sister.

Her brows drawn together, Allie was turning the pages of one of the ledgers. "Huh?"

"You said he looked almost . . ." When her sister didn't answer, she snapped her fingers to get her attention. "Looked almost . . . ?"

"Smug," Stevie supplied.

Smug! Smugness only made it worse! Her gaze shot toward where she'd last seen the cool, arrogant, *smug* man who should be assuring the world she was the last woman he'd fix his interest upon. He was closer now, leaning against a lamppost and looking unforgivably handsome in a white polo and a beat-up pair of khakis. His bare feet were stuffed in battered, navy blue leather loafers.

Golden boy.

My parents wouldn't have approved.

Of course, it was no big shock that the Bennetts had considered her some number of notches below them on the social scale—it had been one of the trigger points of the Bennett-Baci feud for a hundred years, but it had stung to hear him say it aloud. To wonder if he'd considered her beneath him as well and that's why everything had ended so poorly.

Too bad, she thought, anger shooting up her spine. If that was his opinion, then he shouldn't be sauntering about town, *smug*, giving everyone in Edenville the impression that they had something going on again. She leapt over the counter, hearing wineglasses rattle in her wake.

Ignoring the sound, she stalked toward her prey.

He saw her, straightening from his elegant slouch. An expression flickered across his face, come and gone so fast that he was back to being maddeningly unreadable in one heartbeat. Except there was no mistaking the way he started toward her.

"You're ruining my June," she told him, when she was close enough. It was an important month. Maybe the most important month ever.

"How's that?"

She glanced around, hoping she wasn't doing just what she wanted to yell at him about—giving grist for the gossip mill. But the five-thirty crowd had arrived and the place was teeming with people who didn't seem to be paying the pair by the Tanti Baci booth any mind. In the distance, she could hear the faint sounds of classic rock. The chamber of commerce had hired a deejay to play on the far corner of the square.

She stepped closer so she didn't have to shout over the new sound. "The town is buzzing."

Cocking his head, he drew nearer. He leaned close to her. "What's that?"

"Town. Buzzing."

He shrugged without backing away. "It's always buzzing. You've just forgotten after ten years away."

His body was close enough that she could smell him. It used to be one of those nose-tickling boy-soaps that had seemed as foreign to her—with sisters only—as jockstraps. Now, as she'd been noticing for months, he smelled like sliced limes and laundered cotton. Common scents that on him seemed as sophisticated and pricey as the black luxury sedan he drove.

"I was happy in Southern California," she heard herself declare. "It wasn't ten years of misery. I dated."

His jaw tightened. "I dated, too. I had fun times."

Why did the idea of it make her eyes prick? "Good."

"It *is* good. We grew up, Jules. As adult as we thought we were then, we were really just kids. We weren't ready—"

"I was ready!" she said fiercely, her eyes stinging again.

He cupped her cheek with one of his large palms. She held still, determined not to lean into the touch. "All right," he said, ducking his head so his breath brushed her ear. "All right."

It wasn't all right. Not when the goose bumps were cascading down her neck and gathering around her nipples, so they tightened into their own hard points. She remembered the heat of his chest against them, the wet suction of his mouth covering them, the way his long fingers had plucked her there.

Do you like that?

How about like this?

What if I do that and *this?*

Two crazy, hormonal kids. The rich boy, confident in his place in the world. The passionate Italian girl, whose inhibitions fled the instant he unfastened the first button. Had her wild responses turned him off?

"I was so easy for you," she muttered.

He laughed, the sound low. "Nothing about you has ever been easy for me, Giuliana."

His thumb stroked her cheek and her body thrummed. Suddenly, she was aware that they were standing toe-to-toe, nose-to-nose, forehead-to-forehead. Yeah, just how to squelch those rumors. Frowning, she took a big step back, in the direction of the tasting booth.

Liam instantly took up the distance. She shook her head, retreated again. He followed.

"Stop," she said, as her back encountered the corner edge of the winery's booth. She was aware that Stevie and Allie were nearby, as well as a knot of people chatting and waiting to be served, but she didn't look at them. Her focus was trained on Liam.

His glance shifted right and again, for just a brief second, his expression shifted, too.

Curious, her gaze cut that same way. Hell. Allie's display had garnered attention, just as her sister had planned. People were poring over the wedding wine ledgers. She supposed it was mostly innocuous, but still . . .

"Jules." Liam caught her attention again. "I won't stop. Because this hasn't." He gestured between them, as if they could both see that invisible pull of wicked attraction that had years ago brought teenage Giuliana into his arms and into his bed.

Her temper flared. She wanted to stomp her foot, but she wasn't sixteen anymore. Or untouched by hard, harsh, heartbreak. "You have to," she said, her voice fierce again, though low enough for only Liam to hear. "You can't let people believe there's even a remote chance we'll get together again."

"Oh. My. God." A voice pierced the surrounding babble. Stevie, talking in tomboy tones. "Oh. My. God. Jules and Liam."

Giuliana's head whipped toward her sister, who was staring down at the page of one of the wedding wine ledgers. Any last enjoyment she might find in the day vanished. Aghast, she felt the chardonnay-gold air around her turn to molasses. It slowed time, movement, comprehension.

But soon enough, she understood.

Liam didn't try to dodge her accusing stare. The rat! He'd returned the missing book. "People don't need to believe we'll get together again . . ." he said.

Stevie, the brash Baci sister, spoke out in her loud voice. "Liam and Jules . . . they married!" There was a pause. "And are still married?"

Giuliana's husband's lips turned up in a wry smile. ". . . when now they'll know we never really broke up."

~

The whole tribe of them ambushed Giuliana in Allie's office at the winery early the next morning. She hadn't been hiding out, exactly, though her youngest sister usually didn't make it into the office before noon on Fridays. The real reason she'd changed locations was because she was so sick of working and sleeping in the fourteen by fourteen space that had her own nameplate on the desk. To be honest, though, she probably would have slipped away in avoidance of the confrontation if they hadn't caught her unawares.

Sometime around eight A.M., she'd dozed off on the stack of bills she'd brought in to peruse.

When Allie, Penn, Stevie, Jack, and Liam popped open the door, she popped up, embarrassingly aware that she'd been drooling on the envelope from the gas and electric company. Her sisters were gazing on her with consternation. Both brothers-in-law stared at the focal piece of furniture in the small room, wearing odd, bemused expressions.

She glanced between them as she straightened the Tanti Baci logo T-shirt she was wearing. "Uh, Penn? Jack?"

The second man shook himself, then shot his wife a quick, hungry look. His hand stroked a path down her bare arm. "Every time I come in here . . ." He shook his head again. "God, I love that desk."

Penn snorted with laughter, and Allie thwacked him on the arm. "Stop," the youngest Baci said, though there was a gleam in her eye, too. "You guys are terrible."

Her husband curled an arm around her neck and yanked her close enough to whisper in her ear. Allie went red in the face and gave him another halfhearted thwack. "Terrible," she muttered again.

Giuliana couldn't help but meet Liam's gaze. From his place behind the newlyweds, he pretended to hurl in the nearby wastebasket. It was so unlike the stiff, almost stuffy man he'd seemed to be the last year that he startled a laugh out of her.

The couples turned around with suspicion, but Liam was straight and straight-faced again. Giuliana laughed a second time.

At the sound, Allie spun back. "I'm glad someone's in a good mood. We were left a little flat-footed yesterday, Jules."

Her humor evaporated. After the big reveal at the

winery's booth, she'd refused to stick around for all the inevitable questions. Running hadn't solved anything, apparently—because when her glance found Liam's now, he shook his head. Clearly he'd avoided explaining, too.

Stevie laid out the facts. "The entry in the ledger that's just turned up indicates you and Liam married in Reno, Nevada, ten years ago last month."

"And we didn't even throw you an anniversary party," Allie added. Her voice held a slight edge. "The traditional gift is tin."

Sighing, Giuliana figured there was no way out of this now. "Look . . ." Then she stopped, deciding to strip it down to the most basic of truths.

"Eighteen," she said, touching her chest. "Stupid." Not just because of the secret wedding, but because they'd recorded it upon downing a purloined bottle of *blanc de blancs* post-ceremony. Then she pointed toward Liam. "Twenty. Not any smarter."

His usual deadpan expression didn't commit his opinion of her reasoning.

Allie couldn't leave it at that, though. "You tied the knot in spring, hied off to Tuscany in the summer, and by fall broke up—but then never bothered with the legal side of things?"

"You make it sound so . . . slapdash." She tried making light, though in her mind those months were the anchor she'd dragged behind her for the last decade.

"You don't do slapdash, Jules," Allie insisted. "Never in your life have you been reckless."

Probably not. In general, both she and Liam had been the responsible older siblings—whether dictated by nature or nurture, she didn't know. Maybe that had been the dangerous attraction of their youthful passion—the exciting lure of the imprudent.

Stevie took up the assessment of her character. "Yet to let it go all this long! Sure, you have a nasty temper and can hold a grudge longer than a vampire's lifetime, but . . . but . . ."

"Gee, thanks," Giuliana said, her voice dry. "Tell me what you really think."

Stevie took her up on the offer. "Well, I—"

"Could perhaps leave off the recriminations," Liam put in.

All at once, her sisters subsided. Giuliana thought she should be grateful for his intervention, but that nasty temper of hers kindled at the realization that no one was castigating *him*. "Just to be clear," she said. "I didn't force Liam to the altar. *He* asked *me*."

The assembled company swung to face the head of the Bennett family. Instead of hauling his ass over the coals, however, after one glance at his forbidding expression, they turned back to Giuliana.

"What are we going to do about it?" Allie asked.

The same thing she'd been planning to tackle at the end of the month. After years of them both letting the situation remain unresolved, she'd promised Liam at the restaurant that she'd finally deal with the issue of their youthful marriage in four-weeks' time. But now . . . She sighed. Now it couldn't wait even that long. And because her reasoning for putting it off in the first place wasn't something she actually understood herself, she just cut to the chase. "We'll immediately do what it takes to get a div—"

"Don't say divorce!" Allie's eyes rounded. "There can't be a divorce. At least not now. Not yet."

"Why?" Then Giuliana groaned as understanding dawned. "You told the papers, didn't you? You made calls . . . claims . . ." That ridiculous legend.

Her younger sister grimaced, guilt flashing over her face. "Well . . ."

Penn raised his eyebrows at his wife. "That's why you contacted the *Wedding Fever* people."

Jack was the only one who appeared perplexed as Giuliana groaned again. Stevie had to fill him in. "Popular TV show . . . remember I told you how they filmed Penn and Allie's ceremony last year?"

"They saved our bacon then," Allie said, sounding defensive. "They might just do it again."

Bacon with a side of rotten eggs, Giuliana thought, when all was said and done. She sighed. "Allie—"

"They loved the idea of the Vow-Over Weekend," her little sister said quickly. "C'mon, Jules. Don't we owe it to Papa to try our very hardest?"

To save the winery, she meant. They'd made that promise at his bedside and she'd honestly tried. Still . . . Yet looking into her sister's big brown eyes, it was impossible to refuse her. She sighed again, and clearly capitulation was written all over her face because Allie clapped her hands together.

Stevie, much more practical, cast a glance at Liam. "We've still got problems."

Allie shook her head, causing her waving hair to float around her shoulders. "Not when the Three Mouseketeers are on the job."

Giuliana almost smiled. When they were little girls, they'd put their Disney ears on their heads and tie their mother's aprons around their necks by the strings. Then they'd galloped around the house and through the vines, fighting imaginary enemies. Always standing with each other.

She could lose that. But not yet. Not quite yet. Her shoulders straightened. "What's worrying you, Steve?"

"You can't go on living here."

That wasn't good. But Honeymoon Central wasn't an option. And though she could go through the motions of searching for another apartment, it would waste time. Instead of saying that, she lifted the stack of bills and let them fall onto the desk. "At the moment, I'd rather save the money than pay for another place."

"You'll start walking crooked if you spend any more nights on your love seat," Penn pointed out.

Allie chimed in. "And you don't look so pretty with creases on your face after you fall asleep on top of the paperwork."

To seek out embarrassing wrinkles, Giuliana's hand went on a reconnaissance mission. "Where? Here?"

"You're fine," Liam said. "Beautiful."

Her hand dropped. She looked everywhere but at him as the word rolled over her heating skin. "Uh, okay."

"Good," Stevie said. "That was easy."

Giuliana's gaze flew to her middle sister's. "Not okay, I'll sleep somewhere else, but okay . . . okay . . ."

"Okay, Liam thinks you're beautiful," Stevie said, in a no-nonsense voice. "All the better for our purposes."

"I think she's beautiful, too," Jack put in, grinning at her. "Always have."

"Scary, but beautiful," Penn agreed.

She narrowed her eyes at her brothers-in-law. "Cut it out. You do that to embarrass me. Keep it up and you'll be the ones frustrated when I move into the farmhouse and insist we girls have sleepovers each and every night."

They didn't even appear worried, which should have worried *her.* Jack's grin widened. "I'm not concerned about the sleeping arrangements, *ma petite soeur.*"

"There's plenty of room at my house," Liam said.

No! After the fire, he'd made the offer. *Move in. We could finish this thing, Giuliana.* But if they were in such close proximity, who knew what she might risk?

Her palms were starting to sweat at the idea, though she tried keeping her expression serene and her voice out of the shrill range. "I couldn't intrude on you and Seth."

"My brother's in Monterey. Big work project, so he's staying there the next few weeks."

"Anyway, you have to intrude on Liam," Stevie said. "That's the whole point. We discussed it on the way over."

Allie was nodding. Penn and Jack wore faint smiles, indicating their approval.

"Please, you guys," Giuliana said. She loved them all, and might only have the chance to show it for a few more weeks, but this was too much!

"I told them you'd chicken out," Liam put in. His voice was cool, his manner unattached, as always.

Suddenly she wanted to slap that nonexpression expression off his face with the flat of her hand. "What's that supposed to mean?"

"Clearly, if we're going to postpone proceedings in order to keep the no-divorce legend going, we can't be estranged."

Panic clutched at her stomach. "We've been estranged! All this last year when we were both in Edenville and for nine years before that."

"But that can't be anymore. Surely you see that." He spoke to her as if she was a two-year-old.

"Surely you see that I can't just move in and . . . and . . ."

"Live with me? Be my wife?"

"I'm not going to be your wife!"

Liam crossed his arms over his chest. "Giuliana, you *are* my wife."

"The kind that will kill you while you lie in bed." She could see it now. "You heard them. They say that I have a nasty temper and hold a grudge for eternity. And you know me. Think! I might even do it without realizing it. I'll just rise up in the middle of the night and . . . and smother you with my pillow."

They were all staring at her as if she'd gone mad. So? The idea of being that close to Liam again *made* her mad.

Allie stepped forward. "Giuliana." Her voice was kind. "Nobody said you had to actually *sleep* with Liam."

Mortification rushed over her. "I knew that," she mumbled.

"For the good of the winery," Stevie reminded her, "all

you need to do is live under the same roof. Fake conjugal bliss for a few weeks."

As if it would be that easy. Good God. She'd started the day hoping to avoid her family and the fact that she was married, but now they weren't going to let her avoid her husband, either. She slumped in her seat.

Penn had this happy face that under normal circumstances Giuliana found charming. These weren't normal circumstances. "What do they call it?" He snapped his fingers. "I know, a marriage of convenience."

Giuliana slid lower in her chair. She didn't dare meet Liam's eyes, though she couldn't avoid his voice.

"Convenient," he said, and if she didn't know better she'd think he was laughing at her. "I like the sound of that."

6

Kohl dominated one corner of the bar at his favorite nothing-fancy watering hole on the outskirts of Edenville's small downtown. There were more than a few upscale tasting rooms and classy cocktail lounges attached to ritzy restaurants nearby, but the winegrowing business employed plenty of real workingmen and workingwomen who couldn't afford the cost of pricey liquor—even the fermented grape juice they worked their asses off to produce.

Ironic, that.

The world was just full of irony, he thought, his hand tightening on his shot glass. He tossed the contents back, and the tequila burned his throat as it went down.

A body slipped onto one of the empty stools on either side of him—the other patrons were smart enough to give him a wide berth. "Whatcha doing?" a familiar, female voice said.

He let his empty glass clack against the bar before drawing a second, full one closer. "Getting drunk. Avoiding company."

On his right, one of his sisters, the unsinkable Mari, didn't seem put off by his brusque tone. "You should have stayed home then."

Yeah. But he had this rule about drinking alone. He didn't do it, not since his last blackout. The way he figured it, a witness or two might curb his most destructive tendencies. Though tonight . . .

"I suppose you heard," Mari said.

About Jules and Liam. Still not looking at her, he grunted. "It makes me want to kill somebody."

A little gasp had him twitching. It wasn't Mari's gasp. His head whipped to the side and he saw Grace Hatch standing at his sister's elbow. "What the hell are you doing here?" he barked out.

Her big blue eyes rounded. Mari answered instead. "Friday night? Two girls out on the town? We're looking for a good time, Kohl."

He turned his stare on Mari. "And you're looking here? This place is too rough for the little rabbit," he said, indicating the other woman with his chin.

"That's why I'm leaving her with you," Mari said. "I just ran into Pat Rowan and he wants to take me to dinner."

Before he could tell his sneaky sister he wasn't the least interested in babysitting, she was off in a flurry of long corkscrew curls and Grace was taking her place. A faint scent of vanilla reminded him of her cinnamon freckles and her wholesome, boy-howdy features.

It only underscored how he was in no frame of mind to deal with a fresh-faced little girl. "You call a taxi, I'll pay to have it take you home."

Out of the corner of his eye, he saw her fingers lace on the bar top, the little rabbit as teacher's pet. "No, thank you," she said, her voice prim.

The bartender placed a glass of white wine on the napkin he set in front of her. With a swipe of his hand, he removed Kohl's empty shot glass and replaced it with a fresh tequila. Good man.

"Excuse me," Grace said. Though her voice was almost timid, it halted the guy on the other side of the bar. "We'd like to order some food."

Kohl stared at her. *We?* "I'm not hungry."

She acted as if she didn't hear him. "Potato skins, I think," she said. "And nachos and . . . some buffalo wings."

"Who the hell is going to eat all that?" he asked as the bartender hurried off.

Her big blues found his face. "You don't like buffalo wings? I could change the order to calamari . . ." She half rose.

"No." He put his hand on her shoulder, then jerked away as something hot sprinted up his arm and toward his chest. "I'm allergic to calamari," he mumbled.

She settled back on her stool. "Is that right? I get a weird rash from contact with the skin of mangoes—though I can eat the fruit."

"It's the urushiol in the skin—the same oil that causes people to react to poison oak and poison ivy. They're all part of the sumac family."

"Really?" She sipped from her wine. "Do mangoes do that to you, too?"

"No. I just learned all I could about poison oak after it gave me six weeks of hell in sixth grade."

Sympathy crossed her features. "On your face?"

"I wish." He snorted. "On my balls, and the surrounding environs."

A pink flush camouflaged all the pretty freckles. "Oh."

"Camping weekend in the mountains. The only thing worse than eating food from foil packets is eating food from foil packets someplace without an outhouse and where you have to use leaves as toilet paper."

She looked at her wine instead of at him. "I would have thought that Boy Scouts 101 covers dangerous plants."

"Kohlrabi Friday was no Boy Scout. My folks didn't have the money for scouting—and were suspicious of . . . what I'd guess you'd call institutionalized joining." They'd been really freaked when he'd enlisted—though youthful rebellion hadn't surprised two hippies who'd met at Woodstock.

"I always wanted to be a Brownie," Grace admitted. "All those pretty colored badges. A group to belong to."

The little confession dug a hole in his belly that he found himself filling once the food arrived between them. They were silent for a few minutes as they shared the appetizers. On Grace's other side, a woman he'd once had a good time with pawed through her purse. She was laughing too loud as she dumped out the contents and Kohl realized that her blouse was fastened with so few buttons that her big breasts were nearly exposed to the nipple line.

"Where the hell's my cell phone?" she asked her companion, another bosomy female. She looked fairly familiar, too. "Have you seen it?" As she shook her purse, a snake of foil-wrapped condoms fell atop the tissues, lipsticks, and breath mints.

An uncomfortable burn climbed Kohl's neck as he noticed Grace's big eyes were taking in the sight. He ignored the urge to blindfold her with his palms and tried redirecting her attention with a question. "Uh, um, do you have any hobbies?" Shit, he sucked at small talk.

Grace put one of her small hands on his forearm. "Excuse me just a moment." Then she turned back to the bawdy woman on her right. "Your desk. Could you have left it on your desk at work? Beside your keyboard."

The woman blinked. Clearly she was thinking back. "Why . . . why I . . . I think I did!" She stared at Grace from under sticky black lashes. "How did you know?"

The little rabbit shrugged. "Just a good guess." Then she picked up another potato skin and smiled at Kohl. "Hobbies, you were saying?"

"Yeah." He glanced over her head to the neighboring lady—Dawn, he remembered was her name. She was still gazing on his companion in bemusement.

"Do you, uh, sew? Cook? Grow vegetables?" he asked Grace.

"Well, I've done all of those, but I think those fall more under activity than amusement." She smiled self-consciously and he found himself hypnotized by the puffy pinkness of her mouth. "I've always wanted to sing, though."

Dawn leaned over her shoulder. "Then you have to sign up tonight! For karaoke. As a matter of fact, you can have my spot—I'm going second. As a thank-you for nudging my memory."

Kohl almost groaned. That's how deep his bad mood was—he'd been so immersed in it he'd forgotten to avoid this particular joint on this particular night. Fridays and Tuesdays were karaoke. He looked behind him, and sure enough, in the far corner of the tiny dance floor, a guy was setting up the equipment, which included a squat portable stage.

Grace glanced at Dawn, shaking her head even though her eyes lit up. "Oh. Oh, I couldn't take your spot. Thank you so much for the offer, though."

Another groan welled up inside him. He hated karaoke, but with Grace wearing that expression—like a girl offered a turn as queen of the Brownies, which included a handful of merit badges—he couldn't very well run them both out of here before the music started. He edged her wineglass toward her hand.

"Take the offer, honey."

Her head whipped toward him. Pink cheeks, those blue eyes startled. He remembered her memory of him calling her "honey" when she was a little girl. Were casual endearments so few and far between for her? Another hole dug itself in his belly. He glanced at the waiting shot of tequila but ignored it in favor of shoveling another potato skin into his mouth.

"Do you think I should really try it?" she whispered.

No. "Yes." Already the first singer of the night was approaching the stage. "You'd better get on over there. I think you have to look through the songbook and choose your piece."

At that, she appeared more abandoned than the damn mangy dog of hers that he'd stolen away. With a sigh, he slid off his stool. "Come on," he said, holding out his hand for hers.

She stared at his open palm. Then, like the rabbit was expecting a trap, she slowly, slowly, extended her own hand. Before it even touched down, he grasped her securely.

Her fingers quivered.

Something deep inside him did, too.

Clenching his teeth, he ignored all that and led her toward the karaoke area. The songs listing was in a fat binder set atop an elbow-high bar table. She turned the stained pages gingerly, as if touching them more fully might commit her fully as well.

But Kohl found himself determined to have her go through with it. How much pleasure had she had in her life? While the Friday household couldn't afford luxuries, and living down the name Kohlrabi with sisters dubbed Marigold and Zinnia had held its own challenges, there'd been more love than lumps.

The striking fists had been his own.

Truth to tell, now that he thought of what she'd endured at the hands of her father and former husband, he felt a little ashamed of his careless brawling habits.

"Pick a song," he urged.

She bit her lip. "What if I'm terrible?"

He fully expected it. Ninety-nine point nine percent of people he'd ever heard grab the mike and belt one out *were* terrible, except they didn't know it. It was why he avoided this particular night at this particular joint.

"Just have fun." And he'd force himself to applaud, though he suspected that she'd set the dogs in town wailing when she chose one of those songs that all the girls did, like Celine Dion's "My Heart Will Go On" or Carrie Underwood's "Before He Cheats" or anything by Kelly Clarkson. *That* would send the cats screeching, too.

"I don't know . . ." She was gnawing on her pouty pink bottom lip.

He couldn't watch. The first singer was starting his turn. Kohl winced as he launched into something by the Boss. When it came to guys, it was always the Boss. Grace was still dithering over the list. "Just close your eyes and point to one," he suggested to her.

Hell, he thought she just might have followed his advice. But his mind wasn't working too well because she shuffled to the side, relinquishing the song book to another patron, and now was clutching his forearm to bring him with her. She was hanging on to him like a starfish glued to a rock.

He was just that hard with her hand on him.

The wannabe Boss wound down. There was clapping. Grace's hand tightened on him so that he was forced to pry her fingers loose. "Your turn," he said against her ear.

When she turned those big, nervous blue eyes on him, he was sunk. "Good luck," he said, and kissed that perfect, plump mouth.

He might have still been kissing it if the master of ceremonies hadn't shoved the microphone between them. Grace's fingers curled around it, and, face dazed, she climbed onto the platform.

Kohl's heart was pounding. He figured it would go with what his head was going to be feeling any second. Cindi Lauper's "Girls Just Wanna Have Fun," he bet. Look attentive and encouraging anyway, he reminded himself.

Then the music started and there was pounding, yes. From the beat. The rap beat.

Grace was singing "Baby Got Back." No, she was rapping. That Sir Mix-a-Lot song. Good God. And her own "back" was shaking, her booty going from side to side, keeping up with the beat. For the first time he realized she was wearing a pair of tight jeans.

The little rabbit had a cute, heart-shaped ass.

And she was getting into the song, in just the right kind of way, stumbling a little sometimes as the words rolled by on the screen, but obviously having fun. So everyone else did, too. Her joy moved through the crowd until the people in the audience were wiggling their hips or nodding their heads, their gazes glued to Grace Hatch, scruffy little nobody from the 'hood.

The crowd cheered when it was over.

She fist-pumped the air, relinquished the mike, then leapt off the stage, grinning like a seven-year-old. "Well?"

Well . . . He just laughed. "Grace . . ." Shaking his head, he laughed again.

Her grin didn't die. "I've never seen you do that," she said. "I've never heard you laugh."

So he did it again. For her. All the while realizing that though he'd been tasked with taking care of her, it hadn't gone that way at all. Shy Grace Hatch had fed him. She'd made him talk. She'd made him laugh. She'd pulled him out of his sour mood.

The only hangover he suspected he'd have tomorrow was the memory of that startling, might-be-addictive kiss.

~

Kohl ushered Grace back to their stools at the bar. Dawn and her friend gushed over the performance and he bought the ladies a round of drinks. Nice ladies, he thought, ashamed again, but this time of his earlier censure. He realized he was smiling, wide enough to hurt cheek muscles that were unused to such an action. Damn, but he was still under the influence of a drug he didn't recognize—almost a kind of . . . happiness.

Grace's high spirits were contagious. The bartender was grinning, too. Who was Kohl to release the helium from their collective balloon?

"This may be the best night of my life!" she said.

Prepared to follow with some sort of agreeable remark, he was surprised when her delighted expression collapsed. Her hand squeezed his forearm again. "I wasn't thinking. I'm so sorry."

Sorry? Who died? His brows drew together.

"Liam and Giuliana."

He tensed. "Do we have to go there?"

Her gaze met his, eyes serious. "You don't really want to kill either one of them, do you?"

It shamed him, that she had to ask. "I was a soldier, true, but what I do now . . . I'm a farmer."

She blinked.

"Babe, I'm the vineyard manager at Tanti Baci. I'm in charge of the vines, the grapes. It might as well be carrots or cauliflower. Anyone who says differently has bought into the mystique . . . and lost the best part of what we do. I'm in charge of a crop." It was so simple—and he was a simple man. Dressing it up with artistic labels and deciding on price tags was someone else's job. His was watching over the land and its product.

She still appeared worried. "Kohl . . ."

He surprised himself by how much he wanted to reassure her. "It means I grow things now . . . not damage them. And if there's anyone I'm angry at, it's me. Jules and Liam . . . they've had a thing for years. I should have seen it."

Her boy-howdy face, her sweet freckles, her laser eyes presented such an arresting package that he found himself staring at her, his thoughts freezing on one truth. *I've scared her. She actually believes I might hurt Jules or Liam.*

So much for hero worship.

He moved slowly so as not to frighten her. "I should take you home now."

"Maybe so."

He wouldn't let her see the pain that caused, not when he didn't understand it himself.

Before they could move away from their seats, the bartender placed a flute of sparkling wine in front of Grace. Only in the Napa Valley, he thought. There was a burger drive-thru in St. Helena that served nothing more sophisticated than burgers and onion rings but also offered dozens of different wines by the glass, half bottle, and bottle. Even the bubbly kind, like was in Grace's glass. It shouldn't surprise him that you could get something like that here, too.

But they hadn't ordered it. "That's not ours," he said.

"It's hers," the barman answered, indicating Grace with a nod. "Compliments of the guy at the other end of the bar. He said he knows firsthand that baby's got back."

Cold steel replaced Kohl's spine. Shit. His gaze cut right even as he leaned closer to Grace. She was staring in the same direction.

A guy was watching them from twenty feet away. Military cut. Muscles. "Who the hell is that?" Kohl could flatten him in twenty seconds. Kohl wanted to flatten him in ten.

"Daniel." The syllables came out clipped, as if her tongue was dry. "My ex."

Kohl was on his feet. He didn't remember standing, but he was ready to attack. Only the trembling he felt in Grace's body stopped him. He couldn't leave her when she was shaking like an E-1 private facing his first firefight.

Then it was Daniel's move. The SOB was sauntering

down the line of the bar, ignoring the chattering around him. His gaze was focused on Grace.

If she was a leaf on a tree in the wind before, now there was a hurricane blowing through. Kohl held himself still, his hand on her shoulder, but trying to do nothing that would contribute to her anxiety. "He'll have to go through me, honey," he assured her. "You're safe."

Daniel wasn't, as far as Kohl was concerned. Especially when the asshole stopped in front of his ex, an ugly smile on his face. "Hello. I didn't know you could sing, sugar."

Kohl ground his back teeth together. Sugar. No way could her ex appreciate how sweet Grace was. "You didn't give her anything to sing about. Now move along."

The other man's drawl deepened. "I'm just giving the lady a compliment."

It looked like a threat to Kohl, and it made him nuts. He dropped his hand from Grace's shoulder. His fingers curled into fists. "Let's take this outside."

Grace sucked in air. It nearly halted him.

But the primal part of him was firing his blood. He stepped toward Daniel, leaving just inches between their beating hearts. "You're going to leave her alone."

Daniel didn't flinch. "You've got it all wrong." He looked around Kohl and gave Grace another of his chilling smiles. "See you, sugar." Then he pursed his mouth in a kiss . . . and strode away.

Kohl was on his heels, but Grace caught his elbow. "No. Don't."

Nothing could stop him. He wrenched from her, familiar rage burning his skin. Again he felt like the Hulk, muscles going rocky, features turning to granite. He could be green for all he knew.

Then she recaptured his arm. He paused, glancing back. Her eyes were an impossible blue, brightened by a sheen of emotion. Shit.

"Stay with me," she said. "Be with me."

She shouldn't ask it of him, damn it. Sure he'd claimed to be a farmer, and he was trying to be a good one, but that wasn't the same as being a guardian—or a peacemaker. Still, he was stymied.

She'd fed him. Made him talk and laugh. Lifted him out of the mood that the news about Jules and Liam had left him in. And then plunged him into a thornier place.

"I'm no hero," he muttered, sliding onto the stool beside hers. His hands ran through his hair as he took several deep breaths. He could manage containing himself . . . for now. "Don't ever believe I'm any good."

~

As the sun set, satisfaction, and an odd sense of relief, twined within Liam as he drove Giuliana toward his home. She was silent in the passenger seat of his Mercedes, and at her feet sat three grocery bags stamped with the Edenville Market logo, containing a few items of clothing and a smattering of toiletries. Her gaze was trained on the house they approached via the long drive delineated by three-foot-high walls built of locally quarried rock and mortar.

He looked at it through her eyes. It was a showplace to be sure, built by his grandfather and Tuscan-inspired. The Bennetts had always held a fascination for all things Italian, despite, or because of, the ongoing feud with the Bacis. His mother had never cared for it, though, and once his father died she'd wasted no time vacating to colder climes and happier memories in her native upstate New York.

Liam, on the other hand, couldn't imagine living anywhere else. The estate property was nestled against a knoll covered with darkly green firs, the trees providing a contrast with the exterior stucco walls colored the shade of caramelized butter. Arched doorways on the second floor opened onto Juliet-styled balconies. A third-floor square-topped tower drew the eye up, then down to the front door that was a massive breadth of aged, distressed wood. Rather than pulling around to the garages located beyond the house, Liam parked the car in front of the shallow entrance steps.

The slowness with which Giuliana gathered her things made clear she was dawdling. He would have offered to bring in her "luggage," but that would have pointed up how meager were her possessions. Tomorrow, he'd take her shopping, even if he had to kidnap her to make it happen.

He led the way to the porch. She'd been there before—though not often—as their courtship had been carried out beyond prying parental eyes. She hesitated as he pushed on the front door.

It hit him then. A memory of that weekend they'd slipped away to Reno. He'd booked a suite at a nice hotel, and with their marriage certificate in hand, they'd returned to Room 2292. He could see the number in his mind's eye, and then the delight breaking over her face as he swung her up in his arms and carried her over the threshold.

It almost hurt to think of it. How young they'd been! How foolishly certain they could overcome each and every obstacle. It was why they'd entered their names in the wedding wine ledger upon their return to Edenville. Giuliana had written the words with a flourish that gave away their exuberant sense of optimism.

He wondered what it said about him that within hours of her recording the information that he'd removed the ledger and hidden it away. Postponing the inevitable explosion, he'd thought then. Now he supposed it bore witness to his innate pessimism. He hadn't realized it yet, but his father had already done permanent damage to Liam's belief in his ability to be a happy-ever-after husband.

Secrets and memories.

"Second thoughts?" Giuliana asked him now, one brow cocked.

"Not a chance." He made to cup her elbow and usher her in, but she stepped away from his touch and into his house.

Again, that odd relief. It went through him like a sigh as he shut the door behind them.

The round foyer table held an antique ceramic footbath filled with flowers: Peruvian lilies, Queen Anne's Lace, some other fat flower that he couldn't name. The floral touch embarrassed him a little. "We have a housekeeper. She likes to make sure we don't let the place degenerate into a clichéd bachelor pad."

"I know Charlene," she said, her voice cool. "She was a friend of my mother's." *You overprivileged snob,* her expression added.

"Oh? I dated her daughter last year." *To hell with your assumptions,* he shot back.

A silence strung out between them. He finally reminded himself this was his own idea, and shook off his irritation. Hoping he appeared more composed than he felt, he lifted his hand. "There's a guest room ready for you up the stairs."

The second-floor gallery was suspended by columns and could be reached by a spiraling staircase on either end. He moved up the nearest set of steps, listening to the rattle of her grocery bags behind him. When he pushed open the bedroom door, this time he was glad to see more flowers in a vase on the dresser top. Charlene had remembered the mix of pink and purple dendrobium orchids that he'd requested.

Giuliana slowly crossed the room, wearing that short full skirt he'd seen before as well as a skimpy T-shirt that read "You Had Me at Merlot." A wrought-iron, four-poster bed was on her right, a pale pink spread covering its wide surface. Four high windows let in the last of the afternoon light. But she moved with purpose toward the arrangement. She dropped the grocery bags at her feet and then reached out to stroke one curled petal with a fingertip.

"What are you doing, Liam?" Her gaze didn't get anywhere near his.

His motivations were snarled, he had to admit. After the fire, he'd wanted her close, under his roof, compelled to know she had a chance to eat and sleep like a normal person. There'd also been the fear that without a close eye on her, she'd up and go again someday, leaving their situation forever unresolved.

And then there was the hellish, unrelenting attraction that unsettled him, unbalanced him, *obsessed* him, every time he saw her.

Every time he thought about her.

Part of his Plan B was the idea that in close proximity it might . . . go away.

Oh, who was he kidding? He'd wondered if they might do whatever it was necessary to burn the damn feeling out.

Hence the orchids. He had filled their honeymoon suite with them in Reno, telling her their pink to plum shades brought to mind the color of her soft mouth.

On a slow turn, she faced him and she saw right through him, he could tell. "You're not playing fair, Liam." Her voice caught, and she looked away. "I'm not a robot."

No, that's what she'd been calling him for months, when he would have given half his vineyards to turn android, instead of being tortured by the swing of her dark hair, the flash of her brown eyes, the tender wetness of her lush lips.

The plush area rug covering the slate floor absorbed the sound of his footsteps as he neared her. The fringe of her lashes hid her expression from him. He tucked his hand under her chin and lifted her face toward his.

"Really, Liam? Orchids?" She folded her arms over her chest, pretending his touch didn't faze her.

But he could see her pulse raising as the blood beat against the tender skin of her neck. Hot emotion filled him as he stared into her big eyes. They were tilted at their outside corners, giving her face an unforgettable, exotic edge. He let his hand trail down her throat.

She swallowed against his palm. “I'm telling you,” she said, her voicc trailing to a whisper. “This isn't fair.”

And since he could only agree, he lowered his lips to kiss away the complaint.

7

Giuliana should duck his mouth. She knew that. But avoidance of Liam hadn't helped her so far. As time slowed while his head drew closer, her heart pounded harder, trying to break out of her chest.

That's what she wanted to do to him. Break the man. Find equal footing by shattering the maddening self-possession of the husband who was gazing down at her with those so-cool eyes.

But his kiss was hot. So hot.

At the first touch of his lips, her knees melted. She grabbed hold of the dresser top behind her to keep herself upright—and to keep herself from holding on to Liam. She'd never been any good at that.

Her stance pushed her breasts forward, but he kept a decent distance between their bodies. *Still so damn detached,* she thought, woozy with desire as his mouth brushed hers again. *Too light, too light, too light.* Swallowing back a moan, she dug her fingernails into the dresser's sleek wood.

His tongue touched her bottom lip. Stupid tears burning

her eyes, she submitted to the pressure, opening her mouth so he could slide inside. There was no insistence in the move. No coaxing, either. Just: *I'm here; I want in.*

Like he had the right. Like they belonged together.

If it went on like this—Liam controlling, Giuliana yielding—the one to break would be her. But she stayed paralyzed, the beat of her heart doubling and then her blood burning through her veins as he stroked against her tongue. Oh, God. Her breasts swelled; there was an aching emptiness between her thighs. She had to find a way to redistribute the power and survive the need.

Flushed with desire, she went on tiptoe to make the mouth-to-mouth fit tighter. She felt Liam stiffen. And then she knew what to do: *Give in to passion,* a voice inside her whispered. *Give in to passion instead of giving in to him.*

One by one, her fingers released their hold on the wood. Though their mouths were tightly joined now, he was still controlling the kiss, his tongue making sure but measured strokes inside her mouth. Heat was pouring from her flesh and her nipples tightened to even harder points.

Wrapping her arms around his neck, she moved in to rub them against his chest.

He jerked, but she didn't let him disengage. Instead, she pressed closer, reveling in the hard planes of his body along the soft curves of hers. He was aroused, his erection thick and long against her belly. As she pushed her hips forward, his hand speared through her hair to change the angle of the kiss.

His tongue drove harder into her mouth. She writhed against him as he thrust his thigh between her legs. Denim rode against her bare skin and then pressed upward, providing both sweet relief and exquisite torture to the pulsing flesh behind the thin fabric of her panties.

He stepped into her, forcing her backward until the small of her back met the lip of the dresser. She slung a leg around the back of one of his, allowing the most sensitive part of her to more fully meet his uncompromising muscle. Liam grunted, a primitive sound of pleasure, and she sucked on his tongue, thrilled by it.

His hand, hot, hard, crawled along the side of her leg, taking the hem of her short summer skirt with it. His fingers slid under her panties to palm her bottom and his mouth moved, too, breaking free for a breath and then running along her cheek to her ear.

"What are you up to?" he muttered, then bit her lobe.

At the small sting, she bowed into his body. Her clitoris stroked his firm leg. "No good," she whispered. Because she wasn't going to be that—good, subdued, careful—she was going to please herself by letting go and taking him, by hell, along with her. Still riding the sweet, unsatisfying pressure of his thigh, she shifted one hand to the front of his button-down shirt. Blind to anything but the roar of greedy need in her blood, she undid it by touch, her fingertips rasping against his bare skin as she found the next fastening.

His breath was ragged in her ear. *Yes.* When she parted the fabric, she placed her mouth against the slamming beat of his heart at the center of his chest then slid her mouth across to his pointed nipple. With the flat of her tongue, she stroked across it, his groan making the tips of her own breasts tingle.

"Stop," he commanded, his fingers tightening in her hair. He yanked her head back to press his mouth fiercely to hers. Refusing to be distracted, she thumbed the damp protruding nub and then trailed her hand to the button of his jeans.

"Stop," he said once more, his mouth still against hers.

But he wasn't in charge here. Passion was running the show and it was telling her to expose him. Touch him. Take him.

She did that, popping the metal button, finding the zipper's tab, then sliding beneath his boxers to wrap her fingers around his heavy shaft. He dropped one hand to grab at hers, but she ignored the protest and stroked, her palm sliding from the silky head to the thick base.

"Giuliana." His voice was tight. "You don't know what you're doing."

Oh, please. She'd first touched him like this when she was seventeen years old, his breath loud in the confines of his car, her own caught somewhere between her heart and her throat. She'd loved the smooth and strong heat of him against her palm, she'd loved the certainty that she could make him shudder.

"Now is not the time," he muttered, his hand trying once again to brush hers away.

She tightened her hold, and he groaned again. His thigh pushed harder between her legs and she stifled her own sound of passion by leaning into his chest again and fastening her mouth on the rise of his pectoral. As she sucked there, he jerked and his erection leapt in her grip.

In the distance, she heard bells. Ignoring the non sequitur of a sound, she shortened her strokes on his flesh, sucked harder on his chest, rubbed at the ache between her legs by using the strong column of his thigh. More bells. More strokes.

"Hell!" Liam broke away from her. His hands refastened his jeans in a blink, then pushed through his hair. "Didn't you hear the doorbell?" he ground out.

She was staring at his heaving chest, revealed by the open shirt. No, she was staring at the mark her mouth had made on him. "Oops," she said. Liam Bennett. With a hickey.

He glanced down. When he looked back up there was a burn of color riding his high cheekbones. "I'm getting the door." He brushed past her.

She trailed at a safe distance. When he reached the foyer, he glanced over his shoulder and caught her leaning against a wall, her gaze on him. The look he gave her couldn't be any less cool. If she hadn't yet shattered him, she'd at least fractured his unflappable reserve.

Smirking a little, she wiggled her fingers in a little wave. Hah. Now who had the upper hand?

He pulled open the door. A familiar foursome—her sisters and their spouses—stood on the other side, their arms full of groceries. "Hey, there." Stevie saluted them with a baguette.

A new flush tumbled down Giuliana's skin and she straightened. "What . . ." She had to clear her throat while she tugged on the end of her skirt. Was everything in place? At least Liam had half done-up his shirt. "What are you doing here?"

"Dinner." Allie traipsed inside first, the rest of them trailing. "Liam didn't tell you? He invited us to a potluck."

Their noisy takeover of the kitchen covered a multitude of almost-sins. She managed to hustle back to the room she'd been assigned, where she ran a comb through her hair and ensured that her clothes were not askew. The battle between herself and Liam should be a private one.

As head of the Baci family, she had to ensure her sisters knew she was capable of making clear and cogent decisions. They might misconstrue the fiery interlude she'd just shared with him as something showing poor judgment rather than a logical and self-protective attempt to knock away his hard shell and prove that he was human. She had to prove to them both that he didn't hold all the power.

On her way back down the stairs, she glimpsed Liam and Penn on a side patio, hovering around a twenty-second-century barbecue. It had enough dials and burners and grates to fly an entire side of beef to the moon.

She drifted toward the half-open door, amused despite herself by their identical fascination with the piece of cooking equipment. They were so alike in looks and other ways—and then so not. While Penn approached the world with the happy smile of a man with his fingertips on the brass ring, Liam was the kind who sat back on his carousel horse and eyed the prize from a distance, coldly calculating whether the bright piece of metal was worth his time and effort.

Whether it had true value.

Just as she was about to move on, their voices reached her. "I met a woman," Penn said. He was practicing with a pair of long, shiny tongs, closing and opening them.

Liam stiffened, then shot his half brother a glance. "Allie's like a sister to me," he warned.

Giuliana stared at Liam, noticing that Penn did, too. Her Hollywood-handsome brother-in-law was devoted to his wife, and it startled her that Liam seemed to doubt that so easily.

It seemed to jolt Penn, too. "What conclusion are you jumping to?" he demanded of the half brother just a few months older than him. "I could be talking about a bank teller. A TV producer. That crone who keeps trying to give me parking tickets around the town square. She loiters by my truck, you know. I've a mind to call the cops."

"*She's* a cop. Sort of. Sharon Lightwell's been Edenville's traffic enforcement officer for forty-seven years. I bet she just wants to meet you, Penn."

He shifted his shoulders. "She wants more than to meet me. Every time I get near her, she starts unbuttoning her uniform blouse."

Giuliana smothered her laugh. Upon spotting Penn, his fans had an interesting habit of shouting "Build me up!" after the name of his show, then throwing off their shirts in exchange for one of his program's logo tees. He carried a stack of them wherever he went, but since his marriage, he'd taken painstaking care to avert his gaze from any half-dressed female forms.

"In any case," Penn grumbled, "I'm not the least bit interested in any woman *but* my wife."

"Fine," Liam said.

Giuliana almost moved on then, but there was something in the silence stretching between the two men that fixed her feet to the floor.

"But, uh," Penn started. He snapped the tongs a few times as if trying to capture his next words.

"'But, uh'?"

"Does the name Erin Bell mean anything to you?"

Liam froze. "Why did she speak to you?"

"Met her at some tasting room in town. Alessandra introduced us."

"Steer clear." His jaw was hard. A muscle ticked in his cheek.

"I think I already plowed into the garbage. Dear old dad . . . ?"

Liam didn't look at his half brother. The man who'd fathered them, Calvin Bennett, had been considered an upstanding citizen until his death when his will had revealed he'd fathered two illegitimate children from separate relationships outside his marriage. "Why would you say that?"

"Because you look like you're about to explode," Penn said quietly.

And he did. Giuliana's eyes widened. The distant, self-contained man that Liam had become—something she'd first had glimpses of when they were young—was vibrating with suppressed emotion. Fury, she thought. Or maybe disgust.

"She said she was a real good friend of your mother's," the Hollywood star continued.

When Liam didn't answer, he spoke again. "You can talk to me," Penn said. "You're my brother. Let me help."

"Then track down the others and get on with dinner. That's why I asked you guys here."

"You asked us to come over and ease the transition for Jules. Make her comfortable."

"Yeah. So make her smile then, damn it," Liam said. "And pour enough wine down her throat and insist she fork enough food into her belly that she finally gets a good night's rest. She'll resist me if I push, but her sisters, and you and Jack, can make that happen."

Oh. Now *she* was a little rattled. Her family was here because Liam was worried about her. Because he wanted to take care of her. She heard it in his voice. Saw it in the look he shot his half brother.

"Okay," Penn said. "But about this Erin Bell—"

"Don't mention her name to me again." He started striding for the door she was lurking beside, so she had to hurriedly draw back, taking refuge behind the half-closed door of a powder room.

She saw Liam's taut expression as he passed her hiding place, and the view of this new side of him pierced the middle of her chest. Calvin Bennett's nasty past punctured some place in Liam just as deep. Wrapping her arms around herself, she closed her eyes. This was something she hadn't considered in her bid to equalize their relationship and melt his chill.

If she was around him when his brittle composure broke, then she could become dangerously close to him again.

~

The morning after her first night in Liam's house, Giuliana awoke rested. As she'd prepared for sleep she'd also braced herself with the knowledge that a strange bed might keep her awake, but the mattress was so much more comfortable than the short couch in her office that her eyes had closed almost immediately.

The kisses and caresses of the evening before had not even interrupted her seven hours of unconsciousness. Probably because she and Liam had retreated to their own rooms shortly after her family had departed. Clearly, they'd both been keen on keeping to their separate corners of the big house.

She had no idea where he slept, actually, and jumped when she stepped into the kitchen and found him at the table with a mug and the newspaper. His hair was damp and he was in jeans, work boots, and a black T-shirt.

"It's early." Flushing, she pushed her hair behind her ears and tugged on the hem of her denim shorts. Her agenda for the day contained nothing more formal than continuing to clear out obsolete files and sorting through the detritus in her jam-packed office closet.

"I work for a living, too," he said, the briefest expression of annoyance crossing his face. "You'll have to make your own coffee. Charlene only works Monday, Wednesdays, and Fridays."

Thank goodness for small favors. She hadn't even considered confronting the housekeeper. "We'll have to explain to her . . ."

Liam lifted a brow.

To avoid the look, she hurried toward an espresso machine that appeared as if it had the capacity to teleport freshly roasted beans from Ethiopia. Clearly Liam had a thing for state-of-the-future appliances. She just stared at it.

A moment later she heard the rattle of newsprint, the scrape of chair legs on slate, a man's footsteps. Her gaze took in the competency of Liam's long fingers as he brewed her a drink. A latté, her morning beverage of choice.

She accepted it, then listened to him return to his seat. "This is how we'll work it, okay?" The words burst from her mouth. "You do your thing, and I'll do mine."

"Sure," he said, his voice dry. "But let's note you made that edict *after* I made your coffee."

Her cheeks warmed. "Well." The rubber of her cheap thongs flapped against the soles of her bare feet as she crossed to the window over the sink, taking the long way around him. Her big idea to indulge in passion with him yesterday now seemed like just a big, *dumb* idea. "You do your thing, and I'll do mine," she repeated.

He made a noncommittal noise, and it hit her, hard, that she hadn't shared an early morning with him since those love-drenched days in Tuscany. Her heart squeezed and she slid her latté onto the countertop. "I'm off to Tanti Baci."

"You should eat. There's fruit, toast, eggs, yogurt. Everything."

"I ate too much last night." With her sisters and Penn and Jack as buffers between her and Liam, her nerves had quieted enough for her to feel her appetite. Allie had made a simple but filling pasta dish they'd eaten with chicken breasts and halved zucchinis straight off that fancy grill.

"I'll see you, uh, later." She wasn't accustomed to accounting for her days any more than she was used to playing wife to a husband.

But it wasn't going to be like that! He'd agreed. *He'll go his way and I'll go mine.*

His chair legs scraped again. "I'll grab my car keys."

"No!" She quieted her voice. "I mean, I appreciate the offer, but I'll take the shortcut."

The one that had brought him to her when they were young and impetuous with passion. Despite those wild moments yesterday, she knew better now. She wouldn't make the mistake of kissing Liam again. Long ago she'd given up on counting on him.

The early-morning air was bracing and she sucked in lungfuls of it as she set out for the winery. The day's high would hit around eighty, but it started cool, an essential piece of the magic that made Napa wine. Of course, it wasn't magic at all, she thought, as in the distance she saw workers moving through the Bennett vines.

As she passed the end of one row, she paused to lean down and inhale the scent of a deep red rose on the bush growing there. Winegrowing lore said rosebushes were planted to serve as early-warning indicators of sickness in the vines. They supposedly were also a leftover tradition from the days when horse-drawn plows worked the vineyards—the thorns encouraged the beasts to make wide turns and thus reduce the potential damage to the stakes and wires that supported the rows. Neither was necessary any longer.

Now they had other ways to assess the health of the grapes, and four-legged beasts didn't work the land any longer. Some vineyards still cultivated roses, but as Tanti Baci did, for decorative purposes on the rows that lined the winery entrance drive and those that faced the tasting facilities. Apropos to their interest in weddings, the Tanti Baci roses were white. However, the Bennett vineyards, for as long as she could remember, had these same bleeding heart–colored flowers at both ends of each row planted on every acre they owned in the Napa Valley.

With the scent still in her nose, she found her feet on the gravel surface that led to the caves of her family's winery. It was a half mile more to her office from here, and the morning was still. No one was about on the Baci property. Her sisters and brothers-in-law would still be tucked in their beds at the farmhouse that was a quarter mile beyond the administrative offices that still lay ahead.

A breeze brushed across her and she shivered. She rubbed her palms against her bare upper arms, wishing she'd thought to wear a sweatshirt for the trek. But even as the goose bumps on her flesh subsided with the breeze, a new, sudden chill raised the hairs on the back of her neck.

Giuliana's stride hitched. She lifted her chin, and glanced around, seeing nothing unusual.

No one.

But there was a flock of metaphorical geese and they were doing a determined square dance on her grave. Telling herself she was silly, she took another step forward.

And then something whispered in her ear. Intuition, fear, impulse. *Someone is lying in wait*, it said. *Go, go, go!* The family farmhouse was still far ahead. The closest safety was the way she'd come. Her thongs kicked up gravel as she turned and ran.

She was out of breath when she let herself into the Bennett kitchen via the back door. With it closed behind her, she bent at the waist and placed her hands on her knees to catch her breath. Better rejoin the Y, she thought. Sign up for more kickboxing and self-defense classes.

"What's going on?"

Hell. She froze. Liam was still here.

Trying to appear casual, she straightened. Not for a king's fortune would she tell him she'd spooked herself and then come running his way like a scared little girl.

He was standing by the espresso machine. She gestured at it, hoping to distract him from what surely must be her red face and wheezing lungs. "I decided I needed a second cup of"—she had to stop to take in a breath—"coffee."

His eyes narrowed. "You'll have to do better than that. I can hear your heart thrumming as fast as a hummingbird's wings from over here."

Making sure she moved no quicker than a saunter, she made her way to the cupboard by the sink. Hah. Guessed right. She found a glass there, and with her back to him, she filled it with water from the tap.

Still turned away, she drained it down.

Then nearly leapt out of her cheap sandals when his hand landed on her shoulder. "Jules?"

Sighing, she slipped out of his hold. Pressing her back to the countertop, she faced him. "It's silly."

"Yeah? I like a laugh first thing in the morning."

Most of the time it looked as if he hadn't cracked a smile since he'd taken that plane from Tuscany. "I don't want you laughing at *me*," she said. "Promise."

"Pinky-swear?" He held his up.

She wasn't making the mistake of touching him again, so she shoved her hands in her pockets. When his dropped, she shrugged a shoulder. "I get a little . . . alarmed on occasion. I just spooked myself."

"Huh?"

"Only occasionally. Since I was mugged."

His head jerked back. "What?"

"You know." She withdrew her hands to mime a blow across the head, then a shove to the ground. "I lost my purse and my laptop."

"*What?*"

"Don't have a heart attack. My CPR certificate isn't up to date."

"I'm not concerned about *my* health. Jesus, Giuliana." He forked his fingers through his hair.

She frowned. "Are your hands shaking?"

Now it was his turn to shove them in his pockets. "My fuse is real short right now, sweetheart."

Except he didn't look the least bit angry or frustrated. Outside of what she'd *thought* might be a tremor or two, he looked perfectly composed. Unruffled, as always.

"Jules . . ."

There *was* a strangely rough quality to his voice. She shrugged again, a little unsettled by it. "I was walking to my car one night. I'd had a late appointment with an account and the parking lot was dark and my car was on the far side. So . . . You know the rest."

"You were hit in the head and then pushed down?"

"Yep." She tried not thinking of it again, but the memory was there, in the ringing in her ears and the sting to her palms, knees, and forehead. "The EMTs said I was lucky I didn't break my nose. The police said it was good I didn't fight to save my stuff."

She grimaced. "I replay it, though, and every time I hold on tight. It's a total pain in the ass to replace your ID and debit and credit cards. Let me recommend writing all the numbers down and keeping them in a safe place at home."

He was staring at her.

"I didn't lose my mind," she said, frowning at him. "So stop looking at me that way. I just lost my driver's license and some work-related files on my computer. No big deal."

"Except you experience PTSD."

Perhaps. A little. It's why she had that big soft spot for Kohl. She shrugged again. "I'm much better now. You know you mentioned Disney? I had to avoid the park altogether because I would freak a little in the dark rides."

He spun away from her. "Jules . . ." Again, that rough note in his voice.

It only served to embarrass her. What had she been thinking, confessing her weakness? "You tell me something now," she demanded. "Something I don't know about you."

He hesitated a long moment. Then she heard him blow out a breath and he turned back to face her. There was a weird light in his eyes—tenderness?

His gaze dropped to her feet. "I despise those stupid rubber thongs you're wearing," he said.

Tender? He was laughing at her. Feeling heat flush her face again, she stomped toward the coffeemaker. She'd make it cooperate if she couldn't make Liam.

"Okay, okay," he said. "I'll tell you something no one knows."

She stilled.

"Penn." He came up behind her and placed his hands on her shoulders. They didn't caress, they didn't squeeze, they just rested there, solid and warm. "When I first met him, I . . . I recognized something in him."

She breathed lightly so as not to interrupt his words.

"Seth took to him immediately, too," he continued, mentioning his younger brother. "But then, Seth likes everybody."

And Liam had turned more and more wary, something she'd finally understood that summer in Tuscany. There were those dark pools and hard edges that she'd found so hard to breach.

"I've never said, Giuliana . . . I've never told anyone. But he feels like the other half of myself."

Liam didn't stay to register her reaction. "I'll get my keys and drive you back," he said, and then he was gone.

She still felt his touch on her skin. And on her heart. She knew why he cared for his brother so much. Penn was like Liam would be if he let the sun shine on his soul.

A phone rang. A portable handset stood in a base on the granite countertop. When it rang again, and then again, Giuliana crossed to it. Ms. Responsible couldn't just let the thing peal when it appeared no answering machine would pick it up.

"Bennett residence."

"Giuliana? Is that you?" Delight infused the familiar voice.

"Bev?" The wife of Edenville's mayor, Beverly Allen, had a distinctive voice that betrayed her Long Island roots.

"I'm so glad I caught you at home . . ." the other woman started.

When Liam returned, she was just setting the phone back in its base. He quirked a brow. "Everything okay?"

"Oh, sure." As long as she abandoned her you-go-your-way-I'll-go-mine plan. "It was nothing much. Just that we're invited to a party tomorrow night. As husband and wife."

8

If he'd been in his right mind, Kohl thought as he stared at the person on the other side of his front door, he wouldn't have responded to the knocking. But he'd been distracted by the hammers doing their own share of banging around inside his brain, despite the cold shower he'd just taken. On his way to the kitchen, with his towel knotted at his waist and water still running down his neck, he'd heard the rap of knuckles on wood and automatically turned the knob.

Grace Hatch stood there, looking wholesome and earnest in a short denim skirt, a white shirt, and squeaky-clean sneakers.

His instincts screamed to shut the door in her face. "I'm busy," he said first.

Her gaze dropped to his bare skin then jerked back to his eyes. She flushed. "I thought you called in sick."

He had. After waking up for the second morning in a row in the Tanti Baci vineyard with no idea of how he'd gotten there and with a time gap of six hours or so, he'd decided to stay home and nurse the hangover. Grace's stare drifted to his naked chest again. The weight of it seemed to tug on his knotted towel and he put his hand there.

Her gaze followed his movement and her eyes widened, then she dropped back a step. "I'll let you get back to your guest."

His guest? He wished someone would come along and evict the nasty carpenters erecting a village of hurt in his head. "They're clamoring for attention, that's for sure."

"There's more than one?" She took another step back. "I, uh, see."

She was looking at him *there*.

Kohl glanced down. *Shit.* The cold shower hadn't calmed his other morning visitor. As if refusing to be ignored in favor of his erection, the pounding in his head redoubled. He pushed at it with the heel of his hand. "Later, Grace."

She shoved a brown bag through the closing gap in the door. "I think there's enough for two."

He couldn't massage his head, shut her out, and grab the bag all at the same time. "Two?" he repeated, letting go of the knob to take hold of the sack.

Her face took on the hue of sunset. "Three? Whatever."

"Three?"

"Women. Lovers. Playmates."

Kohl blinked. "It's a dozen midgets, honey, and they're not playing inside my skull. They're working on driving nails into gray matter I can't afford to lose."

"Oh." Her expression softened. "Let me make you breakfast, then."

And before he could refuse her access, she pushed past him and was inside the tiny kitchen that was part of the vineyard manager's bungalow on the Tanti Baci property.

"Hey . . ." he protested.

"Hey, yourself. Now go get dressed."

"I don't want company."

She peeked inside his refrigerator. "I'm not company, I'm cooking."

He figured he could get rid of her more easily if he wasn't nearly naked. It took him just a few moments to step into jeans and a sweatshirt with the sleeves scissored off. Back in the kitchen, he saw that she was halfway through coffee prep and decided to let her finish that up before ushering her on her way.

He wasn't fit for company like her.

She glanced around. "'Company like me'?"

Had he said that out loud? But the fact was, he wanted to get rid of her. They had nothing in common and worse, that night of karaoke had been too much work for him. Small talk, song encouragement, and then the effort to restrain his baser impulses.

I wanted to beat the hell out of your ex-husband, he thought. Only the realization that he would scare her had stopped him, but he couldn't count on his self-command forever. He had those lock-ups in the local hoosegow to prove it. Lucky for him, the guys with badges understood he'd had a few anger-management issues after returning to Edenville. And though he hadn't done any damage to himself, others, or property in months and months now . . .

Or so he supposed. Morose, he dropped into a chair beside the table. He just couldn't guarantee anything because of the damn blackouts.

The coffee had started to drip and Grace was rummaging in the fruit basket on the counter. "What are these?" She held up a couple of small round vegetables, their color a pale imitation of pippin apples.

Just another reason to feel effin' sorry for himself. "My namesake. Kohlrabi. My mother keeps me supplied."

Grace ran her thumb over the skin and Kohl gritted his teeth. The damn things always reminded him of testicles and thinking of Grace touching his balls . . .

"You'd better leave." He ground out the words.

"That's nice of your mom," she said, ignoring his last remark in favor of inspecting the vegetables. Her palm cupped the orbs.

Kohl looked away, willing a mug to emerge from the cupboard, fill with the coffee streaming from the maker, and then float its way over to him and his ugly hangover.

Grace sighed. "I always wanted to be one of the Flaky Fridays."

Startled, Kohl jerked his head in her direction, disturbing the carpenters with their hammers and nails. After a second, they started in all the harder. "I haven't heard 'Flaky Friday' since I split the lip of Alan Prescott in eighth grade." Somebody had coined that term for Kohl, his sisters Marigold and Zinnia, and his hippie parents Bobby and June Friday.

"It identified you as a group—a family."

Kohl snorted. "A family of freaks, you mean. You've seen my dad in his dead-rock-star T-shirts and my mom—floating around town like Janis Joplin might if she'd ever sobered up and lived to sixty."

"I love your mom." Grace sighed again. "At least I think I would."

Kohl's jaw clenched. He'd mentioned her meeting both Bobby and June a few days ago—a strategic error. She wasn't going to make the acquaintance of his parents or hang around any more with him. "They're good people," he had to admit to her, however. "Though we grew up in that double-wide they still live in, with the same rusting appliances in the yard and that same organic garden taking up as much of their attention as their kids."

She shook her head. "They love you a lot. Your dad adopting a stray dog that his son brought home. Your mom keeping you in kohlrabi."

That would mean so much to a girl who'd been brought

up without a mother and who'd been knocked around by the one parent left to care for her. Kohl felt the familiar burn of rage start to fire up in his belly. He jumped to his feet and made for the coffeemaker on the counter.

"Were you aware they're responsible for the yellow ribbons all over town?"

Kohl froze, then set the mug he'd pulled from the cupboard onto the countertop. "What?"

"Your parents. Right after you left, they delivered them everywhere, anonymously, I think. Stacks at the library, on the counter at the post office, held down by a rock on a bench in the park. Everybody took a few and tied them to doorknobs, to their car antennas, and anywhere else you can think of."

He'd seen the tattered remnants of them once he'd returned. "How do you know this?" he asked. "My parents were completely against me enlisting. 'Make love not war' and all that."

"I could catch a ride with a neighbor to school, but it meant I got there really, really early. So I'd hang around downtown—which means I saw a few things." She shrugged. "I know who doesn't scoop up after their dog during walks and which boys snuck out of which girls' houses in the mornings."

He could see it. The little rabbit observing the world around her from the safety of a doorway. Happy to be out of her father's range. The idea of it wrenched at his heart as much as Mom and Pop delivering secret stacks of yellow ribbons around Edenville. It was so like them. Loving the sinner if not the sin. Loving the soldier if not the fight.

And instead of getting the warm fuzzies from the feeling, his hand lashed out and he brushed the mug off the counter so that it shattered on the linoleum below.

Grace stilled.

Closing his eyes, he realized he couldn't move. Not yet.

Her hand touched his arm. "Kohl?"

His muscles tensed beneath the pads of her fingertips. "Go."

She didn't obey. He could still feel the gentle contact of her hand. Her breath blew against the skin of his bicep. "What happens?" she murmured.

She wanted to know about his PTSD. He didn't know which he wanted to go away more: the symptoms or the woman asking about them. His chest tight, he forced out the words. "I don't relive experiences, as a general rule. My symptoms mostly fall into the emotional numbness and withdrawal category, with some outbursts of anger to spice things up."

"Are they getting any better?"

They had been getting better. *He* had been getting better. The work in the vineyard, the trust that Jules had in him, both had reconnected him to the world in a powerful way. But Giuliana had always been tangled with Liam—he'd known that on some level from the beginning—and that left him with this big-eyed, soft-mouthed little rabbit, who was likely ready to hop out of her skin at his next burst of temper.

Why wouldn't she just *leave*? That soft breathing of hers was getting on his nerves, grating them rawer than ever. Her cinnamon sugar smell was too sweet for the bitter, dark man he'd become. Pulling free of her soft hold, he stepped away. The broken ceramic cut into the bottom of his bare feet, and he welcomed the sharp sting.

Her gaze dropped to the blood he left on the floor. "Kohl . . ." He saw her swallow. "Tell me where the elastic bandages are."

"They're not going to fix what hurts me," he said, his voice harsh. She wasn't leaving! Why wasn't she running from the blood and truths that were leaking out of him? He gulped a breath, and over the coppery scent oozing from the bottom of his wounded feet, he could taste that confection smell of hers.

Suddenly he wanted to eat it. He wanted to eat her up.

Reaching out, he took hold of her upper arms with both hands. His grip was careful, though, because he saw in his mind's eye those rings of black bruises she'd once worn on them. Still, he brought her closer. Her tennis shoes crunched on the pieces of broken mug. "You should have run," he said, pulling her so close that he could see her pupils expand into the bright blue sea of her eyes. "I wanted you to go away."

Her human warmth reached out and wrapped around him as certainly as he was holding her. Her soft pretty lips parted. She wasn't afraid . . . she should be afraid!

So he kissed her, kissed her like he was some kind of demon out to steal her breath. Maybe he did, because Grace went boneless against his chest. But her mouth was alive, working against his as he sought the right fit. There. There!

His tongue surged into her mouth, and hers didn't play dead. Instead, she dueled with him, giving as well as getting, exchanging sweet for bitter, light for dark. She tasted like sunshine and he swallowed it down.

Lightheaded, he had to break the kiss for air. Her golden red lashes had half drifted over her magnificent eyes. She looked languorous. Seducible. No, already willing.

It tore at him again. Why hadn't she left?

"Kohl . . ." she whispered.

And he had to tear away from her. With a wrench, he did it, leaving her swaying on her feet. "I have one other symptom," he said, his voice rasping. "They call it something like the limited-future syndrome. I don't want a wife and kids. I don't expect to live a normal life—or even have a normal lifespan."

Her eyes were wide now. She had to wish she'd run the moment he'd opened the door. In the silence, he saw her swallow.

"I understand," she finally said, her voice as hoarse as

his. "For a long time, I thought one of them—my father or the man I married—would kill me."

And then she was gone. Kohl dropped his aching head to his hands. Jesus, Jesus. The one he really wanted to get away from now was no one other than himself.

~

The evening of the dinner party, Liam's gaze followed Giuliana's passage down the curved stairway. He caught a glimpse of her black open-toed shoes, the high heels accentuating the length of her calves. The hem of a dress skimmed her knees. Then she disappeared around the bend and he had a moment to breathe before she reappeared again. The shoes, the calves, the knees, the hem, and then all of her.

The dress was satiny, the color a dawn-pale pink splashed with tropical flowers in black. It was close-fitting, following the curves of her hips to her small waist, up her rib cage to the wide, U-shaped neckline cut low enough to expose the rise of her breasts. Narrow straps clung to her shoulders and he could tell it dipped low in the back, too. Her hair, shiny as a crow's wing, hung in a straight waterfall.

Long jet earrings hung from her ears. Her eyes were made up to look more dark and mysterious and her mouth shone a sheer pink color.

At the foot of the staircase, she looked up at him, a black clutch purse in her hand and some sort of matching wrap folded over her arm. She took him in, too, but he was nothing as exotic as her in his summer-weight ivory trousers, open shirt, and blue blazer. Another long minute stretched by while he continued to stare. Her brows drew together. "Aren't you going to say something?"

"I can't," he answered, honest. "Because there aren't words that would do you justice."

She pressed her lips together and a little dimple winked

out, evidence of the smile she was working so hard not to release. "Okay then."

A hint of a spicy-sweet perfume drew him forward. He took the wrap off her arm and dropped it over her shoulders.

She quirked an eyebrow at him. "What nice manners you have."

Little Red Riding Hood to the wolf. Oh, little did she know how wolfish he felt tonight. Right now he was itching to take a bite. "I was raised to know what fork to use," he only said.

They headed toward the foyer. He'd pulled his Mercedes up to the front. As they crossed the threshold it struck him—how weird as hell it was to be going to a dinner party with Giuliana at his side. As his wife. They'd had that passionate weekend in Reno and then those too-short weeks as newlyweds in Tuscany. But like this . . . in his house in Edenville . . .

This is how it could be, he thought, taking in another breath of her tantalizing perfume. Maybe it was what they both needed to experience before being able to move on.

He looked down at her dark head and put his hand at the small of her back as they descended the porch steps. Her dress was sleek; her body warm. He felt another rush of that weirdness that wasn't weird at all, he realized. The thought struck him again.

This is how it could be.

"Speaking of manners," Giuliana mused, as he reached for the passenger door, "I would have thought His Honor the Mayor and Bev Allen would have given more advance notice of their party tonight."

He frowned down at her. "I've known about it for a month. I already had it on my calendar."

"Oh." Her gaze dropped. "Maybe . . . maybe I shouldn't come. I wasn't invited."

"Of course you were invited. You talked to Bev yourself yesterday morning."

Embarrassed color flagged her cheeks, and she worried her small purse in a nervous gesture. "Because they think I'm your wife now. Before—when I was just a Baci, I wasn't on the guest list."

He wanted to groan. Instead he kept his tone reasonable. "Well, you are my wife. Now, before, for the past ten years."

"It wasn't real—"

"It *was* real. It's always *been* real." Okay, he had to keep his cool, but his movements were jerky as he found the door handle and yanked at it. He wanted her with him tonight, damn it.

"Get your fine ass inside, please." Even to his own ears he sounded as frustrated as he felt. So much for cool.

She obeyed, sliding into the seat but keeping her profile to him when he took his place on the driver's side. "It's just that my fine ass doesn't feel like being a second-thought, second-class-citizen fine ass," she said.

She wasn't second to anyone, and she should know it. "Your fine ass isn't invited to more parties because you're a pain in the ass," he muttered.

"That's not true," she protested. "Face it, the Bacis have never existed in the same social strata in the Napa Valley as the Bennetts. You're the Haves and we're the Have Too Littles."

"You're ridiculous."

"You're blind to the truth."

This is how it could be. The words came back to smack him in the face. Yeah, they could be going at each other like this twenty-four/seven.

A half mile of silence later, she spoke again, her voice small. "Do you really think I have a fine ass?"

He sucked in his cheeks so he wouldn't smile. "First class all the way. Nobody in Napa has one better."

"It's Allie's dress," she said. "So tight I had to go commando, but for that compliment it might be worth it."

His hands jerked the wheel. The Mercedes pulled right, and he tightened his hold to wrench it straight. A lesser car would have fishtailed from his lack of finesse. "For God's sake, Jules." Commando!

"What?"

He gave her a sour glance. "You haven't been able to manage that innocent look since you let me get to second base on New Year's Eve eleven years ago. Remember—"

"I remember! I remember!" She whacked his shoulder with her hand. "Yeesh. You don't have to play dirty like that."

"You started it." He shook his head. "Commando, Jules. C'mon. Give me a break."

"Fine." She humphed.

The bounce she made against the leather seat made him think of her naked behind again and he almost lost his hold on the wheel for the second time. *This is how it could be.*

Still, he discovered he was smiling as he pulled up to the mayor's house. Pulling her hand to the crook of his arm, he led her from the car to the door. "For the record," he whispered, ducking his head against hers, "I like playing dirty with you."

She was smiling, too, as they walked into the party, the couple everyone was eager to see.

Yeah, he didn't fully realize that until they'd made their way to the living room. He had a hell of a lot more sympathy for Giuliana's nervousness now, as he saw that they were the focus of every eye. The place was full of two dozen or more movers and shakers of Edenville and its environs.

"My youngest sister is married to a TV star," he heard her murmur, and he suspected she was giving herself a little pep talk. "My other sister is an Ardenian princess."

"Even better, Stevie knows how to adjust a carburetor," Liam pointed out.

Giuliana stilled. Then she looked up and flashed him a

brilliant smile. "I take back some of the mean thoughts I've had about you."

"Some?" That sounded like progress. "Exactly how many?"

She mulled a moment. "Two," she said, and then she was moving away from him to hold out her hand to the mayor and then his wife. Her smile continued on its full-wattage setting and her earlier nervousness must have evaporated because she exuded confidence while mingling with the others in the room.

Nursing a glass of a Russian River Valley pinot, he watched her from a spot by the bar. She had a killer body. Now womanly and ripe. He couldn't look away from the changing expressions on her face. She was shaking her head sometimes, chuckling softly at others, on occasion flicking him a glance over her shoulder. People were grilling her on their marriage, he realized, as he caught snippets of the conversation even at this distance.

. . . youthful impulse . . .

. . . too long apart . . .

. . . came to our senses this last year . . .

With the exception of that last one, she spoke the truth. And even then, well, they had to come to their senses and do something about the situation, didn't they? She threw another bright glance at him over her smooth-skinned shoulder. He smiled at her, toasting her performance with his glass.

He was so damn proud of her.

Her lashes fell and rose just a little, the look flirtatious now. His belly tightened, and he thought about walking over, putting his arm around her waist, and heaving her across his shoulder, caveman style. They'd go home, he'd peel her out of that dress—wait, she was commando, he'd shove up the hem of that dress—

And it hit him again. *It could be like this.*

"I'm so happy to see the two of you together," a female voice said at his elbow.

Resigned, Liam turned. He shouldn't have expected to duck all the relationship flack. Rex and Janice Sandburg stood beside him, both beaming. They had kids the same age as Liam and Giuliana and he'd known the entire family all his life, just as they'd known both his parents and Mario and Elena Baci.

He shook hands with Rex and leaned over to brush a salute on Janice's cheek. "How are you both? Sunny and Dan?"

They were distracted by telling him of their recent trip around the Greek isles followed by a detailed account of the marriage of their daughter, Sunny, in Kauai. "She thought about the Baci winery, but there wasn't an open date that worked."

"It's a popular spot," he agreed. A year ago he'd had doubts, but the Baci sisters—as Penn would say—were scary. What they wanted, they got. His eyes lifted to find Giuliana still working the crowd.

"So it's really true?" Rex asked, following the direction of his gaze. "You two kids eloped and then had a falling out?"

Liam nodded. "That's right."

"It's so romantic." Janice sighed.

Ten years apart? Sure. "Like *Titanic*," he murmured.

"What's that?" Janice tilted her head.

"I was just agreeing with you. Romantic."

Rex sidled closer and lowered his voice. "So . . . what went wrong?"

He'd made so many mistakes. The thought of them sent his stomach pitching. He should never have left her in Tuscany. He should have told her what was going on at home. Afterward, he should have found some way to tell her everything he was feeling.

Why hadn't he done that? Why hadn't he *been able* to do that?

And why were all his missteps so easy to identify now?

"Liam?" Rex prodded him with his elbow.

"I . . ." His hand tightened on his wineglass and he searched the crowd again, his lurching stomach subsiding as he once again identified her dark head. While he saw Penn as the sunny twin, the opposite of his grimmer personality, just the sight of Giuliana seemed to balance him.

It could be like this . . .

For the rest of our lives.

Rex and Janice were staring at him, he realized. "I'm sorry." He swallowed some of the spicy pinot. "What were we saying?"

Janice had a misty look in her eyes. "I'm just trying to wrap my mind around the fact that one generation of Bennetts and Bacis might finally get the love they want."

He was trying to wrap his mind around that as well. But he attempted to keep it light. "So you suppose my great-great-grandfather and Giuliana's great-great-grandparents would approve?"

Janice ducked her head to stare into her glass of straw-colored wine. "I'm actually thinking more of your father, Liam."

"Dad?"

Rex cleared his throat. "Janice . . ."

"The boy has a right to know," she answered her husband. "I think there's been too many secrets between the two families."

Liam couldn't refute that. He grimaced. "Plenty of Dad's came to light when he died." Infidelity, illegitimate children, enough truth had come out that people realized that Calvin Bennett wasn't the straight arrow he'd fooled the world—though not Liam—into believing for so very long.

"Your father was unhappy—not that it gave him the right to do what he did to your mother, that's for sure."

Liam let go a short laugh. "Screwing around on his wife bummed him out?"

"He was in love with someone else, Liam," Janice said. "He'd been in love with one person since he was as young as you were when you married Giuliana."

Yeah, he was in love with his own reflection, the selfish bastard.

"It tainted him, I think," she continued. "He didn't know how to love her generously—and the way to do that was by letting her go."

"I don't know what you're talking about." The women who'd born the illegitimate Bennetts had not known Calvin when he was that young. Neither could be the object of his father's unrequited—and alleged—romance. "Who do you mean?"

"You know the rosebushes you still plant at the beginning and end of each row in a Bennett vineyard?"

They were a dark red, the color of a wounded heart. "My father insisted. It's even written into his will, that tradition."

"One your father restarted as a young man. There'd been no roses in Bennett vineyards for years before that. He had them planted as testament to his undying love—a love he would never let her forget."

Tainted, undying love. Uneasiness crawled down Liam's spine. "Undying love for who?"

Janice hesitated. "Surely you can guess."

He shifted his gaze away, moving it around the other partygoers. Then, and as if he'd summoned her, a woman emerged from the milling guests and started walking toward him. A beautiful woman. His wife, coming closer. Soon, he'd be able to reach out and stroke her silky hair, her warm cheek.

"Who?" he asked Janice again, his voice rough. "My father had an undying love for *who*?"

Another woman was heading off Giuliana, touching her arm just as Janice whispered into his ear.

"Elena Baci," Janice murmured. "Your father was in love with Giuliana's mother."

Elena Baci? His fingers closed into a fist as Janice's words echoed in his head. *It tainted him, I think. He didn't know how to love her generously.*

It couldn't be like this with Giuliana, then. He wouldn't let it.

9

Giuliana had felt Liam's gaze following her since they'd parted ways. It had warmed her and she'd looked around more than once to share a glance with him. Those . . . warmed her, too. Now she headed his way, drawn by the appreciative light in his eyes and the open expression on his face. But before she got to him, another partygoer snagged her.

"Come with me," Sally Knowles said. "There's someone you need to talk to."

Giuliana found herself being pulled in the opposite direction of her husband. A glance over her shoulder made her frown, the starkness that had returned to Liam's face puzzling. When she tried to catch his eye, his gaze purposefully shifted away from her.

Giuliana felt like the bodice of Allie's dress had shrunk two sizes. He was sliding away from her again. Since the day before when she'd shared with Liam about the mugging, their relationship had taken a new turn. There'd been more ease in the atmosphere inside the house. They'd had another dinner together and he'd made her another latté before he'd driven her to work that morning.

Sue her, she'd been thrilled at his notice of her "fine ass." She'd wanted to laugh when he'd claimed to enjoy playing dirty with her.

They'd been getting close again, and she couldn't make herself regret it. At different times in her life he'd been her playmate, her co-adventurer, her first love. They'd always be the oldest siblings of their respective—and eternally entangled—families. Their unhappy breakup couldn't erase all that, and it didn't take a shrink to realize it would be healthier for them both to be . . . amicable.

Sally tugged her forward again, and Giuliana let herself be moved, even as she took another backward glance at Liam. His face was shuttered and she couldn't guess what he was thinking, though there was a new tension in every line of his body. Maybe it was her Ms. Responsible attitude again, maybe it was the memory of all the good times they'd had when they were young, but she hated seeing him like this.

Where did he go and why? She wanted to find that place and yank him from it, bringing him back to the world of flesh and blood.

She wanted to be with him. "Sally . . ."

"Here she is," the other woman said, pushing her toward a small knot of people, which included a thirtysomething man with longish hair and an arty stubble around his mouth. "Alexander Murphy, meet Giuliana Baci, who has saved her family winery."

Alexander Murphy was a journalist. Sally let her know he'd won prizes and wrote travel pieces as well as reports on the economy. The article he was researching was a twofer, which would include information on how the Napa Valley was faring in this particular financial climate.

"So we want to give him good news," Sally said, smiling. "He talked to my daughter Clare about her boutiques.

My son-in-law, Gil, told Alex that his car-repair business is busier than ever."

"But there are a lot of properties for sale in the valley," the writer pointed out. "Homes. Vineyards. Wineries. I don't believe it's all pop-culture memorabilia flying off the shelves and endless queues of autos lining up for oil changes."

Alex Murphy had a cynical edge to him, but she couldn't fault him for that. "We've weathered the phylloxera epidemic, Prohibition, and all kinds of pests," she said. "I'm sure we'll weather this." *Some of us.*

"You and your sisters are stabilizing Tanti Baci by adding a new revenue stream with weddings, I hear."

She shrugged. "We decided to give it a year."

"Culminating in something called the—" He glanced at Sally.

"Vow-Over Weekend," the older woman supplied.

"I'd like to know more about that," Alex said. "Can I visit sometime?"

Allie would have her head if she heard about this request and Giuliana hadn't extended a welcoming red carpet. At the end of the month she'd have enough to atone for. "Of course." She smiled at him. "One of us will give you a personal tour."

His gaze dropped for just a second to her cleavage. It was a glance more appreciative than lascivious, so she didn't move away. "What about you?" he asked, that appreciation gleaming in his eyes. "Can I put in a special appeal to have you assigned as my private guide?"

Her mouth opened. Then a hand covered the cap of her shoulder. Male body heat radiated at her back. "Sorry to interrupt, Giuliana," Liam said. "They're calling us to dinner."

"Sure. Right." Embarrassment wrapped the back of her neck and traveled upward like a burn. She supposed he felt it as he rested his hand lightly on her nape to guide her toward the small tables set up on the terrace. Did he think she was flirting with the journalist? She hadn't been, of course, but maybe she looked guilty because she hadn't introduced the two men.

She slid Liam a glance, trying to explain. "Allie will squeal with happiness. That guy's with the media and he's interested in Tanti Baci."

"I see." His voice stayed even, his walk sedate. "She won't be so gleeful if you demonstrate interest in a man besides the husband with whom you just reconciled."

Demonstrate interest! She hadn't been doing any such thing, not in the way he meant. Was he . . . could he possibly be jealous? "Liam—"

"Think of the winery," he said, in that maddeningly dispassionate manner of his. "Think of your sisters, me, my family. We've all got a financial stake in it—so let's try to keep this farce going until the last weekend in June—all right?"

All wrong! She was *always* thinking of the winery, thank you very much, and the financial pressure both families were under as a consequence. And . . . Her Italian temper caught, then flared hot. "*Farce?*"

"Calm down." He pulled out the chair at the place assigned to her. "We agreed to keep up the appearance that we've reconciled and that we're glad we're married. The legend, remember."

"But 'farce'?" she said to him under her breath as he took the seat beside hers. "A farce implies some kind of fun, and FYI, I'm not having fun. Furthermore, let me give you a tiny bit of advice. Never, ever tell a woman to 'calm down.'"

"Relax."

She stared at the lovely silverware, gleaming in the light from votive candles flickering in centerpieces of ivy and gardenias. *Relax.* Somebody ought to give her a medal, she decided, for not stabbing him with her salad fork.

But now he was back to appearing supremely untroubled, again, his posture relaxed, his attitude courteous as he spoke with the other four who joined them at their table. So she decided to act as unperturbed as he. With a winemaker's conviviality as part of her DNA, she chatted, she laughed, she even got up to visit a few other tables between courses. Without even glancing at Liam's reaction, she paused beside Alex Murphy and made a point to tell him the directions to Tanti Baci and their hours of operation.

By the time the final course, coffee, and dessert wines were offered, she was feeling pleased with herself and the entire evening. Her initial nervousness was gone. She could manage anyone and anything, including the ice-filled crevasse that separated her from Liam. Just a few more weeks of this "farce," and then it would all be over.

After she and Liam said their good-byes to the host and hostess, Giuliana decided to make a stop at the powder room. Another woman was waiting for it to open up. Sally Knowles smiled at her. "Enjoy your evening?"

"Absolutely."

The older woman looked at the still-closed powder room door, let out a little sigh, then turned back to Giuliana. "Stevie's feeling better?"

Giuliana started. "What?"

"She and Jack were on the guest list for tonight. I heard they begged off at the last minute because your sister wasn't feeling well."

Giuliana's mouth was dry. "She's pregnant."

"It's all over town." Sally was nodding and smiling again. "I—"

The rest of the sentence was lost as Giuliana rushed toward the entrance, where Liam was waiting with her things. Another time she might have giggled—men always looked so hopelessly helpless with a purse in their big hands.

But she was the one feeling hopelessly helpless as she

snatched it from him. Did he sense it? Liam caught her, his big hands warm on her cold shoulders. "Jules?"

"Stevie isn't well." The words came out with odd clicks, because her mouth was still so dry. "She couldn't come to dinner. I need to call." Her fingers trembled on the tiny latch of the satin clutch.

But when she had her cell in her hands, Liam plucked it away. "No," he said, ushering her out the door with an arm behind her back.

"I have to call!"

"And alarm her with your panic?" He inserted her into the passenger seat of his waiting car.

"You don't understand," she said, as he settled beside her. She pressed her fist to her heart to ease its agitated fluttering.

He gave her a look. "I talked to Jack earlier tonight. Your sister was tired and didn't feel up to a long evening."

"I want to talk to her." Her phone was in his pocket.

"In the morning," he said, composed as always.

He was right. She supposed he was right. But her spine didn't touch her seat back as they made the short drive to Liam's house. Her heart continued to pound.

She slid a glance at Liam's profile, edged with the light from the dashboard. He was impossibly handsome, completely remote, and she wondered if he even had a pulse. Nothing, she thought, nothing ever really touched him.

He parked beside the front steps. His hand was hard on hers as he pulled her out of the car. They mounted the steps together. She tried to appreciate his steadiness. A rock might be cold, but it was solid, wasn't it?

With his hand on the surface of the door, he hesitated. Then he half turned, his gaze in the direction of the vineyards that surrounded the property. "God."

Giuliana straightened, her eyes riveted to his face. Liam Bennett never betrayed any kind of mood and she hesitated to speak, fearing to interrupt the moment when she thought he just might.

"Ghosts. Legends. Lost loves," he murmured.

She held her breath. Was he finally going to reveal some of his thoughts? Was he going to let her into his inner sanctum? She'd been waiting for an invitation for longer than a decade but now stayed silent, unsure if he was even aware of speaking aloud or that she was still beside him, her hand in his. Then he turned his head, his gaze pinning her.

She felt her heart pound even harder, wondering what truth he might reveal and wondering how it might affect this new relationship she'd thought they were building.

"Giuliana," he said, in a musing tone. "Do you ever get the feeling that we're cursed?"

~

Kohl walked out of the Baci vineyard, following his habitual morning survey, to find two of the three Baci sisters set up on one of the tables in the picnic area, going over paperwork. He didn't blame them for the location. Tanti Baci didn't open for tastings or tours until eleven A.M., and this peaceful early morning should be enjoyed out-of-doors. It calmed the hell out of him. He'd stayed out of bars and kept clear of Grace Hatch for the last couple of days and now he felt almost normal.

Ordinary. He smiled at the thought. Maybe everything was getting back to ordinary.

He approached Stevie and Allie across the gravel parking lot. They looked up and smiled as he stood beside their table. "How are you, Kohl?" Steve asked.

Ordinary. "Good." He remembered Giuliana encouraging him to engage a little more in social niceties and he figured that's what an ordinary guy would do. "Uh, how are you?" He made a vague gesture. "And what's-it?"

She laughed, looking down at the slight curve of her

belly. "We've been trying to come up with names. I'll add What's-It to the list."

Allie cast a glance at her, then at the nearly full bottle of apple juice beside her. "Well, you and What's-It better start downing the liquids. Jack's decided you're dehydrated and that's why you're so tired all the time."

"Jack's suddenly become an expert on all things pregnancy," Stevie said. "It's endearing, but suffocating at the same time."

Kohl sympathized with Stevie's husband. Like every other male he knew, Jack was a man of action, and being at the mercy of some tiny creature growing inside his wife's womb had to take a hell of a lot of patience.

Then his own voice echoed in his head: *They call it something like the limited-future syndrome. I don't want a wife and kids. I don't expect to live a normal life—or even have a normal lifespan.*

Grace had taken his harsh words without blinking. As if they were ordinary.

As if it was an ordinary action for a man to push her away like that. Guilt slugged him right in the solar plexus, because, of course, being pushed around by a man was exactly what she was accustomed to.

She exited the doors of the administrative offices just then. In a Tanti Baci T-shirt, jeans, and tennis shoes, she looked like just an average young woman. Run-of-the-mill.

Kohl breathed out a little sigh, then the morning sun struck her hair. The light brightened the gold and burnished the red and she was transformed into something extraterrestrial—a full-sized fairy or maybe a dragonfly in human form. He choked at the fanciful thought.

Christ, he did so not do whimsy.

But she had him thinking that way, didn't she, with her rose gold hair and her summer-day eyes? She was making a point of not looking at him, he could see that, as she walked toward the wine caves on some errand of her own.

He glanced away, too, his gaze catching on Giuliana . . . and a man.

"Who's that?" he asked her sisters. "Who's with Jules?"

Allie didn't glance up. "Say again?"

Kohl watched the couple disappear into the wine cottage. "Is it another of her clandestine meetings?"

Two pairs of Baci-brown eyes snapped to his face. "What clandestine meetings?"

He shuffled back. "I don't know . . . I . . ." This is why he shouldn't do the chitchat thing. Sooner or later he did something, said something, that women found alarming. His gaze jumped from their concerned faces to the ground to the gravel drive. "I, uh, have to go . . ."

Liam appeared in the near distance, striding along in jeans and his scarred work boots. His mouth moving, he appeared to be arguing with himself. Kohl retreated from the sisters a few steps, but it was odd enough behavior for this ordinary day that he found himself staying within earshot as the other man approached Stevie and Allie.

"Where the hell is she?" he demanded.

Allie played innocent. "'She'?"

"That damn sister of yours."

"You mean your damn wife?" the youngest Baci asked, sweet as you please.

"My damn wife who left this morning before I could get up and drive her here." Liam drew in a deep breath. "Look, I've been sleeping like crap and she got away because I finally dozed off at dawn." He blew out another gust of air. "She should have woken me."

Stevie lifted one shoulder. "She had an important early appointment. I'm sure she didn't want to disturb you."

"She disturbs me every minute of every day!"

A little cat smile came and went as she absently smoothed the slight swell at her waist and sat back in her chair. "Now, Liam—"

"Who the hell is that?"

They all turned their heads. Giuliana and the stranger had exited the cottage, but were paused beside the flowering rosebush at the corner. The man had his back to them, but was standing close enough to Jules that when he plucked a bloom from the bush he could tap the white petals playfully against her nose.

Maybe Kohl did whimsy after all, because he could swear he saw steam come out of Liam's ears. He allowed himself a smile at the other man's discomfort. Payback was *such* a bitch. "You okay, pal?"

The head of the Bennett family didn't even spare him a look. Instead, he strode off toward the cottage, his walk purposeful, his face granite-hard.

"Uh-oh."

Kohl's head whipped right. Grace was at his elbow. Her blue eyes flicked to his face, then went back to the potential disaster of Liam descending on Giuliana, his hostility barely concealed behind a stony face and steely spine.

She drifted in the same direction, a breeze tugging at the ends of her vivid hair. Kohl reached out to catch her sleeve. With it pinched between his thumb and forefinger, she halted. "Where are you going?" he asked.

"Toward trouble."

"If so, it's not your trouble," he protested, but she slipped free of his hold and made for the cottage.

Shit. All right. She wasn't ordinary in this. Kohl couldn't deny that Grace likely had a finely tuned instinct for violence-in-the-offing—just like he couldn't deny that he wouldn't mind seeing Liam Bennett with someone's fist planted in his face. But he wanted to be sure Grace wasn't in the way of that, so he hurried after her.

As they approached the bottom of the cottage steps, Liam reached Giuliana and the stranger. Maybe their alarm was off the mark, because Liam smiled and reached out his hand to the other man. He didn't break the guy's fingers. Instead, he turned to Giuliana and bent his head to kiss her. Except he bypassed the usual destinations—forehead, cheek, lips—and pressed his mouth to the side of her neck.

He lingered there. It wasn't perfunctory—it was possession. It was a blatant statement of intent, but Liam delivered it coolly, as he did everything else. Somehow, the banked fire inside the man made it only more intense . . . and intimate.

"Uh-oh," Grace said again, as Giuliana flushed red and shoved at him. Liam rocked back, only to ease forward again, using the momentum to drape his arm over her shoulders.

Kohl and Grace drew near enough to hear Giuliana speak through gritted teeth. "Give me room to breathe."

Liam was smiling again, that imperturbable flash of perfect white teeth that had made Kohl want to punch him a dozen times himself. "Babe, I gave you ten years of breathing room and what did that get me?"

Giuliana's eyes flashed. "This is a journalist, Liam. I'm giving Alex Murphy an interview. About winemaking and the Napa Valley."

"Then your new friend, Alex, should know about us, don't you agree? Why don't you tell him that story?"

Still red-faced, Giuliana opened her mouth, but the writer guy slid smoothly into the conversation. "No problem, Ms. Baci. I'm sure I have all I need."

"Mrs. Bennett," Liam corrected, in a pleasant tone.

"Baci," Giuliana insisted.

The journalist pasted on a noncommittal smile. "Thank you so much for your time." Then he looked down at his hand and the white rose he held. He lifted it toward Giuliana. "Let me give you—"

Liam's fingers closed over Alex Murphy's wrist. "My wife doesn't accept flowers from other men."

"Liam!" Giuliana said, clearly appalled.

Baring his teeth, her husband didn't spare her a glance. "You understand, Alex?"

The journalist was already backing away. Liam released his wrist but followed his retreat. "I'll walk you to your car. Jules, you stay here." More teeth baring.

Grace gave the men a little distance, but then followed. Kohl trailed her, not sure who he felt the need to protect. Okay, so it was a weird blip in his ordinary day, but he breathed another sigh of relief as the journalist shut his car door behind him. So what that Liam's pat on the vehicle's roof was more like a pound?

As the sedan accelerated away, it was again that mundane morning Kohl had so appreciated. Inhaling another calming breath, he turned to head back to his usual duties. Surely Grace Hatch had her regular tasks to accomplish as well.

"Kohl." Liam called his name.

He disguised his groan with a cough. "What?" he asked, turning back.

Liam's eyes glittered. "Am I going to have to take you on next?"

Jesus. For months they'd been bristling at each other, but he wanted to brawl *today*? He glanced toward Grace. No way would he subject her to brutality on what was supposed to be a perfectly normal morning. "Go home, Liam," he said, shaking his head. "Do us all a favor. Go home and take your commotion with you."

"You're damn right I intend to take her home."

His commotion, Kohl thought, amused despite himself, was Giuliana. "Good luck." And as his eye caught that bright color of Grace Hatch's hair, he realized he sincerely meant it.

"Oh, hell." Liam looked around him. "She's gone."

She'd poofed, all right. But that just showed how ordinary this day really was. It was Giuliana's regular MO to run from the man she'd married. Barely suppressing a little whistle, he smiled at Grace. "Did anyone make coffee?" he asked her.

But she was biting her bottom lip, her eyebrows peaked over her cinnamon-dusted nose. "You've lost her?"

His jaw hardening, Liam turned in a circle. "More than once," he muttered.

Grace ducked her head, was quiet a moment, then she lifted her chin. "The northwest corner of the vineyard."

He whipped his gaze to hers. "You're sure?"

"I'm sure."

Without another word, he took off at a run.

Kohl didn't watch him go. Instead, he stared at Grace Hatch, the daughter of a diviner. He'd seen the old man work once, his rod of polished wood held between two hands. It had trembled at a certain point, shaking Peter Hatch like a dried leaf on a valley oak, but Kohl had called bullshit on the performance . . . even though water had been found where he'd indicated.

Grace didn't betray a quiver. But he remembered her knowing the location of Allie's watch. At the bar, she'd spoken up about the missing cell phone. Now it was a missing wife.

The mundane morning went eccentric on him. The sky was still blue, the air warming with sunshine, the breeze the one he would expect on any normal summer day. But Grace Hatch . . .

A shiver rolled down his back. Grace Hatch wasn't ordinary at all.

10

Giuliana escaped to the vineyard. She didn't know what she wanted to flee more, the embarrassment of the scene between Alex Murphy and Liam . . . or Liam himself. In either case, his kiss stayed with her. Her skin throbbed where he'd pressed his mouth to her throat. She touched it with her fingertips as she watched the Tanti Baci rust-colored dirt kick up with every step.

She'd eschewed her rubber thongs for the sake of the interview. The day before, Liam had insisted on driving her to a local mall. Insisted was not quite the word. He'd practically inserted her into the car and then remained silent after telling her she needed more clothes.

If he'd demanded she shop at a hoity-toity department store his mother favored, she might have balked. Instead, he'd merely followed her around as she made her sale-priced—and spare number of—choices at a discount place. The khaki-colored cotton skirt was layers of ruffles to the knees, the last of lacy cutouts. She'd worn it with a sleeveless spring green cotton shirt and gold stud earrings to match the bracelet of blue glass and gold beads she always wore on her left wrist. Her sandals had ankle straps decorated with sequins in the same colors.

Today, Liam hadn't even spared the new clothes a glance. He'd only been interested in staking his claim, which she found . . .

. . . annoying and . . .

. . . exciting, God help her.

Guilty at the thought, she glanced around, finding herself still blissfully alone and about a quarter mile into the vineyard. With a little more time away from the winery, she should be able to regain her sanity and face her family and friends without a still-racing heart.

Through the cover of the lush vines, she spied movement. Her heartbeat hiccupped. Liam? But he wouldn't sacrifice his glacial dignity by going to the trouble of tracking her down in the vineyard. So . . .

That itchy sense of inherent danger came over her again—just as it had a few mornings before. Her pulse began racing, and she found herself crowding closer to the vines, leaves seeming to reach out to brush her cheeks and pat her hair. She couldn't be threatened here, surely, amidst her hundred-year-old legacy.

But she *did* feel threatened, her blood rushing to the surface of her skin so that Liam's mark took on a new sting. She heard footsteps. Deliberate and measured, they were almost lost in the sound of her rattling heart in her ears.

"Giuliana?" a voice whispered.

She jerked, setting the leaves to twitching like her nerves. *Be still,* she told herself. *Stay silent.*

"Giuliana?"

She realized that the speaker wasn't whispering, but the voice only seemed quiet because of the internal racket of thundering heart and jangling nerves. It meant she couldn't tell how close or how far he was from her, either.

Be still. Stay silent.

Despite the admonitions, she peeked around the foliage surrounding her and glanced down the row. A long leg. A muscled forearm.

Liam!

The knowledge shot through her, bursting the bubble of fear but leaving behind a giddy liquid that ran drunkenly through her veins. He'd sacrificed his glacial dignity after all.

Yet everything inside of her still signaled danger. Operating on impulse, she exploded from her hiding place and took off in the opposite direction of where he'd been, the soles of her new sandals sliding on the soft dirt.

"Jules!"

She ignored his voice, sprinting two rows over and then pressing close to the vines again. They'd played games like this as children a hundred times, and she knew not to press too close to the berries, clustered pale and green under their leafy protection.

She was glad of her tan legs, her earth-toned skirt, her shirt that blended in with her surroundings. A laugh swelled, but she held it back with a hand at her belly and one over her mouth. Glancing around, she didn't see a sign of him, so she was on the move again, racing farther into the family acres.

This time she heard his footsteps, clapping heavy on the ground in the distance behind her. "Jules!"

Her laugh broke out, free as the child she'd once been, wild as the teenager who'd fallen into untamed passion with the boy next door. Then she ducked around another row and hunkered down.

"I'm going to get you," he called out.

He'd gotten her when she was sixteen years old. Before that, maybe, with his golden good looks and his competent air. Number one children appreciated that. Even though they were both first-borns, they'd complemented each other, what with his natural reserve and her Italian emotion. As a pair, she'd thought they had an effective balance of personalities, even as he grew older and quieter, his silences darker.

That shadow in him hadn't stopped her headlong rush into love. She'd assumed her unfailing, unflagging passion for him would keep him close to her forever.

"I'm going to get you," he called for a second time.

"Why?" she questioned back, then scurried off so her voice wouldn't give her location away.

"Because it's time," he said, implacable.

The sure tone of his voice made her shiver. Danger again, she thought. *Be silent. Stay still.*

"We can't go on like this, Giuliana. I'm not sleeping. You don't eat. We're making our families as crazy as we are."

Oh, sure. Bring up the families. Theirs were so tangled in so many ways.

On soundless feet, she shuffled down the row.

"Tell me yes," Liam coaxed. "Jules, tell me yes."

This new, soft tone was just rough enough to rob her breath. It was his assurance that had always been her undoing. *We'll wait to make love until we're married. We'll tell them we're husband and wife when we get back from Tuscany. I have to return to California, but I won't leave you alone for long.*

The memories made her eyes squeeze shut to hold back childish tears. She'd cried when her mother died, in her father's arms, and then in Liam's. Afterward, she'd vowed to be strong. Her sisters had needed a maternal figure and her mother said it was up to her—and that she'd be a good one.

So the last time tears had flooded down her face, she'd been alone in the bed she'd shared with Liam in Italy.

Leaves shook around her at the same time a hand shot through the row at her back to grab her wrist. "Gotcha."

Her jolt of surprise released her from his grasp and she went on the run again, zigging and zagging with speed fueled by a feeling that was part desperation and part exuberance. Who could analyze it? She was panicked . . . and panting with desire.

"You can't win," Liam said, and she sensed him gaining ground.

"I will win!" But it was futile, she knew, as his fingertips grazed her shoulder and then tangled briefly in the ends of her hair. Her last burst of speed made her feet cycle, cartoon roadrunner style, as the new soles lost traction on the soft earth. Her legs were churning but no ground was covered, and then he had an arm slung across her chest.

A laugh rang out—hers—and she threw her weight back so he was off balance. Then they were going down, Liam cushioning her fall. A breathless jolt as he hit and she was cradled on top of his hard body.

Another laugh bubbled up and she dug her elbow into his ribs to get leverage. Sitting up, she started to scramble away. Then Liam, a veteran of skirmishes with a younger brother, stretched out a long arm and caught her ankle.

"Mine," he said, hauling her back. He wasn't laughing.

She slid along the dirt and was tipped on top of him again. Her chin tilted up and the crown of her skull met the jut of his chin with a *thwack*. They both moaned.

"That hurt me way worse than it hurt you," he groused, but he used his free hand to rub at the spot on her head. "Okay?"

She couldn't speak. Her backside was pressed to his front and she could feel the stiff column of his erection against her butt. It locked the breath in her lungs and made her nipples clamp into tight points. In a breath, she was that passionate hedonist, the Italian girl who wanted more than anything to push her steel-willed boyfriend down the path of sexual pleasure.

He'd been more experienced . . . but committed not to rushing her along. While she'd been in her own rush—

when it came to him, she'd always wanted so much, everything, all.

The balance between them—which she'd thought had been so right—prudence to passion—had actually always been off. He'd held back, while she'd flung every emotion his way. Smarter about that now, she attempted, again, to get free.

"No," Liam said. He twisted, so that it was her back in the dirt and his weight atop hers. Her eyes closed, the sensation so luscious, but then she wiggled, her sixth sense whispering to her again. *Danger, danger, danger.*

"You're not getting away from me now," he murmured. His mouth brushed her temple, her eyelids, the curve of her cheek.

She gave way for a moment, and then recalling the lessons of childhood, she scissored her legs around one of his. Frontier wrestling, they'd called it, and the surprise of it worked, because she flipped him to his back and leapt once again to her feet, liberated. A dozen strides later, she looked back, then paused.

Still lying on the ground, his chest heaved with heavy breaths. Nothing else about him moved and he watched her out of glittering eyes. There was dusty dirt in his air, a streak of it on his chin, a bead of sweat rolling down his temple. He looked nothing like Liam Bennett, self-possessed scion of one of the wealthiest families in the Napa Valley. He looked like the playmate of her childhood, the one who snuck over on summer nights to play games with her and her sisters in their vineyard.

He looked like the adventurer she'd first encountered as an adolescent, who'd kissed her softly, then with more recklessness, until she'd twist against him in need. His soft laughter at her frustration had been only another turn-on.

He looked like her first love, the man who'd married her and who'd then, finally, *finally*, made love to her. Her own chest labored to bring in more oxygen, but the added

O^2 didn't bolster her common sense. Instead, she . . . she yearned to touch him.

That yearning had her moving again—but toward him. She sprinted the ten yards and then skidded to a halt inches from his prone body. His expression was watchful, as usual giving nothing away.

It was her choice now. He'd pursued, she'd run, and now he'd left the next move in her hands.

"Do you want me?" she whispered.

Now he laughed. Still splayed in the dirt between the rows, he let it all out. The sound tugged at the corners of her mouth. When the laughter subsided, he ran his hands through his dirty hair and looked up at her, amusement still lighting his face. "Sweetheart, what do you think? I've just been chasing your ass like a randy teenager."

"My *fine* ass," she said primly.

He grinned, and it was as if an anvil had been lifted from her heart. "Your *fine* ass."

But it was still her choice, because he added no further persuasion. Liam Bennett was nothing if not stubborn. So was she, of course, which was why neither had done anything about that wedding certificate for the last ten years. They were staring at each other, she realized.

Still a game of who will blink first.

And then she did. She lowered her lashes at the same time that she lowered her hand to pull him to his feet. But Liam being Liam, take-charge, I'm-in-control-always, used the offer to yank her back down to his chest. Then he rolled again and she was underneath him, his mouth fastened to hers.

Caught!

~

Liam should have bet on it: Giuliana's yielding only lasted a brief moment. Then she wrenched her lips from his. "We're in the vineyard," she cautioned. "Workers."

He drew his mouth along her jaw. "There's no one out here this morning."

"Kohl—"

His head shot up. "Forget you ever heard his name."

She made a little face. "Be reasonable."

The admonition riled him. He'd been reasonable every damn day of his life—weighing options, making the smartest decisions under the circumstances, using a level head instead of listening to his heart. Always trying to do the best for his family. Where had it got him?

Where the fuck had it got him?

Fury he'd been banking for years leapt into a full-fledged fire. Liam's arms slid around Giuliana's body as his muscles tightened into uncompromising cords, binding her to him.

Her eyes widened. "What are you doing?"

Sending my common sense on vacation, he thought. But he pulled her to her feet without answering. Then he swung her up in his arms and found her mouth again, kissing her and kissing her as he set off for his house. Finally carrying off the spoils of a war he'd been waging with himself for far too long.

He might have stayed in the vineyard and got her naked in the dirt and under the sun. It appealed to him right now, the primitiveness of that, but there were too many ways he wanted to have her.

Her arms wound around his neck even as she laughed against his mouth. "Liam, don't."

Liam would. Liam would do anything and everything he wanted this time, damn logic and consequences and even Giuliana Baci, who'd crawled into his being as surely as he'd crawled into her bedroom window when she was seventeen years old. Unless and until she said no, he was going to take and take and take from her until all his lustful wanting of her body was wrung out of him.

It was a contradiction, God, he was aware of that. But

their relationship had always been a contradiction. Push-pull, Baci-Bennett, infatuation–pretend indifference.

"I hope you're ready for me," he said, his voice rough. "Because I'm going to be inside you for hours."

She twitched in his arms.

It didn't put the slightest hesitation in his stride. She was the captured prize after a long, hard battle and should know what lay ahead for her. "I'm going to bathe myself in you."

She groaned, a sweet, sexy sound. "Liam . . ."

"Are you wet?" he whispered against her ear, feeling her shudder. "Because I want to write my name on your belly with your come. And I want to bite your nipples into hard berries and then string kisses between your hipbones before I bury my tongue—"

Hers slid between his lips as she angled her head to instigate a lush mouth-to-mouth. Heat flashed over his skin and he lengthened his strides as his feet found the path he'd worn between their homes. He hitched her higher in his arms, taking charge of the kiss.

She broke free to suck in air. "I'm too heavy."

She was light as a cat, lighter, because he would swear she'd lost a dozen pounds since returning home last year. It worried him, how delicate she'd become, as if she might float away from him at any moment. The thought caused him to adjust his hold, bringing her even closer. She shifted, too, winding her legs around his waist.

"God," he muttered. The new position pushed the folds of her skirt between their bodies, leaving her panties to ride the tip of his erection. He slipped his hands beneath the ruffles in back and then under the elastic edges of her panties so his palms were filled with the sleek curves of her ass. Her *fine* ass. His cock surged and he hastened his speed toward home.

The path allowed him to avoid the workers in his own vineyard, and he blessed the fact as each footstep brought the aching head of him against the sweet heat between her thighs. He could hear her breathing, and even though he was doing all the work, hers was quickening. Her inner thighs tightened on him and she buried her face in the crook of his shoulder and neck.

"Liam." It sounded like a plea and then she licked him like a kitten, a delicate lap along his throat that went straight to his groin.

His hands tightened on her ass. "Hold on."

"I can't," she whispered against him, as her pelvis tilted toward his body. "Every move . . . It's so good, Liam."

He groaned, yanking her even closer. "Soon, sweetheart."

She was ablaze in his arms, her flesh hot, her hips plastered to his so that his jeans abraded her with each tiny jolt. She sank her teeth into his neck and fire shot up his spine. He had to get her naked.

Pausing, he got one hand between their bodies. He yanked at the buttons on her shirt, feeling them pop free or pop off, he didn't care which. It only mattered that his fingers could travel along the silky skin covering her ribs and then up to her bra. It clasped in front and he twisted it open. The cups sprang free and he brushed them off her breasts, the edge of his hand catching on nipples that were already hard.

Her hand fisted in the fabric of his T-shirt at the back of his neck. He grasped there, too, and between them they pulled it over his head. Then torso met torso and they both closed their eyes.

"Hurry," Giuliana said.

He jogged forward. She moaned and he knew that this only brought her closer, the jerkier movement causing her tight nipples to rub his chest and her clitoris to pulse against his hard, jean-clad cock. It was agony for him, too, because she was the beautiful, willful girl of his memory here, finally, in his arms. Giuliana Baci, unafraid of her passion and with her black hair gleaming in the sun, her tanned skin a golden hue that made her appear part goddess.

She rolled her shoulders and her blouse and bra dropped to the bend of her elbows. One impatient arm at a time, she released her hold on his neck. The clothes dropped and he kicked them aside and kept right on moving. He didn't look where he was going, mesmerized instead by her naked shoulders and naked breasts, curve upon curve that led his gaze to the plum pink hard centers.

She reached up to kiss him again, all the while rubbing herself against him with tiny pulses of her hips. He saw her cheeks flush and the blush spread across her breasts. "Oh, no," he said, wrenching his mouth from hers. "You wait."

His fingers felt thick as he fumbled with the latch. Giuliana had her eyes closed now, dark lashes fanned against her cheeks, and she was still moving on him, the little hedonist. Taking what she wanted, pleasing herself, proving she didn't need him.

"Don't wanna wait," she whispered, confirming his thought. Her hips rolled against his in more frantic circles. She was close. About to take off without him.

He couldn't have that. When he kicked open the courtyard gate, his gaze focused on the center fountain. Its pool was flush with the terra-cotta pavers and six feet across, with eight inches of standing water. In the middle, a carved stone base stood, taller than he was, supporting a shallow stone bowl. Water jetted from it, then fell back into the dish where it cascaded over the dish's lip in a shower of drenching water.

He glanced down at Giuliana. Bending his mouth to hers, he thrust his tongue inside. She sucked, clearly frantic with desire, and her nipples pressed into his chest, hard brands of lust. Oh, yeah, she was ready to detonate.

Fire flared up his spine like a lit fuse. Skirting a grouping of patio furniture, he walked them straight to the fountain and climbed in. Cool water rained down. Instantly drenched, Giuliana jerked away from the kiss, sputtering and struggling against his hold.

"What?" she demanded.

"Cooling you off." He was the captor, the rewards were his to bestow or withhold.

When she struggled again, he let her slide down his body. Her feet splashed into the fountain, found solid ground, and then he bent his head again to take one wet, naked nipple into his mouth.

Her hands forked into his hair. For a moment he thought she'd push him away, but he curled his tongue around her peak, rasping over it with steady strokes, and her fingernails dug into his scalp. Another flame rocketed up his spine.

He lifted his mouth from her and slid his wet cheek over her taut flesh. She made a noise, a plea, he thought, and he squeezed her abandoned nipple between his thumb and forefinger as he closed his mouth over the other. Giuliana went rigid, and his free hand found the small of her back, holding her close. Her desire was rising again, he could feel it in the quivering of her muscles and in the urgent clasp of her hands on him.

"Please, Liam," she murmured. "Please."

But he'd been at her mercy for far too long to give in so readily. Payback necessitated protraction, he thought through a haze of lust. He'd promised her hours and it was going to take at least that long.

Her wet skin made her slippery, though, and even as he tried to grip her, she escaped him. She took a step back, and he stared at her, hypnotized. Her wet skirt hung low on her hips, the sodden folds wrapping her thighs. She was naked from there up, rivulets of water running down her gleaming torso and over her swollen breasts. Her hair clung to her neck in black waves.

From beneath her spiky lashes, she stared back, her dark pupils nearly overtaking her brown eyes. He saw the pulse in her neck throbbing against the thin skin.

He jerked himself free of her spell. "You'd better not run again," he warned.

Licking water off her lips, she shook her head. Wary, though, he braced himself for her next move. Then she dropped to her knees and his heart crashed against his ribs. His captive, transformed to fallen angel.

His brain scrambled as she leaned forward and opened her mouth against the length of his cock, hot breath penetrating the wet denim. Damn! He reached for her hair, intending to pull her away . . .

. . . But it was too good, and his sense was long gone, just what he'd said he wanted.

Her hands had him naked then, too, his cock free to her touch, and he gritted his teeth as her lips caressed his flesh. Giuliana's tongue slid along the rigid column and his head dropped back, lust overwhelming him. Yeah, he was definitely beyond thinking now.

Her mouth closed over the knob of his shaft, its suction as sweet as the sting of her fingernails digging into the back of his thighs. He palmed her wet hair, and she sucked harder, her gaze lifting to his.

Jesus. Lust redoubled as he remembered that he'd taught her this himself. Giuliana had always been an eager, willing, and generous lover, and they'd played like lusty, unself-conscious animals before and after they'd married. Watching her pleasure him like this twined memory, fantasy, and reality into a braid of heated gratification that wrapped around his chest and pulled tight.

"Stroke yourself," he said softly.

She paused, her nostrils flaring, her tongue still on his flesh. Her lashes dropped, hiding her eyes.

"Look at me." He added a hint of command.

Her lashes rose. Her tongue swirled.

He didn't allow himself to be sidetracked. "Touch your nipples." This had been part of their play, too. "Show me how you like it."

Slowly, her hand left the back of his leg. Her tongue lapped at him as she brought her fingers slowly toward her breast. An inch away, her movement froze. Her hand dropped as tears sprang to her eyes.

The sight slapped at him. He'd taken the game too far, too soon, and made her feel vulnerable and exposed instead of sexy and confident.

Cursing himself, Liam moved swiftly, yanking up his pants then capturing her once again in his arms. She was trembling now, and he could only make it as far as a wide chaise lounge before he collapsed onto the cushions. He made the struggle to remove their remaining wet clothes as quick as possible, and then he had her against him, flesh to flesh, letting the sun warm her. He stroked her hair back from her face and laid a gentle, comforting kiss upon her forehead.

Once upon a time she'd been his sweet playmate, his innocent lover, and he'd just pushed too hard. She was quivering under the hand he stroked down her arm. Her mouth turned up to his and he kissed it, gentle again, but she didn't move away. Instead her tongue came out, painting his lower lip. He groaned, common sense ready to make another escape. He held on to it with both hands. "Jules . . ." he groaned.

And then she was kissing him harder, writhing in his arms. His fingers flexed and he felt his good judgment slip through them. He drew her higher in his arms, bringing her nipple to his mouth, and he played there with tender licks and delicate laps. Her hips moved, and he took his cue, his fingers finding their way to the slippery folds between her legs.

"Liam," she whispered. "Liam."

He knew what she liked, because he'd taught her this, too, once upon a time. He opened her with his hand, spreading the pretty, glistening folds to the sunshine. When she closed her eyes, he kissed the lids, and slid one long finger inside her. She bowed into his touch, and he kissed her cheek, rolling his thumb around her clitoris.

Her mouth was swollen and half open to take in panting breaths, and he thought he'd never seen anything so beautiful as Giuliana responding to his hand. But then her body seized, shuddered, and her flesh tightened around his penetrating finger. As her skin flushed and she moaned, sweet and familiar, Liam felt, oddly, like he'd been freed.

She was still recovering when he made a quick trip into the house. He came out with a dry towel hanging around his neck and a warm, wet washcloth in his other hand. Standing over her, he took a memory snapshot of the sight. This was the post-orgasmic Giuliana he remembered. Limbs splayed, eyes languorous, a cat smile turning up her mouth. He smiled, too, the male animal in him damn satisfied with his work.

He propped a hip on the cushion beside her, coming to grips with the return of his good sense. He didn't welcome it, but he couldn't help it, either. Clarity was rushing in with a sharp focus.

He drew the warm cloth over her intimate flesh, soothing the sensitive skin. It had been one of their lovers' rituals, and he'd delighted in this kind of aftercare, knowing it bespoke of a deep trust.

Now she allowed him to spread her legs wider. He touched her with near reverence. Chasing her through the vineyard, he'd supposed that sex with Giuliana would purge her from his system. They'd left their relationship unresolved and he'd counted on the act bringing it down to a level he could dismiss. It would be something to kick aside as easily as those clothes they'd dropped on the way here.

He'd told himself this story: they'd been horny young people who'd loved too easily, married too soon, and paid the price. He'd told himself it would just take some wrap-up sex to finally write "The End."

Except now he knew differently.

Giuliana's legs shifted, restless. He saw her eyes were

no longer closed, but at a sexy half-mast. Her gaze was directed at his cock, still hard, still stretching up his belly. He swiped at the flesh of her pussy again, and saw that she was becoming once more aroused.

He threw the cloth to the ground. She gave him a sleepy smile. "What are you doing?"

No longer a conqueror, but just a man, he took her into his arms and started for his bedroom. "I promised I was going to be inside you for hours."

His level head silently worried that it was going to take much longer than that, much longer than he'd ever expected, to get her outside of his life.

11

Giuliana slipped out of Liam's home as quietly as she'd slipped out of his bed. In her own room, she showered, then stepped into a pair of Stevie's old sweatpants she'd cropped herself just below the knee. The T-shirt she'd pulled on was one she'd found in Liam's room and had worn for her dawn dash down the stairs. Soft from washing, it was the glacial blue of his eyes. In an act of rebellion, before heading out of the house, she'd dug out the rubber flip-flops he so despised from the back of her closet.

She didn't need to please him, she told herself, although he'd seen to her pleasure time and again since capturing her in the vineyard the morning before. *I'm going to be inside you for hours.* He'd made good on the promise, and the memories of it tickled her skin, still sensitive from his mouth, his hand, the possessive strokes of him on her, everywhere. There'd been hours during which he'd just held her, too. They hadn't spoken much—she'd been glad for that. When he'd finally fallen asleep hours after midnight, she'd remained beside him until she was sure he wouldn't awaken when she left.

It was a relief to walk into the cool Napa morning. There was the smell of summer sunrise in the air, that buttery Chardonnay scent that landed like a sip of gold on the back of her tongue. She greedily swallowed it down like someone about to give it up for Lent. These tastes of home would have to last her for a lifetime.

On the shortcut to the winery, she found the abandoned clothes. Her face burned as she balled in her hands their shirts and her bra. The evidence of her complete abandon embarrassed her now, though it had always been like that with Liam. He'd been the patient tutor and she the avid student, her physical ardor for him as fiery as her temper. All these years later, she'd believed she had both under control.

But no.

His Bennett restraint seemed to set her Baci passions ablaze. Maybe they were cursed after all.

Squeezing the clothes between her hands, she refused to believe the thought. Wasn't she walking away from him? Hadn't she done it before and didn't this prove she could do it again?

Liam had said it was "time." He'd implied that the tension between them was making themselves and everyone around them nuts, and he was right. She'd been crazed with desire for him, but yesterday and last night the flaming sex had burned away the last threads of connection between them.

Surely it had . . . right?

She squeezed the clothes again. No one would be up and about Tanti Baci this early, but she'd stash them in her office closet the minute she got in. Then she'd go back to the task of purging the unnecessary files. It wasn't only wanting to get away from Liam that had her heading for her desk at this hour. As a precaution, she was clearing out the bulk of the paperwork when family and staff weren't around. They might ask questions she wasn't yet ready to answer.

In the distance, she saw the roof of Anne and Alonzo's cottage. Though she felt herself smile, her heart ached a little at the sight. Allie and Penn had worked so hard, a year ago, to get it ready for that first wedding. Then Stevie had pitched in to make sure the winter nuptials were carried out. Her sisters joked about purchasing a unicorn to graze on its front lawn, but her mind's eye always saw her mother there, her daughters surrounding her during some long-ago picnic tea party.

Her footsteps took her closer and her smile died. The grass was littered with things, but not dolls and bears and tiny plates. Instead, it looked like torn cushions, ripped curtains, and smashed perfume bottles. Her throat closing down, she ran closer and saw that the entrance doors hung open and shards of glass littered the porch beneath the broken front windows.

She froze. Though she didn't see or hear any movement from the cottage, latent fear held her by the throat. Panic fluttered in her belly and her mind silently screamed, *Liam!*

His name snapped her free of the paralysis. She was on her own, she told herself, forcing her feet forward. She knew better than to depend upon him.

One step, two. Then a voice shouted her name. She spun around, her shoulders sagging. *He's here. He's come.*

Liam's gaze was on the cottage as he ran up. "Jesus. What happened here?" An absent hand slid over her hair to cup her cheek.

"I don't know," she choked out. It took everything she had not to step into his body and hang on. "I just got here myself."

His eyes flicked to her as his jaw hardened. "You were heading inside."

"I had to see—"

"I'll see." He shoved his phone in her hand. "Call the police."

Her heart tried lurching after him as he headed up the walkway and into the house. Despite a couple of deep breaths, her fingers fumbled on the keypad of his phone. He was on the porch again before the dispatcher picked up. "Tell them there's no hurry," he said. "No one's here—just the damage."

Her knees crumpled. She sank onto the grass. Liam rushed back to her and took over the emergency call. Standing beside her, he pressed the side of her head against his thigh. She leaned on him, allowing herself these few moments to absorb his strength.

She was back on her feet by the time an Edenville patrol car drove up. It was still too early for her sisters or any of the other winery staff to be out and about.

"Call the farmhouse," Liam urged. "Get everybody over here."

She shook her head. "Not yet. I have to clean it up first."

"Jules, you can't go in." He sounded impatient. "The PD is sending a team to take photos and fingerprints."

She didn't want anyone cataloging the havoc. It would only seem more real then. "How could that possibly help? It's a public venue. A zillion people have been in and out of there since last summer."

"And another zillion before that," Liam acknowledged on a sigh. "Even the cop told me he brought his wife here when they first started dating."

"Just like everybody else in Edenville." The location had held a cult status for area lovers since before her own birth. It seemed as if you couldn't call yourself a couple unless you'd necked at least once in the Tanti Baci cottage. "Stupid legend," she grumbled.

"I have a few fond memories myself."

She refused to look at him. Looking at him would make

her remember her own memories—stolen kisses, kisses given freely, more intimate lovemaking that she'd demanded from him but that he'd not allowed until they were married . . . and then again yesterday, in those long hours in his big bed.

"I have to ask, Jules . . ."

"It was great, okay? It was great when we were teenagers and it was great last night." She glared at him. "Does that satisfy you, Mr. Ego? Can we drop the subject now?"

He went still. Then he lifted a hand to draw his palm along his whiskered cheek, creating a sandpapery noise that sounded loud in the quiet morning.

Her skin prickled in response, everywhere that he'd left a burn: on the lower curve of her breast, the tender skin covering her pelvic bone, the soft flesh between her thighs. She refused to look away in shame, though. When she thought about it, she was damn glad the day and night before had been so wild. She could hope that the wild had been burned out of her as well as the bonds between her and Liam.

That wildness had led her to rash decisions and deep regrets ten years before.

He was still looking on her with that annoying, bemused expression. Her skin prickled again. "Fine. The earth moved. Several times. Happy now?"

"I was going to ask you why the security alarms didn't go off."

"Oh." And all she'd talked about was how *she'd* gone off. "Well."

He cocked an eyebrow.

This was almost more difficult to confess. "I cancelled the contract two months ago. We couldn't afford it. I've been relying on the window stickers and those little staked signs they gave us when we signed up to act as a deterrent."

He gaped at her. "For God's sake." He then snapped out, "What the hell were you thinking?"

"Didn't you hear me? *We couldn't afford it.*" More embarrassed heat crawled up her neck. "I've been doing my very best, but we still struggle with cash-flow issues."

He took a jerky turn on the path in front of the cottage. She stared, because he didn't do jerky very often. "Are you . . . uh . . . okay?"

"No, I'm not okay," he said, halting in front of her. "Why didn't you come to me? Or Jack or Penn?"

"I ran it by Seth—"

"I'm going to *kill* my brother."

"He didn't exactly recommend it, either," she confessed.

"*Giuliana* . . ." He pinched the bridge of his nose, then spoke again, quieter now. "I would have floated you the money. Not to mention your brothers-in-law. Penn and Jack would come to the rescue, you know that."

She was coming to the rescue. Her plan was just a short time away from fruition. "My sisters and I agreed that we would handle this on our own—it's our place, our problem to solve."

He studied her face, then sighed. "You are one stubborn woman."

His recognition of that loosened some of the knots in her belly. "So you'll stand clear while I go into the cottage and—"

"If you dare, I'll tie your hands behind your back and haul you home."

Outraged, she flushed. "You wouldn't—"

"Oh, I will. I want to." A smile twitched the corners of his mouth. "As a matter of fact, if memory serves me, I have."

Heat flooded her skin. He was trying to distract her, unnerve her, *infuriate* her. And it was working, because she remembered another dark night, a wrought-iron bed, scarves . . .

Exasperated by how easily he could turn her mood, she spun away from him. This connection was supposed to be gone! The tension, the awareness, finally in ashes after all they'd done the day and night before. But he had only to simply mention . . . She pressed her palm to her head as if that could force everything they'd once been to each other back into the farthest reaches of her mind.

His hands closed over her shoulders. "Jules . . ." He started up a tender massage. "I'm sorry. I'm sorry about this mess."

She didn't know if he meant the cottage, their stale marriage, or the way she worried they might have complicated all their problems by having sex again. "I just want to clean it up before Allie and Stevie get a glimpse—"

"No." His hands continued their gentle kneading.

She blinked the sting of tears away. "They were married there, Liam."

He pulled her back against him and crossed his arms around her waist to hold her close. His head tucked so his scratchy cheek was aligned with hers. "I know, sweetheart." He rocked her gently. "I know."

Her nerves steadied. "How did you come to be here, anyway?"

"I woke up. You weren't in bed. I missed you."

After one night in ten years. Tears stung again and she closed her eyes. Then she walked out of his arms. To prove she was strong, she turned to face him. "Sorry to have troubled you."

His eyes narrowed and he cocked his head. "It's going to be okay, Jules."

"Sure."

"Your sisters, you, you'll all survive this just fine."

"Of course."

"Tanti Baci will go on, too."

See, this is why reestablishing distance between them was imperative. He made her want to agree with him. She wanted to say that yes, they would all survive just fine.

That the winery would last forever. But no one knew better than she that it wasn't going to happen.

~

Since returning to civilian life, Kohl didn't always understand what motivated his own actions and reactions. He'd find himself enraged, arms corded, fists clenched, and not quite know what exactly had set him off. Like last night, he could lose chunks of time that he could never account for. He was growing accustomed to bewildering himself.

So he didn't think too hard about why, upon learning about what happened at the wedding cottage, that he'd rushed to find Grace at the vineyard that morning. By the time he tracked her to the tasting room, he was breathing hard and his hangover headache was throbbing at the base of his skull in time with his speeding pulse. In the doorway, he stood for a moment, silently taking her in.

She appeared harried as well, sweeping the floor of the tasting room with the kind of vigor usually reserved for scouring a sticky pot. Her pretty hair was caught in a lopsided ponytail that bobbed with every one of her overenergetic arm movements.

He pointed to the Tanti Baci logo painted onto the wooden surface. It was coated with polyurethane, fortunately. "I don't think you'll get that up."

Letting out a shriek, she jumped, and the broom flew from her hand, its wooden handle crashing against the floor with a loud clack. Those summer eyes of hers went round. "You scared me," she said, pressing her hand to her chest. "I didn't hear you come in."

"Lots of surprises around here this morning."

She bent for the broom and he noticed the way her jeans clung to her butt. He remembered her shaking that cute little booty when she'd been rapping along with Sir Mix-a-Lot. Rubbing the back of his neck, he wondered if he could blame his behavior on the song. Maybe it had been some sort of incantation. A spell that caused him to want to seek her out. He suspected she had special powers, didn't he?

She glanced at him through those reddish gold lashes as she straightened. "What's going on out there?"

"Fingerprints have been collected and photographs taken. All that's left is the cleanup."

"Maybe I should . . . ?"

He could tell she didn't want to and he didn't blame her. The damage to the pretty place had bothered him, too. "It's not as bad as you might imagine. A few lamps and windows bashed and the curtains and couch cushions will need to be replaced or repaired. Giuliana's already making calls. The display case that held some of Anne and Alonzo's things was broken, but the stuff is all there—including Anne's diary."

"That's good." She was back to sweeping again.

"I only wish I'd heard when it was happening." So far no one had asked him what he'd been doing that he'd missed the sounds of destruction from the vineyard manager's bungalow. Prevailing wisdom supposed it must have happened before midnight, when the two couples who were residing in the farmhouse were out to dinner and a movie. Likely they assumed Kohl had been out, too—which he had, in a sense. He'd broken his own rule about drinking alone and spent a lost evening with his friend, José Cuervo.

He thought he could quit the boozing, and he thought he would, from time to time, but the appropriate incentive had been lacking. Sometimes avoiding the present was just too tempting. One drink became four became six became . . .

A big ol' chunk of blown time.

He shook his head. "I missed the whole damn thing."

"I'm glad." Grace propped the broom in a corner and then took up a cloth to dust the shelves of stemware. "You could have been hurt."

"Me? I made it through a war. And if you hadn't noticed, I'm kind of a big guy."

Her hand stilled. "I noticed."

Okay, there she went again. Two words from her soft pink mouth and he was on his way closer to her, like a fish with a damn hook in its cheek. But smelling her on this summer morning suddenly seemed imperative, too, for whatever crazy reason.

Peaches. Today she smelled like peaches. Fruity, fresh, and cinnamon dusted. Her flesh would taste like that, he thought, a sexual fizz charging through his bloodstream. He could imagine peeling away those clothes, slow, just as he removed a peach's fuzzy skin, before he took a big, juicy bite. His mouth watered, and below the waist, his penis started thinking about its own appetite.

"My ex is a big man, too."

Her ex. Kohl moved back. Talk about a buzz kill. The woman had a big, violent ex-husband, which made her the exact wrong candidate to satisfy Kohl's cravings. Worse, he would likely scare the hell out of her if she thought he was even thinking of her in those terms. Sure they'd kissed that one time, but he'd been careful it didn't happen again.

He'd rescued her dog. He'd tended to her injuries when she was seven years old. Likely she considered him as some kind of vet-cum-EMT. Or a big safe teddy bear. Not a man.

Didn't that just piss him off? "What the hell were you thinking to hitch yourself to a loser like that?"

Immediately, he regretted the question. He leapt toward her and grabbed her free hand. "Grace. I'm sorry, I—"

"You don't have to apologize."

"I do. I'm a beast—"

"That's why I brought Daniel up. I can recognize one of those beasts now, Kohl, and you're not close to that category."

Right, he thought, looking down at his feet. He was the pet and people rescuer, to her mind. Warm and fuzzy like a stuffed toy, he supposed. Remember? Not a man.

"I married him to get away from my father, of course. And because he was the only person who ever told me I was pretty."

Kohl's head jerked up. "What? The only . . ."

A clear wash of pink overlaid the cinnamon snowflakes on her cheeks. "The kids at school always teased me. One person said that people with red hair smell funny."

They smelled good. Kohl took in another breath of her peachy scent and squeezed her hand. Oh. His gaze jumped from her face to their fingers. They were still holding hands.

Another woman with her background probably would have run screaming if a rough guy like Kohl had his hold on her. But she trusted him, and that . . . that felt good. Even as his blood started zinging around his body again, Kohl tried looking cuddly instead of bulky and brutish.

Grace's brows drew together, her expression slightly alarmed. "Do you feel okay?"

The alarm registered. Clearly cuddly wasn't working for shit. He dropped her hand and moved a decent distance away. "I should leave you alone." Why wouldn't this sink into his brain?

She made a little movement of her shoulder. One of those "I don't care" gestures that meant she really *did* care. He sighed. "Are you afraid to be alone? I'm sure the vandal is long gone now, but if you need me to hang around . . . ?"

Her smile had a little sad in it. "You're a very nice man, Kohl."

Uh! Enough of that! He found himself beside her again. This time he grasped her shoulders and spun her to face him fully. "I'm not some freakin' saint, Grace. As a matter of fact, I—"

Brain cells sizzled then smoked as he looked into her beautiful eyes. There was something in them, something he couldn't quite decipher but that destroyed his ability to tell her just exactly how demonic he'd become. Demon enough to want to have sex with a woman who had very strong reasons to be suspicious of men.

"You're so lovely," he heard himself say instead. His hand reached for her cockeyed ponytail and he pulled the elastic band confining it free, so that her rose gold hair fell around her shoulders. He took it in his hands, letting the silky locks slide through his fingers. They caught on his calluses and he worked them gently free. "So damn lovely."

That clear, watercolor pink washed over her face again. "I wish you wouldn't have said that—though I suppose it seems as if I was asking for it."

He frowned. "Huh?"

Her blush brightened. "Just because I told you I didn't get a lot of compliments growing up, I wasn't fishing for fake ones, okay?"

His smoking brain was still struggling to catch up. "Huh?"

"Fake compliments . . . you know. As in, not true."

She thought he was bullshitting her, Kohl realized. He blinked, trying to imagine a world where anyone would imagine him capable of that kind of pretense. For God's sake, it was his personal brand of hot-headed honesty that had gotten him into barroom brawls with bad men and kicked out of the beds of good women.

Grasping her by the shoulders, he shook her a little. "I'm truthful to a fault, my friend."

She made a little face. "As if we were friends, either."

Well, hell, what could he say to that? He didn't want to be her friend any more than he wanted to be her teddy bear. So he avoided that subject altogether. "Let's get this looks thing settled, all right? I don't know what people saw when you were a kid—I know I went through a phase when my neck was longer than my legs and my Adam's apple seemed to be the size of a soccer ball—but now . . . now you're just what I said. Lovely."

"Kohl . . ." Again with that little face.

Frustrated, he looked around. "Here," he said, spotting a small display of coasters. There were cork ones in the shape of grape leaves, square ones that depicted labels from local wineries, and round ones that were, in essence, silver-framed mirrors. With one in hand, he spun Grace around so her back was to his front. Then he held it so her reflection filled the glass.

"Here's what I see." He slid his hand through her "red" hair again. "A color like gold and rubies melted together."

She straightened, her sharp shoulder blades poking his chest.

"No BS, Grace," he said, guessing that would be her first response. He brushed his thumb over the soft arch of one brow. "Shall I talk about your eyes? They put the sky to shame."

She was leaning slightly against him now and he tried ignoring how the warmth of her body made a fire inside of his.

"And this nose?" His fingertip followed its straight line. "Not much to talk about, truthfully, except that it leads to such a pouty, kissable mouth."

Her breath exhaled on his hand as he pressed against the center of her lips. "Kohl—"

"Shh. This is about what *I* say, what *I* see." He let his hand fall. Touching her was torture. "As for your creamy skin and its—"

"Creamy!"

"Milky, then. Milk with cinnamon sugar floating on top." He leaned over to whisper in her ear, "You know what those freckles do? They make a man want to spend a lifetime trying to taste each and every one."

A trill of nervous laughter broke from her then, and she

stepped away. She wrapped her arms around herself, not looking at him.

Kohl lifted an eyebrow. "Do I have to go on about your body?"

Grace glanced at him, glanced away. "P-please don't."

That break in her voice told him he'd gone too far. Damn! Wary Grace Hatch didn't need a man telling her how drool-worthy she was. "Hey," he mumbled. "Sorry."

She shook her head wildly. "No, no! I . . ." Her hand gesture told him nothing. "Like I said. Kohl Friday, you are a very nice man."

Back to the teddy bear!

Like that, the anger came over him again. He wanted to hit something, no, hit someone. Grace's ex, or her father, or maybe even himself, who couldn't settle for being her soft and gentle comfort object.

"I am not a nice man," he bit out.

"Kohl."

"A nice man wouldn't be thinking about you when I'm in bed at night. A nice man wouldn't be thinking of you when I'm brushing my teeth. A nice man wouldn't be thinking of you even when my cock aches so damn bad that I want to break it off and beat myself with it . . . so I have to beat off instead."

She was staring at him, that ordinary nose of hers flaring, but he didn't regret sounding crude and rude. Hell, he *was* crude and rude.

"I've been thinking of you, Grace. I've been thinking of those freckles and wondering where they stop. Do you have them on your breasts? On the tops of your thighs? Are they sprinkled on the backs of your knees?"

She was still just staring at him.

"Tell me to stop, Grace. Tell me to go away and stay very far away from you."

"No." Her chest moved in and out with quick breaths. "I don't want you to go away. To stay away."

Shocked to the core of his dark heart, Kohl stared at her. What? There was a look on her face, it had been in her eyes before and he was certain he couldn't interpret it. Because it couldn't mean, she didn't mean . . . She wanted him. That's what his gut was telling him, but his head just couldn't wrap around the thought. Wary Grace Hatch wasn't looking at bad-ass Kohl Friday as if he was a gentle friend . . . but as a lover, a man she wanted.

And because he had no idea what to do about that, he did exactly what she didn't want. He rushed away from her just as quickly as he'd rushed to her. And didn't understand why he did that, either.

12

When Liam opened the door that evening to Giuliana's sisters, he had to agree with Penn's oft-spoken assessment: the Baci women were scary. Taking a step back before they plowed him over, he gestured them inside. "She's taking a shower," he said. "You might want to go easy on her. It's been a long day."

"We'll wait for her in the living room," Stevie said.

He pulled two bottles from the fridge, a sparkling water and a New Zealand sauvignon blanc. Along with the beverages, he brought some wineglasses and a bowl of nuts to the table that sat in front of the couch where the young women had taken a seat. When he caught a look at their expressions, he frowned and raised a brow.

"Why are you giving me the stink eye?"

"Stink eye." A reluctant dimple dug itself into Allie's cheek. "I haven't heard that in a billion years."

Liam had known the Baci sisters for a billion and one. His parents had discouraged contact with the Italian family—and now that he knew of his father's feelings for their mother, he figured he finally understood why. Still, living in a small-town rural setting, they'd been childhood playmates. With his mother most often in a darkened room with a migraine headache and his father pursuing pretty young things far and wide, Liam and Seth had often found their amusement next door at Tanti Baci.

Stevie had made a damn good pirate. Alessandra could always be counted on to play the damsel in distress—her easy tears legend even then. Giuliana . . . Giuliana had been as good as he at organizing and planning, whether it was an elaborate game of cops and robbers, keep-away, or flashlight tag.

Which made him realize she wouldn't appreciate being blindsided by her siblings like this.

He glanced toward the stairway. "Perhaps I should let her know you're here."

Stevie's eyes narrowed. "Perhaps you should tell us what you're after with her first."

He tried giving her the I'm-older-and-I-know-best stare, but she only drummed her fingertips on the opposite arm she had crossed over her chest. Hell. All the Baci girls were harder to deal with now that they'd grown up.

"I'm waiting," Stevie said.

"I'm thinking," he countered. The fact was, Giuliana's sisters had practically rolled her into his house by wheelbarrow. Once the truth was out about the marriage, they could have encouraged a quickie divorce, but instead they'd played the save-the-winery card. He knew that was important to them—but more important than their older sister's welfare?

"Don't drive her away again," Allie said softly. "Please, Liam."

That wasn't what he was after! He'd forced her into his house and seduced her into his bed in order to drive her out of his head—not out of town. Somehow they needed to unfasten the tether they'd recklessly tied between them when they'd tied the knot in Reno. Maybe this stab at cohabitation wasn't the best way to go about it, but he'd been desperate.

"Look. I—" But hell, he didn't think it would make sense to them if he said it out loud.

"What's going on?"

His head whipped toward the stairs. Giuliana was peering over the balustrade, a sleeveless, lacy white top cut low across her breasts. Her hair wasn't styled in that sleek fall that he thought of as her LA look. It appeared shorter now, with the natural bouncy waves curling around her face. She might as well be seventeen again, and lust grabbed him around the throat with the same intensity that had driven him to marry her the minute she'd been old enough to sign the paper.

"Allie? Stevie?" As she walked into the living room, her bare feet and jeans only sharpened his memories of those young years. Giuliana, her mouth reddened by his kisses, her nipples the same dark blush as he'd unfastened her bra and then pulled denim free of her legs. She'd had a pair of panties—

"Liam?"

Her voice jerked him back to the present. "They just showed up," he said. "I don't know what's going on any more than you do."

Giuliana switched her attention back to her sisters and there was an edge of anxiety in her voice. "You're okay? Everyone's okay?"

"We don't need a mother hen," Stevie said, in her usual direct fashion. "We came here to make that clear to you, Jules."

The oldest Baci slowly approached the high-backed chair across the table from her sisters. When she sank down on it, Liam moved forward to pour her a glass of wine and put it in her hand. She swallowed down a gulp. "What exactly has your hackles up, Steve?"

Allie scooted forward on her cushion. "You should have called us right away when you discovered the vandalism."

"It was early. You guys—"

"That's exactly our point, Jules!" Stevie put in. "*You* decide it's too early. *You* decide we shouldn't see the full extent of the damage. *You* try to direct everything and everyone and it's got to stop."

Allie was nodding. "We're partners. We're in this together."

"And you're wearing yourself to nothing by holding on to all the worries and responsibilities. Yeah, Allie and I work hard, too, but you won't share where your head is, and it's not in a good place, Giuliana. We can all see that."

Whoa. These sisters were rough, Liam thought. They wanted to haul out all the evidence and then examine it in public. He preferred the way he and Seth handled their differences—in silence, until whoever was angry had their ire bundled into a tidy package that could be stuffed into a remote closet.

Giuliana took another quaff of her wine. "I look so bad?"

"Don't take it like that." Stevie rolled her eyes. "You look beautiful, you always do, but to be honest, you could probably do with a month's worth of meals and maybe a funny movie or two."

"Some time off," Allie added.

"When we're done with the Vow-Over Weekend," Giuliana said quickly. "There'll be freedom then. For all of us."

Liam cocked his head. *There'll be freedom?*

"We don't want freedom, Jules." Allie set down her wineglass. "You're not getting what we're talking about. When something happens like that vandalism today—or when a decision needs to be made—like who to call about the curtains and the cushions—we need to be consulted.

Together we can divvy up the tasks instead of you taking them all on yourself."

Anger sparked in Giuliana's eyes. "Sort of like how you consulted me about leaking the no-divorces story?"

Allie flushed. "I'm the PR person. Getting us press attention is actually part of my job."

"But according to you, you should have consult—"

"You're being deliberately obtuse," Stevie said. "We're *worried* about you."

"And I'm worried about the two of you, but that makes me interfering and overbearing and—"

"Ah!" Stevie leapt to her feet and pulled on the ends of her hair. "You're not listening!"

Liam froze, not sure whether he should interfere or not. He suddenly remembered the flameouts the two oldest Bacis had engaged in when young. He would have let them at it again, but there was something—something almost frantic—in the expression on Giuliana's face. It drew him close enough so that he could sit on the arm of her chair. He laid a hand on her tense shoulder.

Allie tugged on her pregnant sister's arm until the other woman sat down again. "Jules, we're just saying that Tanti Baci belongs to all of us."

"Not the land." Giuliana's body vibrated beneath Liam's hand. "Don't forget that the land is mine."

Oh, God. Not a good time to bring that up, he thought, noting Stevie's answering glower. Though it was true, that in usual Baci style, the inheritance matters were snarled. He wasn't sure he had all the details straight—or if anyone did—but the vineyard acres were in Giuliana's name alone, while other parts of the holdings were split between the sisters . . . with the Bennetts thrown into the mix as well.

"The land is mine," Giuliana repeated, her voice softer now.

Stevie was back on her feet, clearly frustrated. "I can't

talk to you right now." She headed for the foyer, Allie trailing behind. Manners made Liam follow, and he saw them out the door and then sighed. Maybe Penn or Jack could be interested in heading out for a beer about now.

No. The doting newlyweds would likely be busy soothing their spouses after the altercation with their sister. With another sigh, he headed back to the living room and was relieved to see that Giuliana wasn't in sight. He liked licking his wounds alone as well. But then his gaze caught on her figure. She'd retreated to the adjoining terrace and was standing there looking out over the Bennett vineyards in the direction of Tanti Baci. He sighed again, supposing he couldn't leave her looking so sad like that.

With the bottle and his own glass in hand, he joined her. Silent, he topped off her wine, then set the remainder on a nearby ledge. He sniffed, swirled, took a sip that he pulled through his teeth. "A bright little upstart, perhaps lacking in character, even shallow can we say, but the flinty finish gives it more finesse," he said, impersonating one of the snobby—and often nonsensical—wine critics that they used to laugh about when they were young. "Has a grassy nose, with maybe just a hint of petunias and new pennies."

She didn't even smile. She didn't even seem to notice his performance at all. "Did I screw up? Today, in terms of my sisters, did I screw up?"

His gaze ran over her bouncing hair and tense body. "It depends on who you ask. I get that it's not easy to go to them—you're used to being the one they go to."

Her gaze flicked down to her glass. "Allie, anyway, though she held a lot inside after Tommy died. Stevie's always been more independent."

"And you've never been completely honest with them, have you?"

She slid him a look that said, *Uh, secret marriage?*

And of course there was yet another secret. Hell, he

thought. He didn't blame her for keeping some things private. "You want to protect them. I get that, Jules."

"You're close to your brother, Seth. Now Penn, too. Are there things you've kept from them that they might believe they deserve to know?"

He hesitated, then found himself telling the truth. "Big things."

Her eyes went wide and she stared at him. "Liam?"

He stayed silent.

"Liam?" she asked again. "Big things like . . . what?" There was doubt in her eyes. "Your dad fathering illegitimate children has been out since the will was read."

Shame made him shift his gaze from her face. "I . . . uh . . ." He was regretting like hell he'd even said anything. But it had popped out and he didn't know how to stuff those "big things" back.

He cleared his throat. "I knew about my father's affairs long before he died. I kept them a secret. He used me as an excuse—'Liam needs some sessions at the batting cages'—and his alibi—'Liam and I are going to the movies'—on many occasions."

He heard her quick indrawn breath. "Oh."

"The first time, I was ten."

"Oh." She sounded strangled.

"He insisted I not tell my mother. And how could I? It would have humiliated her and broken up the family—he told me that, too. I don't know how many times I lied for him, all to keep Mom from finding out and Seth from learning the ugly truth. Which they eventually both did, of course, but I never want any of them, including Penn, to know . . ."

"That your father blackmailed a little boy. His own little boy."

He'd blackmailed his grown-up son, too, but Liam couldn't confess that without getting into darker territory he didn't want to travel to tonight . . . or ever.

Then she had her hand on his arm. "Come over here." With the wine bottle in the crook of her elbow, she pulled him toward a wide chaise lounge that was similar to the one they'd made love on the day before. But she didn't look like she had sex on her mind, even though she stretched out on the cushions and patted the space beside her.

He settled in, unable to resist the invitation.

She was quiet a minute, then she took a sip from her glass. "A surprisingly long wine. I agree on the copper undertones but can't get behind the petunias at all. Maybe a little . . . pea gravel?"

His smile felt good. He knew he didn't do it all that often these days. But for the first time since she'd returned from Southern California, he felt that he and Giuliana had found a small measure of peace between them. They understood each other on this level, because they both felt fierce protectiveness and deep responsibility.

He slid his arm beneath her head and she leaned against him, a little sigh traveling through her body. No matter what happened in the future, no amount of drama, no bout of fiery sex could affect this very real connection they had. They shared a past as well as a loyalty to their families and to their land in the Napa Valley.

An errant snippet of conversation whispered again through Liam's head: *When we're done with the Vow-Over Weekend, there'll be freedom.* But he packed the worry away with all the other baggage he had in that subterranean storage area at the back of his mind.

As he'd said, it had been a long day and they both deserved a little peace.

~

A few days following the vandalism at the cottage, Giuliana, Allie, and Stevie were ensconced in cushioned chairs beside the pool at the Bennett house. Beyond the pool deck, Liam, Penn, and Jack were playing some sort of game on the half basketball court situated there. Shirtless, and in bright board shorts, the men were showing off both their muscles and their athletic prowess.

Her gaze on the sweaty torsos and roped arms, Stevie sighed. "I know what you're doing, Jules. You think you can get around my mad by giving me eye candy. Dessert even before the pizza you promised."

Though she hadn't arranged for the display of masculine beauty, getting back in her sisters' good graces *was* Giuliana's plan. They needed to be in sync these last weeks leading up to the Vow-Over Weekend. What happened after . . . She didn't know what would happen to her relationship with her sisters after, but while she was here in Edenville, she couldn't take them being angry with her. To that end, she'd laid out the bait of pizza while they worked at Tanti Baci that afternoon. Liam had made a call to Penn and Jack, and she was given the chance she needed.

Stevie lifted one sandal-shod foot. "If I was wearing better shoes, though, I'd be out there myself, showing them I haven't lost my jump shot."

"You can't," Giuliana instantly said, alarm tightening her belly. "You should be taking it easy. You should be—"

"Stop clucking, mother hen," Stevie replied. "Especially when I've not yet decided if I forgive you for being such a damn bossy know-it-all. Don't push your luck."

With a reluctant nod, Giuliana subsided.

"Speaking of luck . . ." Allie leaned in. "You should hear how lucky Stevie got last night when Jack did his best to put her in a better mood."

"I didn't tell you anything about it!" Stevie protested.

"I *heard* you, didn't I just say that?" Allie rolled her eyes. "We live in the same house and even the floor between us couldn't muffle all your moaning and groaning."

"He was giving me a massage." Stevie slid lower in her chair and her face went a bit red. "And speaking in French while he did it."

Giuliana found herself grinning. "If the guys in Monsieur Green's class at Edenville High had only known what a few *merci*s and *s'il vous plaît*s could get them."

Stevie dipped her fingertips in her water glass to fling a spray at her sister's face. "FYI, I'm the one with the please and thank yous. Jack just demands or provides."

Allie groaned. "Don't—"

"As if you and Penn are oh so innocent. Or quiet, yourselves, I'll have you know. You left off being the Nun of Napa a year ago, and from what Jack and I have seen, you've been making up for lost time by—"

"Stop!" Giuliana put her hands over her ears. "Stop talking any more about this."

Her sisters exchanged sly smiles. "Okay," Stevie agreed. "As long as you tell us everything that's going on between you and Liam."

Giuliana blinked. "What?"

"That's how it works," the middle Baci said. "We tell you about our sex lives and you tell us about yours."

"*What?*" Her face heated. Maybe because she'd considered herself their second mother, that kind of conversation with them just didn't feel right.

"We'd settle for the relationship details," Allie offered. "We'll be happy to know if you like the same television shows or if you're arguing about replacing the cap on the toothpaste."

"We don't argue." Which was funny, when she thought about it, because they had argued, a lot, over the year she'd been living in Edenville but not living with him. The sharp barbs and skewering looks of the past few months had disappeared. In their place was . . . kindness. Caring. Sharing.

She remembered his clear concern the morning when she'd told him about her mugging and subsequent fears.

Then she thought about their conversation the other evening. She'd struggled to hide her surprise at his openness and then her shock at how his father had emotionally manipulated him. Since he was ten years old! Those shadows she'd sensed in him had begun to make more sense.

"We get along fine," she murmured. Fine enough that they'd been in silent agreement about the sleeping arrangements. They'd been going to separate bedrooms without a word about it. "But neither one of us watches much TV. I'm reading a good book."

Allie straightened. "That reminds me." Dipping into the tote at her feet, she came up with a package wrapped in a familiar scarf. "After what happened at the cottage, I think you should have this for safekeeping."

Giuliana fingered the paisley silk wrapping the rectangular object. "Where'd you get this? It was Mom's, wasn't it?" A hint of their mother's signature scent wafted from the fabric.

She breathed it in, and just like that she was facing her mother again, feeling frightened by her bloodless lips and shadowed eyes, but pretending she wasn't. Giuliana had pretended to be strong and capable and that she believed everything her mother said.

You'll have to take good care of your sisters for me.

Don't worry, you'll be a wonderful mother.

"Jules. Jules!"

Her name came to her from far away. She shook herself, then glanced up from the scarf to find her sisters staring at her. "What?"

"Where'd you go?" Stevie asked.

"Uh, I . . . Never mind."

Her middle sister shook her head. "Giuliana . . ."

To get away from the censure in her gaze, she returned her attention to the package. Inside was a leather-bound volume, Anne Baci's diary, that Jack had found hidden in the wedding cottage six months before. Her fingers caressed the embossed leather. "This should go to you, Steve. You're the one who always believed in the old legends."

Allie sighed. "I admit I had a hope or two myself that

there'd be a hint about the treasure in there—if not the out-and-out location."

"She never even mentions it." Stevie gave a sad shake of her head.

"Still, I'm glad we have it." Allie settled back in her chair. "What if it had gone up in flames with the rest of the stuff in Jules's apartment?"

Which popped a thought into her head. "Oh—"

Each of her sisters sent her an inquiring look.

"Uh. Oh." Damn. Maybe she shouldn't say anything.

Stevie frowned. "What are you holding back now?"

"Nothing, nothing. I, um, I was just going to tell you that the police called yesterday morning. There was nothing new to report."

Allie's eyebrows drew together. "What? They called just to say 'hi'?"

Hmm. She beamed a high-wattage smile. "Advantages of a small town."

"Not buying it." Stevie's gaze narrowed. "Despite your practice at keeping secrets, Jules, you are a truly terrible liar. Why did they really call?"

"Fine." She sighed. "There *is* nothing new about the cottage, per se. They just asked me if I thought the trouble there could be related to the arson at my apartment."

The nearby sound of a basketball splatting against terra-cotta tiles had Giuliana turning. Liam was staring at her from a short three feet away, the orange orb at his feet. She'd not noticed that the men had finished their game.

"Why didn't you tell me this yesterday?" he asked.

She shouldn't have to feel guilty! "I'm telling you now. I'm telling you all right now. The detective asked if I could fathom a connection, I said I couldn't, and he said have a nice day, and I said you, too, and then he said good-bye and I said—"

"We get it. We get everything." Liam gave her a long look, then skirted her chair to dive into the pool. The resulting splash sprayed her bare legs and dampened her shirt. She figured *he* was telling *her* something with that.

The mood of the evening seemed to sour. Pizza was delivered, wine was opened, laughter ensued. But there was something simmering under Liam's surface and she internally railed against it. She didn't have to tell him everything the moment it happened. He was only her temporary husband, after all.

When she followed him into the kitchen with the empty pizza boxes, she said as much.

He spun to stare her down. "'Temporary' husband. Jesus, Jules, we've been married a decade."

Defensive now, she muttered, "Ten years of wasted time."

His expression instantly shuttered. Without another word, he took the boxes from her hands and systematically crumpled them between his big hands. She puttered about the kitchen as well, arguing with herself about apologizing. Taking a peek at him, she still couldn't decide. If they'd been discussing rainbows and puppies he couldn't look any more peaceful.

How did he *do* that?

She poked at a chair with her toe. "All right. I'm sorry. I shouldn't have said wasted time."

He glanced over. "It was wasted. Don't think I don't regret every moment of that."

Meaning he regretted every moment of being tied to *her*. Her face burned. To maintain a semblance of dignity, she stalked back to the pool, glad that the landscape lighting wasn't bright enough to give away her expression. She didn't have the gift of Liam's stony face.

Even so, Stevie sensed something was wrong. "Jules? What's up?"

"It's just another couple of weeks until Vow-Over Weekend," she said.

"Yeah . . ."

Liam came into view and she followed him with her gaze. Her chest hurt as he dropped into a chair and made some remark to Penn—something that made them both smile. A couple of weeks . . . and suddenly she didn't know if she'd ever smile again.

She pivoted toward Stevie and put her hand on her sister's forearm. "Steve . . ."

Her sister's free hand closed over Giuliana's. "What?"

She had no right to ask. Any promise she extracted now might be one Stevie would ultimately want to break. Still, glancing at Liam again, she couldn't help but beg. "Don't be mad at me anymore."

"Jules—"

"Don't turn your back on me, please." When this ended, when she and Liam ended, she just knew she'd need her sisters more than she could imagine. When her mother had asked her to watch over them, she hadn't understood how much their love would come to mean to *her.*

Stevie squeezed her fingers. "I'm right here. Allie's right here. But I think we might need to ask you not to turn from us."

Giuliana closed her eyes. Because that was true. She was already on that path. Still, she savored being—for the moment at least—in her sisters' good graces. She needed that, after losing her newfound peace with Liam.

13

In the weeds on the side of the road between his place and Edenville, Liam had to face the ugly truth: he'd lost every shred of serenity. His hand squeezed the metal of the wrench and he slammed the toe of his work boot into the rubber of his flat tire. What had getting Giuliana into his house and into his bed—once—bought him? A mere few days of calm, and now this.

Ten years of wasted time.

"Shit!" He flung the useless wrench away, sending up a poof of dust just as another vehicle pulled up behind his. His half brother Penn climbed from his truck, his gaze taking in the tire, the discarded tool, then Liam himself.

Penn's eyebrows rose. "Lookin' frustrated, bro."

"Yeah." He tried blowing it out with a long breath. "Stupid lug nuts won't budge."

"You want me to give it a try? You're not known for your brute strength."

"Fuck you." Liam realized Penn was joking around, but he wasn't in any kind of mood for it.

"Ouch." Penn cocked his head, clearly more amused than insulted. "What did I do to deserve that?"

"I don't like the way you look."

His lips twitched. "According to most everyone, I look a hell of a lot like you."

"Impossible. The only way I could look as goddamn cheery as Mr. Build Me Up is if I was getting regular sex from a beautiful woman."

Penn grinned. "Okay, you got me. It's a situation I highly recommend."

With a shake of his head, Liam turned back to his car. "Go away, Penn. I'm not good company."

"But I am, given my ready availability to, uh, conjugal pleasure. Hop in. It's past lunch. We'll blow this pop stand and find a beer somewhere."

Liam kicked the offensive tire again. "There's this small problem."

"Call Gil at Edenville Motor Repair. We'll drop your keys with him on the way into town. He'll tow it to the shop and take a hydraulic wrench to the lug nuts." Penn barely held back his smile. "Or just use his own brute strength."

Liam flipped his middle finger at his half brother but made his way to Penn's passenger seat anyway. What better revenge than subjecting his relative to his lousy mood?

"Is there something besides a beer you might like? Maybe I can find a place where you get to tear pillows in half with your bare hands."

He slid Penn a look. "Beer will be fine. Remember, I'm weak."

"You said it this time, I didn't."

Liam ignored this latest dig and stared out the window as they made their way into Edenville. It only took a moment to set up the tire repair at the auto shop and then they were on their way again.

The truck slowed as they turned a corner. The burned shell of Giuliana's apartment building stood on the right.

Ravens perched on the charred beams like vultures. Penn let out a low whistle. "This is the first time I've been by since the fire. Lucky thing that everyone got out."

Liam couldn't look away as they passed, his neck craning to keep the remains in sight. Maybe this was what was wrong with him—it was a delayed reaction to the understandable stressors of the close call at her apartment and then the vandalism at the wedding cottage.

Not a reaction to what she'd said that night. *Ten years of wasted time.*

Hot emotion spiked like a fever through his blood and he squeezed shut his eyes. "Get me to a beer, ASAP." As Penn kept driving, Liam tried bringing his temperature down. This was what he hadn't wanted—and what he'd hoped he'd outgrown—the way the woman could invade his system and short-circuit his good sense, his good intentions, his very sense of self.

He was civilized, he'd settle for staid, even, and life at the mercy of Giuliana tested his control. If he couldn't contain himself, then he was no better than his father, who indulged his every appetite and who had ruined so many lives.

It wasn't until he was seated on a stool at a high table in a downtown Edenville bar with a sweating bottle of Negro Modelo in front of him that he felt a bit more sane. He wrapped his hand around the cold glass and then wiped his wet hand on his forehead. After another moment he felt calm enough to meet his half brother's curious gaze.

"I know," he said. "I'm acting crazy."

Penn shrugged. "You're not acting like an ice cube. Don't know that it qualifies you as crazy."

"An ice cube?"

"Listen, bro. Anybody would be struggling right now. You and Jules have been at each other's throats for a year. It's got to be hard to live with her."

He shook his head. It wasn't hard to live with her. What

he couldn't come to grips with was how she hadn't come to him when she couldn't pay the security company's bill or shared with him the police's suspicions. What made him want to strangle pillows and socket wrenches was the way her comment—*ten years of wasted time*—had stung. Why the hell was that?

"You could talk to me," Penn offered. "I'm actually a good listener and I know what it's like to be involved with a Baci girl."

"I'm not involved with a Baci girl!" Then he realized how ludicrous that sounded. "God." He thumbed his eyes. "When haven't I been involved with that particular Baci girl?" His co-captain as a child. His lover as they moved into adulthood.

But opening up to Penn could give rise to topics that he'd been steering clear of since the other man came into his life. He didn't want the one who seemed like the happy twin to know all the ugliness that came along with the paternal half of his DNA.

"It must be my lucky day," a female voice purred. "By all that's handsome, Liam and Penn Bennett."

Liam's hand dropped. His muscles hardened to concrete, even as bile sloshed in his belly. Standing beside their table was a fortyish woman, sleek and well tended.

Penn got to his feet, an easy smile on his face. "Erin, isn't it? Erin Bell." Glancing over, he appeared to note Liam's distinct unwelcome. Eyes narrowing, he returned to his high stool.

Erin turned her attention to Liam, her smile still at full wattage. "I had the pleasure of meeting your half brother just the other day."

"Move along," Liam said.

Her nostrils flared. "I could join the two of you. I'll even buy the drinks."

"*Move along.*"

She laughed, though he didn't think he imagined

the strained note. "Don't be surly, Liam. So you're husbands. Why, I'm sure your wives—those cute Italian girls, right?—"

"Don't mention our wives." Liam shot to his feet. "Don't speak of them, don't speak *to* them."

"Liam." She had the gall to appear hurt. "Who I really want to speak of is your father. It would be lovely to have a chat about him with his sons—"

He had her elbow in his grip. "Good-bye, Erin."

Penn put out a hand. "Stay cool, bro."

Ignoring the warning, he used his hold to propel the woman in the direction of the exit. "Don't bother me and mine again."

Once the bitch was out the door, Liam's half brother allowed him a few minutes to reseat himself and down two-thirds of his beer. It didn't do much for his temper, but it allowed him time to consider his options. Penn was going to press him for info. When he glanced up, it was to find Penn waiting.

"Interesting woman," the other man said.

"You need to steer clear of her." He decided to reiterate the warning and leave it at that.

"You've said that before. Why?"

Liam gulped another swallow of beer. "You don't need to know."

Penn cocked his head, then shook it. "Must be hell to be you."

Liam choked on his next swallow. Coughed. "What?"

"I figure it's gotta be uncomfortable, walking around with a big stick of noble shoved up your butt."

"Noble!"

"It's what's keeping your spine so stiff, right? And it reminds you to be the decent and dignified Bennett brother, setting a fine example for his family and the community."

"You're just trying to piss me off," Liam said.

"Maybe." Penn shrugged. "Maybe you're already pissed

off. And keeping all that pissiness inside and under a veneer of calm and upright integrity is starting to wear on you."

"Fuck off." He wouldn't be goaded.

"I admire you, man, I do. It must have taken a boatload of control to spend the last year living half a mile from your wife, patiently waiting for her to find the time to face up to your marriage."

Penn was trying to provoke him. Liam told himself that, yet it didn't stop the words from dropping like lit matches onto dry tinder, starting fire after fire in his head. He took another swallow of his beer, trying to douse his temper. "Don't push me," he said.

"Maybe someone needs to." Penn smiled, then leaned close and lowered his voice. "Civility is for sissies."

Liam's hand slammed onto the tabletop so hard their beers jumped. He felt the eyes of the few other patrons in the bar jump to him, but he ignored the sensation. "Screw you," he said to Penn, in a harsh whisper. "Screw you and your talk of civility and decency and fucking nobility."

"Yeah?"

"I'm none of those things. *You're* none of those things."

Penn spread his hands. "I don't pretend to be. I'm the Bastard Bennett, remember?"

"*He* was the bastard," Liam spit out. "Dear old dad. All his stinking affairs—I knew about every single one since I was a little ten-year-old kid lying to my mom about going to the movies with the old man. Instead he'd drop me off so he could bang some bimbo at the No-Tell Motel the next town over."

"I'm sorry." Penn was silent a moment, his gaze watchful. "I'm sorry for that. I hate what he did to you."

Liam's laugh tasted bitter. "Everyone around Edenville regarded him as this successful, stand-up family guy when he was hopping into the beds of his best friends' wives—and into the bed of his wife's best friend."

"Ah." Penn glanced toward the door. "Erin Bell."

"Yeah. She was younger than my mother but they did everything together. It would have killed my mom to know—so when Dad called me in Tuscany and begged me to come home . . . I went. He said that Erin was going to break the news of the affair to my mother and he needed my help to persuade her against it."

He dropped his head to his hands, his guts twisted in knots of anger and sickness. All this was better left in that dark closet in his head, but it was out now, and he couldn't stuff it away. "She had a price for her silence—something, *someone* to replace the man who was ending the affair. I was twenty years old . . . and the price of her silence was me."

"Jesus," Penn said, his voice soft. "Jesus, Liam."

"I didn't touch her. I swear to God I didn't touch her. But for a long time I felt so dirty I didn't want to touch anyone." He looked up and almost smiled at Penn's appalled expression. "So noble, decent, upright? I don't think so. Our gene pool is more like a cesspool."

He shoved back from the table so abruptly his stool's legs screeched against the floor. "I need fresh air." Three feet from the entrance, the door opened and the outside light silhouetted two newcomers.

He knew their outlines.

He could find her mouth in the dark.

Giuliana walked in, her arm linked with Kohl's, her face turned up to his. She was laughing, then she went on tiptoe to kiss the other man's cheek.

Kohl put his hand on her shoulder.

Rage wooshed up inside Liam like an overfed fire. He remembered what she'd said in his kitchen two days before. *Ten years of wasted time.*

He heard Penn's words repeat. *Civility is for sissies.*

He saw Kohl's hand on his wife. For the first time in the last few days he wasn't confused or frustrated or struggling to restrain himself. He knew just what to do. Fuck serenity.

Like a jackhammer, his arm shot back and then rocketed forward, catching Kohl square on the jaw and knocking the man on his ass.

~

After the punch, sensory details sharpened so vividly that Giuliana had to wince. The tree-fall thud of Kohl's body hitting the ground jarred her bones, the smell of tap beer was lip-pursing sour, the flash of ferocity in Liam's gaze hurt her eyes.

She swung toward the downed man, but Penn was there, pressing a set of car keys into her hand. "Get Liam out of here," he said. Then he pushed her and his half brother in the direction of the door.

It all happened so fast. One second she was walking into the bar with Kohl—he'd said he wanted some advice—and then *ker-plow*, he was on the ground and she and Liam were outside, squinting against the bright sunlight. He looked over his shoulder, as if debating a return to the fight.

She grabbed his arm to tow him in the direction of Penn's truck. "This way."

He resisted her encouragement, his expression set. Then his gaze jumped from the bar's door to her face. The sight of his eyes, still that furious blue, made her belly jolt.

"Fine," he bit out. "I want to fight with you, too."

The raw sound of his voice made her insides twitch again. But then he had her hand. When they made it to Penn's truck, she realized he'd gotten her where he wanted her *and* he'd taken possession of the keys to the vehicle.

Goose bumps jittered across her skin as she climbed onto the bench seat in the warm cab. Liam shut the door behind her and she instantly curled her fingers around the handle, instinct telling her to run again.

But another part of her—somewhere below all the jolts and flutters—was breathless and paralyzed by the harsh glitter in his eyes. She'd seen Liam collected, impassive, silent, controlled.

Now she couldn't miss the emotion roiling beneath the surface of his skin.

His gaze caught on her hand as he slid into his seat, the one still clutching the handle. "Let go," he said.

Let go. It was what she'd always wanted to see Liam do, and this might be as close as she'd ever get.

"Let go," he ordered again, and she uncurled her fingers.

He started the engine, and then he stretched one long arm across the back of the bench seat as he reversed. His fingertips brushed her bare shoulder. Her nipples instantly hardened, and she slid down in her seat, hoping to hide the reaction by creating folds in the soft cotton of her sleeveless shirt. Under her light skirt, she pressed her knees together.

It didn't alleviate the sudden ache between her thighs.

They were out of town in no time. She couldn't guess exactly where he was heading—except that it was into the hills. In the ten years since she'd been gone, vineyards had crept up these elevations as well, the value of the crop worth the cost and toil of removing trees and rocks.

But the mood inside the truck's cab didn't match the lovely surroundings. Over the soft exhalations of the air conditioner, she could hear Liam's heavy breaths. Hers began to sync with his, and each time she drew in a gulp of air, she felt her breasts swell. Every inch of her skin felt ready to burst.

Face burning, she turned it away from him, but it didn't help. He pulled off the paved road onto a dirt track and they were surrounded by overhanging oaks. The rutted road caused her to bounce on the seat, her body jumping as roughly as her heartbeat.

Then he pulled off the path to nose the truck into deeper shade. The trailing branches of trees lightly scratched the roof and windshield like fingernails. Giuliana shivered.

She shivered again as Liam punched the controls and the windows rolled down. Cool air blew across her sensitized skin and it smelled like fresh creek water.

Just like that, she knew where they were. A make-out spot he'd known about and taken her to shortly after they'd gone from playful shoves to tentative kisses. Squeezing her knees together again, she slammed her arms over her chest and shot him a nasty look. How many women had he brought here after her that he would remember it so well?

He was staring straight ahead, a muscle ticking in his jaw. His fingers strangled the steering wheel. The tension in the cab could be served over pancakes.

She broke first. "Why the *heck* would you hit Kohl?"

His head turned, and he merely looked at her out of those hot, glittering eyes.

She squirmed as a bubbly thrill shot through her bloodstream. Bad Giuliana, liking that buzz of danger in the air. "There's nothing going on with me and Kohl," she said. "You know that."

"For the last year I've put up with him bringing you coffee, giving you back rubs, acting like your personal errand boy—"

"He works for the winery!"

"Keep away from Kohl."

The steel in his voice electrified her. Her ankle bones met each other in a hard kiss. "You don't make the rules!" Her neck went hot with her awareness that she sounded as if she were eight years old, a child objecting to whatever boundaries Liam was setting for the current game.

Lowering her voice, she unfolded her arms to wipe her damp palms over her cloth-covered knees. "I can see any man I want."

The air crackled. "How many have there been?" he demanded.

His jealousy set hers free. "You answer that question first." But she'd die if he did, she thought. She'd just curl up like a diseased leaf on the vine and drop to the ground. "Erin Bell's one."

In a blink he'd slid down the bench seat. Her shoulder harness snapped free and he made her face him, her upper arms in his firm grip. "Did she speak to you?" A little shake. "Did you see her on your way into the bar?"

Swallowing, she wet her dry mouth. "No. I ran into her in town a few days ago. She told me I was a fool to have left you alone for ten years."

Liam's hands fell away. "She's nothing. Don't listen to her."

So she hadn't been a fool? Because she felt like an idiot now, hot and bothered and her heart beating against her chest like the *boom-boom-boom* of doom. Surely only a fool would feel stirred up by the way his very presence was crowding against her, even with his hands no longer touching her.

But she was, and he was. Liam, usually so remote, was surrounding her with the force of his personality. If another man's energy had pushed at her like this, she would have been out the passenger door on the instant. In LA, whether during a casual cup of coffee or on a more serious dinner date, she'd been always poised to step back, disengage, flee.

"Tell me about the men," he insisted.

Movie stars, she thought. *Tell him you dated famous men at Hollywood parties. Stunt pilots who wowed you with their tricky maneuvers. An ER doctor who saved lives every day.*

"They were nothing," she said instead.

"They're nothing now," Liam added.

His certitude should offend her. She should object to his tone, balk at the order, make her own demands. *Take me home. Stop being so . . . so . . . deliciously forceful.*

Ducking her chin, she glanced at him through her lashes, noting the strain on his face and the taut line of his neck.

Quit all the passionate engagement.

Instead, biting her lip, she shivered. Liam reached over and picked up her hand. With slow movements, he threaded her fingers with his. The slide of his larger, longer digits against the inner surfaces of hers, spreading her for his possession, was like a sexual act in and of itself. Her breasts tingled, the tight tips hurting as they constricted. She couldn't breathe.

"This is how it's going to be," he said. "Until Vow-Over Weekend is behind us, there'll be no journalists, no Kohl, no other men."

There'd never been any other men that counted, but she averted her eyes so he wouldn't see the truth of it on her face.

"For the next two weeks, you'll be in my bed and I'll have you there—and any other place I feel like it."

Her gaze leapt to his and her temperature spiked. He hadn't just said—but he *had* just said, and the unbending intent was clear in the simmering blue of his eyes and the rigid set of his muscles.

She didn't follow orders, she wouldn't follow orders . . .

But, Bad Giuliana, she *so* wanted to follow this order. Her mouth was dry again as she tried to reason it out. Was it because she'd had those years of being in charge as the little mother, tasked with caring for her younger sisters and keeping up her father's spirits after their mother had died? Was there some flaw in her that made her aroused at the idea of being overwhelmed . . . overcome?

Or was it because she wanted Liam to want her just that much?

For two weeks . . .

"And I've decided I want it right now, Giuliana," he said, as if she'd already agreed to his demands. Releasing her hand, he shoved back on the seat until his spine met the driver's door and the rest of his long body sprawled against the leather. "Take off your clothes, baby."

Here? Now? Heat flared on her flesh, hot enough to burn away the material that covered it. She swallowed hard, her brain wading slowly through her jumbled thoughts.

Was this a dare? Some kind of backhanded attempt at pushing her away? Was he trying to assuage his conscience by an offer that gave her a chance to reject him?

Except she didn't want to reject him. Why couldn't she—for two weeks—let Liam set the rules?

Still, she hesitated, her brain on stall, her breath caught somewhere between her lungs and her throat.

"I said I want you naked, Jules."

Her gaze jumped to his. He was focused on her, his attention not wandering from her face, his blue eyes resolute. A shiver wracked her body and she licked her lips, hot everywhere, inside and out.

His right hand shifted to his left cuff. He unfastened the button there and slowly folded back the fabric to his elbows. Mesmerized by the ropey muscles he revealed, she watched as he did the same with the other cuff. Then he linked his hands over his flat belly, right above the rigid length she could see beneath his fly.

Her gaze landed there, lingered, and she thought she saw it flex. "Jules," he warned, and one palm rubbed that fascinating ridge. "Clothes off."

The sensualist inside her skin couldn't take the confining brush of the material covering it another second. Her hands went to the bottom of her tank top.

"Skirt and panties first," he said.

Her cheeks burned. "Liam . . ." she whispered, glancing at his face.

His jaw hardened. "Skirt and panties first."

Oh, God. Ducking her head, she placed her palms over the cotton. There was six inches of stretchy ruching from waistline to hips, and she pushed it down. The elastic edges of her panties got caught in the movement, and her blush seemed to slide lower as they did, all the way to her ankles.

She wiggled her feet to free them from her pull-on flats and the folds of fabric.

She glanced at him. His face still set, he gestured at her with his chin, not having to use words to direct the next part of the disrobing. Hands shaking, she pulled her tank over her head and released the catch on her bra. The two pieces joined her other clothes.

"Now come here," he said.

Oh, my. It was daylight, in the front seat of a truck, in the location where she'd once—more than once—begged him to make love to her. He'd taken charge then, too, and her passion had been able to persuade him only so far. They'd touched and teased each other to climax, but this—this he'd held back from her.

Through the screen of her lashes, she glanced over at him. He was freeing the metal buttons of his fly. The knuckles of his right fingers were swollen and red from the punch. Both of his hands were shaking.

A surge of power shot through Giuliana. A little smile curved her mouth and she turned, trembling herself, to crawl over his long legs. He caught her naked bottom in his hands.

She slid from his hold, rubbing her belly against the hard column of his flesh that he'd released from his clothes. Her eyes closed, reveling in the satiny feel of him against her. She caressed him by undulating her pelvis, and his hands stroked over the curves of her hips, controlling her rolling body.

"Now," she said, already eager to join with him. Edging her knees higher, she poised herself to take him inside. "*Now.*"

He held her off. "No."

"Yes." She could tell he was as into the moment as she, his palms were burning, his eyes so tightly closed that fine lines fanned at the edges.

"No condom."

She froze. This was cruel! He was cruel! If he'd known he had no protection with him, he shouldn't have started this game. A younger Giuliana might have considered taking the chance, but the woman she was now wouldn't ever.

"No," he said again, sounding tortured. Liam wouldn't risk it, either.

He brought her mouth up to his. "We know how to do this, baby," he said against her lips. Then he slid his tongue inside and put downward pressure on her hips so that she stroked his heavy shaft with her body. Stroked it *there*, along her soft and wet layers of flesh and against the aching, pulsing nub at their apex.

"I couldn't wait," he said roughly. "I had to have you now."

And then their bodies moved together, her nakedness against his rough clothes, but their hot and straining parts meeting, over and over and over. His hands were tight on her skin, still controlling, still making sure they were both safe.

This was their unique balance. How they meshed. His tight restraint, her willful pleasure-seeking. Combined, the experience was made better for both of them.

Command and acquiescence. Now and yes.

Heart and soul.

It felt like that as they both cried out. Climaxed.

"Two weeks," he ordered again, as he took her mouth with another hot, wet kiss.

Yes. Two weeks was what she had left for all of this.

14

Kohl squared his shoulders, smoothed his palms over his hair, then approached the Tanti Baci booth set up for Market Night in the Edenville town square. His new shirt felt too tight around the neck and he worried about the amount of aftershave he'd spread onto his face, but he didn't let those concerns slow his steps. He had a date. And a promise to himself. For the duration of the evening, he was going to be the epitome of the three Cs: charming, considerate, and civilized.

It was what Giuliana had advised, right before his jaw and Liam's knuckles had their humiliating meeting. "Invite the girl out," she'd said. "Then remember the three Cs. Show you can be social through dinner and a movie. Food, anyway, followed by some form of entertainment." She'd followed that up with a kiss on the cheek, and then—

Liam's fist came out of nowhere.

Kohl touched his chin with his fingertips. For Grace, he'd shaved so close that the bruise he'd been hiding behind a couple of days' worth of whiskers was in evidence.

He figured she was too polite to ask about it, though he hoped it wouldn't put her off. Damn, he thought, his mood swinging low. If that was the case, he should have at least pounded on Liam in return.

"Kohlrabi."

He groaned, and didn't immediately turn in the direction of the pleased voice. Only two people called him by his full first name. "Hey, Mom, Dad," he said. Though it was his mother's voice, his parents were permanently joined at the hip.

Taking in a breath, he spun to face them. All his life he figured he'd been a disappointment to them, so when in their company, he felt soaked in guilt. Leaning down, he kissed his mother on her thin cheek and shook his father's lean hand. Dedicated vegans, Bobby and June Friday's spare physiques made him feel only more guilty—the night before he'd had rare steak for dinner.

His mother looked up at him then looked him over, her maternal gaze cataloging his every feature and every limb—though she kept her judgments on them to herself. Once he'd grown up, he'd realized they probably hoped he'd use his great size to a certain kind of advantage. Like chaining himself to the gates of a pesticide plant. Or battling whale hunters from the decks of a Greenpeace ship.

"I'm sorry," he said, a catchall apology for his multitude of sins and disappointments.

"For what, son?" his dad asked, smoothing his hand over the face of Jerry Garcia on his Grateful Dead T-shirt. His dad considered the band a talisman of sorts. Bobby and June had met at Woodstock under the benevolent gaze of Jerry et al—from the stage overlooking the four hundred thousand or so concertgoers, anyway—and they'd fallen in love grooving to the tunes during three days of music, mud, and bliss.

They were card-carrying members of the Make Love Not War generation . . . and then he remembered Grace telling him about those anonymous yellow ribbons they'd delivered around town. His chest tightened, mimicking the squeeze of the collar around his throat. They were such good people. Weird as all get out, but they delivered yellow ribbons and nurtured stray dogs and raised three kids who'd survived their hippie-given names just fine—in large part to these two kind souls who still danced to the beat of drummers they'd first heard in the 1960s.

"Kohl?" his mother prompted. "Why are you apologizing?"

He smiled at her, filling with a love for them that seemed to open up new spaces in his heart. He put an arm around each parent. "I'm sorry because I don't have more time to talk. I have a date." Then he wiggled his brows because he knew it was the kind of light touch that would delight them both.

They laughed, as he knew they would. "Who is she? When can we meet her?"

He hadn't told them about other women before, those he'd boffed with the same intent and the same care with which he took ibuprofen, and he felt only more guilt about that.

"When, Kohlrabi?" his mother insisted.

He gave her a squeeze and didn't dare look in the direction of the Tanti Baci booth. "In good time." But not this evening. Introducing Bobby and June to Grace would give himself an unfair advantage. Tonight he was determined to rely on himself to follow through with the three Cs.

As he waved his parents on their way, though, he thought he could be something more than charming, considerate, and civilized. Thanks to this chance meeting with his folks, he felt downright cheery.

He ventured closer to where Grace was pouring tastes for the tourists. They were on for five P.M., and he'd planned to be early enough to allow himself a few minutes of watching her without talking. He still had to work himself up to the social niceties, so while gazing on her, he practiced them in his head.

You look beautiful. And she did. So far he'd only seen her in casual clothes, jeans and shorts, but she had on a dress. The woman had worn a dress because she was going out with him! He swallowed, his gaze taking in the eggshell blue color, the halter top that revealed a slice of freckle-dusted cleavage, the kicky skirt that ruffled around her knees in the breeze. And her hair . . . she'd left it down and he found himself rubbing his fingers together, remembering the feel of his hands sliding through a liquid sunset.

You smell nice. From this distance, he had to imagine that part, but there would be a cinnamon sweetness to whatever scent she wore. God, he loved her freckles.

I've been looking forward to this evening. So much so that he'd been holding an ice pack to his jaw when he'd called his sister's house and she'd answered. Once galvanized by Giuliana's advice, even a sucker punch couldn't keep him from taking this step.

He took more of them now, pacing toward the booth. When he was still eight feet off, she glanced up. Their gazes met and then she quickly ducked her head, giving her attention to the tasting glass in front of her. He didn't miss the blush spreading across her face or the little smile that curved her mouth.

The three people in front of him took their time, but he didn't mind waiting the few moments it took for him to belly up to the counter. He nodded at the other cellar rats doing their time in the booth—the Baci sisters would arrive soon to take over—and then his focus shifted to Grace. *Remember,* he told himself, *charming, considerate, civilized.*

A last-minute onset of nerves thickened his vocal chords. He had to clear his throat to get a word out. "Hi."

Her head ducked again, then her chin lifted. "Hi."

He curled his hands around the counter instead of curving them around her face and drawing her forward for a kiss. What was he supposed to do next? Say? Then he remembered, and he tried mimicking Penn Bennett's charming smile. "You look pretty good."

The minute the words left his mouth he wanted to bang his fists on his forehead. Not pretty good! Beautiful! "That didn't come out quite right," he said swiftly. "I meant to say . . ."

Her big blue eyes distracted him. She'd darkened her rose gold lashes somehow—though he had sisters, he'd never understood the tools of the female trade—and now they deepened the blue from summer sky to azure mystery. He swallowed, feeling like a clumsy ox. "I meant to say . . ." he started again, wracking his brain for the phrases he'd practiced. One flitted through his head and he made a desperate grab for it. "I meant to say you smell."

Oh, God, oh, God, oh, God. He went from behemoth to the size of a flea in the space of a breath. He should have introduced her to Bobby and June. He could have hidden behind them and let the Flaky Friday parents do all the talking.

Dad could have waxed on about his beloved dog. Mom could have chatted about the beneficial effects of kohlrabi.

Something had to convince her to give him a chance tonight and it didn't appear it was going to be him.

Then Grace was pouring out some of the cabernet sauvignon she was holding in her hand. She filled up the small glass, rather than the customary two-ounce taste. Smiling, she held it out to him. "I'm nervous, too."

He tossed the wine back like it was a harder liquor. It steadied his brain. "Are you ready? I've been so looking forward to this evening." It came out as smoothly as the wine had slid along his throat, and he smiled.

She smiled back.

All right. Breathing now. Charming now.

Air was still moving in and out of Kohl's lungs as she collected her purse then sketched a good-bye to the others in the booth and slipped through the gap in the back counter. He met her there, and they exchanged another smile. Then he held out his palm and they both looked at it.

Big. Rough-skinned with calluses from physical work. Men had, on average, fifty percent more upper-body strength than women, and that difference and every other male-female gender distinction seemed embodied in his hand, the one that could stroke her soft skin.

Or strike it.

Caress her delicate body.

Or crush her delicate bones.

He felt himself closing down and moving away—without moving a muscle. *My symptoms mostly fall into the emotional numbness and withdrawal category, with some outbursts of anger to spice things up.* He'd told her that himself. Maybe she'd understand if he made his excuses and left.

Then her fingers touched down on his open palm, like a butterfly landing on a flower. His heart rocked in his chest and he came whooshing back into his body and into the present. He was going out on a date with Grace Hatch and she was holding his hand.

He closed his fingers over hers, and clasping them, felt even steadier. A breath of air silently slid from his easing lungs. "Ready?" he asked.

"Absolutely," she answered.

They took the long way out of the town square. Grace sniffed the handmade soaps on the table outside the bath shop. He took the chance of spoiling his appetite by buying plastic-wrapped Rice Krispies treats being sold by the Brownies. Though he wasn't a huge fan of the sugary things—Bobby and June had a way of influencing a guy—he'd remembered Grace's wish to be one of the little girls in their brown shorts and sashes and with their fancy badges and pins. Feeling her gaze on him, he turned and smiled at her. "Getting in your good graces."

Grace grinned at the little bit of word play and he slung an arm around her shoulders. This stuff was coming back to him. He hadn't been a caveman his entire life. Once upon a time he'd been a favorite of women. Now he just wanted to be the favorite of one.

Could that be true? Steering her away from the crowd and down an empty street, he dropped a kiss on the top of her head. He inhaled with appreciation her cinnamon-laced scent. Yeah, it could be true.

A man suddenly stepped out from between two buildings. Even in a ball cap pulled low, he recognized Daniel, her muscled ex. Kohl froze. Grace hadn't seen him yet, and kept walking. Using their joined hands, he reeled her close, then pushed her behind him.

She clutched his waist, squeaking a little.

"Shh," he said, turning his head to whisper to her, while keeping his eyes on the threat ahead. "Just back away from me, honey. Go back to the square."

"No." Her fingers tightened on his sides.

"Honey. Please."

"No."

Frustration surged inside him. It pitched his stomach and swelled his muscles until he was hard on the outside and a mass of churning aggravation on the inside. The other man took a step and Kohl couldn't help himself. He softened his knees in a fighter's stance and lifted his arms. His curled fingers twitched in a little "come and try it" gesture.

To hell with civilized.

Grace squeaked again and he felt the pinch of her fingers on his skin. "Don't, Kohl. Please don't."

Oh, God. Just like that, the distress in her voice tempered the fight in him. His hands dropped from their challenging posture to cover her icy fingers. "All right. Okay."

He didn't take his eyes off the ex, but he gentled his voice and shuffled back a step. "We'll go."

"Together?"

"Together." The belligerence drained out of him at the word. More backward steps and they were close enough to the public square that he could breathe again. He pushed her around the corner.

"Grace!" The ex had advanced a few steps. "Grace!"

Kohl gave her another push. "Don't—"

"What?" She peeked around the edge of the building. "Just say it, Daniel."

The man had his hands up. "I just want to tell you somethin', sugar."

"Tell me what?"

"I don't blame you. It's not your fault you left me." And then, as quickly as he'd appeared, he was gone.

Kohl didn't hesitate to hustle Grace farther into the center of the square. With his arm around her shoulders, she curled into his chest, snuggling against his warmth. She was trembling a little, but he couldn't describe how much satisfaction he felt in the way she turned to him for strength and comfort.

God, he'd done it. After a shaky beginning, he'd dredged up some charm. More important, when faced with her freakin' ex, he'd gone all Incredible Hulk, but then, with her touch on him, managed to bring himself back to the more civilized Dr. Bruce Banner. Her Beauty had controlled his Beast.

Reaching the flagpole at the center of the square, he stopped. He put his hand on the solid metal to steady himself, then looked down at the incredible, gentle yet strong woman beside him. "You okay?"

Her gaze jumped to his. "Maybe . . ." She bit her bottom lip, then let it go. "Maybe we should try this some other time."

Kohl stared into her heartbreakingly blue eyes. He'd started out the evening promising to be charming, civilized, and considerate. With a long breath, he made a decision.

Two out of three ain't bad.

"No," he said, and swung her up into his arms.

~

"Is Liam meeting you here later?" Allie asked Giuliana as they tied matching aprons around their waists. Their shift in the tasting booth began at five P.M. and ended at eight P.M.

"Mm," Giuliana answered. She stepped into place beside Stevie, who was already pouring.

"Well?" Her youngest sister cocked her head. "Is that a yes or a no?"

"Why do you care?" she snapped.

Allie's eyes widened. "Because Penn and Jack are meeting me and Steve later. I was going to ask if you two want to catch some dinner with us."

"Why does Liam's presence matter? Can't I come with you by myself? Do I automatically have to be part of a couple?"

Stevie gave her a soft kick. "Scaring the tourists," she murmured. Then she smiled at the next woman in line. "What would you like to sample? We have an unoaked chardonnay. Our cabernet sauvignon is known for its smoky flavor."

Embarrassed by her outburst, Giuliana pasted on a smile and applied herself to the short line of visitors in front of her. A few minutes of chitchat and pourings passed before they hit a lull. Then she busied herself with the glassware on the countertop so she wouldn't have to meet the gazes of her sisters.

A few tense moments of silence passed. "I haven't been sleeping well," she finally said. It was true. You'd think she'd be exhausted by the sex. She'd return to Liam's house after a long day at Tanti Baci and they'd start out like mature, polite adults—a glass of wine, some appetizers left by the housekeeper. And then, like kids whose parents went away for the evening, they abandoned the platter of crudités and go straight for the Twinkies and Ding Dongs—in a metaphoric sense, that is. Oh, they'd make it back to the kitchen eventually, so you'd think she'd fall asleep sated in every way.

Instead, she lay awake in Liam's arms, putting off dreamland because being with him like that had for so long been one of her fantasies.

Even with that time limit on their togetherness, she was becoming afraid of enjoying it—him—too much.

"Jules—" Stevie started, a frown on her face, but she was forced to stop when a young woman came running up.

"A baby bump!" the young blonde crowed. "Am I seeing things, or is that a bona fide baby bump?"

"Gertie! Your vision's twenty-twenty. Jack and I are expecting." Stevie's smile bloomed, so brightly it almost hurt to look at her.

Giuliana couldn't look away, though. At first blush, Tomboy Stevie and her Ardenian prince might seem a surprising pair to rush into parenthood. They'd only been married six months, after all. But she'd never seen two people happier about their impending future and family.

Allie nudged her with an elbow. "Imagine that. Our Steve, running carpool and baking birthday cakes."

Tearing her gaze from her pregnant sister, Giuliana opened another bottle of wine. "Imagine that."

"I think we should schedule a huge baby shower for right after the Vow-Over. And you and I should find a free day to explore every baby store in a fifty-mile radius. It will be so much fun to buy little clothes. I already ran out and found a yellow onesie and some tiny slippers with ducks on them." Her little sister sighed. "We're going to be aunts."

"Yep."

Allie sent her a sharp look. "You're good with that, right?"

"Of course—"

"Because I remember you saying last year, right when Clare was getting married, that you never wanted to be a mother."

Giuliana couldn't meet her sister's eyes. "An aunt is different. And I said I liked kids. I don't think there's anything wrong with kids."

"Okay. So let's talk names. I heard your husband joking around with Jack that he thought 'Liam' has a fine ring to it. Do you think—"

"I've got to go do something," Giuliana said. She had to get away because her heart suddenly seemed to be splintering. "I'll be back later. Right now I need some . . . air."

"But we're outside," Allie pointed out.

Giuliana ignored her and fought the knot on her apron as she exited the booth. She flung the fabric down on the counter and then turned back to her sister. "If my husband does happen by . . ." She couldn't see him right now. "Tell him . . . tell him I have something to do tonight."

A movie, she decided, as she strode off, intent on putting space between herself and talk of motherhood, onesies, and baby names.

Liam. God.

After her shift, she'd sit in a dark theater and pretend to be somewhere else and be someone else until she could go to Liam's house and face being Liam's temporary wife without thinking of motherhood, onesies, and baby names. Without breaking down.

Passing the sidewalk eating area of a small café, she heard her name. Glancing over, she felt her stomach flip. But she couldn't avoid the pair of diners at the bistro table by the railing, so she approached them, smile in place.

One of the men stood and waved her over. "Join us!"

She shook her head but stepped closer to give her excuses. "I'm sorry. I have to get back to the tasting booth."

Vern Bristol and his brother Rand were good-looking men of late middle age. They'd made a fortune in something telecomm related—it was never quite clear to her what—and used their time and money to become passionate about unusual hobbies. It had been ballooning and flying fixed-wing aircraft until their wives had put their Pradas down. The men needed to find a new obsession. An old family friend had introduced them to Giuliana.

Vern rubbed his meaty palms together. "Can we come over tomorrow? I just have to see the Tanti Baci caves again."

Giuliana went on tiptoe to peer toward the tasting booth. Her sisters were both busy. "I think it would be better if we put that off until—"

"Please." He could wheedle like a little kid wanting cookies. "A quick visit. We'll be in and out in no time."

She sighed. "Quick," she agreed. "Don't come to the offices. Meet me outside the caves at seven A.M."

When the older men nodded, she waved good-bye and hurried off. Seven A.M. Her sisters and their husbands would still be sleeping at the farmhouse. She'd slip out at dawn from her place beside Liam.

Her stomach flipped again. What would he think about her plan? And why did it matter? He'd only wanted these last two weeks with her anyway.

Reaching a narrow side street off the square, she leaned against a warm brick storefront and took in that air she'd claimed she required. It was going to be okay. She didn't need to hang on to her composure or her secret for all that much longer. Once the latter was revealed, she could take herself someplace private and allow the former to fall apart.

She dropped her head in her hands.

"Hey, are you all right, ma'am?"

The Southern-accented voice had her looking around. A big man in a ball cap stood on the sidewalk. She thought he might look familiar, but she couldn't place him. A lot of different people came through the winery for tastings and tours. He was positioned outside the same shop as she, only on the other side of the recessed entrance door and in front of the second of two plate-glass windows.

The shop was closed, but a ladder stood between herself and the stranger, as if he'd been working on the sign above the doorway. She glanced up at it. Mystical Meanderings. Her gaze took in window display: a selection of books on ghosts, palmistry, and tarot reading. Decks of fortune-telling cards were spread on a cloth, their intricate illustrations glowing in the late afternoon light. A sign taped to the glass listed the hours a psychic was available for appointments.

"Ma'am?" the guy in the hat asked again.

"Oh, I'm fine." She looked at the ladder, looked again at the man. "New shop?"

He smiled. She couldn't see much more than half his nose and his mouth with his hat pulled so low on his forehead. "I wouldn't know. I've got a creepy aunt in Louisiana who practices voodoo, so I keep myself clear of the black arts."

He said "Louisiana" like Lose-E-ana, and to her, his accent sounded straight out of the bayou—though the closest she'd ever come to an alligator was at the zoo. "I thought this might be your store."

"Nope. You have one in the area yourself?"

She shook her head. "Family has a vineyard. And a winery."

"Must be nice."

Until it had become the albatross that dragged them all down. Right now it was the anchor that kept her in Edenville when her survival meant getting away from Liam.

Her husband. In her mind's eye, she saw him as he'd

been that morning, sprawled on his stomach on his big mattress, the white sheets yanked low to expose the long, golden valley of his spine and the top rise of his butt. He'd turned his head on the pillow, his blue eyes finding her dressed and almost out the door.

"Sweetheart?" he'd called, his voice rough with sleep. "Running?"

She worried it wasn't fast enough.

His gaze had focused more sharply then, humor sparking in those blue eyes even as his voice gained that sexy edge of command. "I don't remember saying you could leave so early. I have something you need to take care of."

A hot shiver had zigzagged down her spine. That game. They'd played it all the night before. It didn't matter, because at that implacable tone, her will melted. So did that suddenly aching place between her thighs. "Liam . . ."

"Are you sure you're okay, ma'am?"

She jerked back to the present and tried to smile. "Sure. I—"

"Then let me show you something," the man said. "Look over here." A movement of his head indicated something on the other side of the window he stood beside.

Giuliana hesitated.

"It's interestin'," he said, in that laidback Southern accent.

A bit curious, but mostly polite, Giuliana stepped forward.

"No!" the man barked out.

She rocked back, startled.

"Sorry," he said. "Sorry. You were about to walk underneath the ladder. Don't want to disrupt the spirits."

"You think it's bad luck?"

"Oh, more, ma'am. My voodoo aunt told me all about it. An open ladder like that—it forms a triangle which is a symbol of life."

He sounded completely convinced. "Okay," she said.

"You walk through it, and you risk wakin' up the souls that live inside. You don't want to annoy any evil spirits, ma'am."

"Ghosts," she said.

He nodded. "Them most of all."

Hair rose on her arms, though she told herself she wasn't superstitious in the slightest. "Well . . ." She laughed a little, eyeing the ladder. "I should get going."

His voice hardened. "You have to let me show you this first."

She stepped back. She didn't have to do anything.

"Giuliana!"

Her head whipped around. At the mouth of the street, half a block down, stood Liam. Relief washed over her.

"Come on," he called. "I've been looking for you."

Worry chased the relief. Another one with orders. Memories from the night before flashed like neon in her mind. *Undress me,* he'd said. *Touch me. Taste me.*

She'd complied with such eagerness.

What if Liam's order, one day, was *Love me*?

"Giuliana!"

Squaring her shoulders, she left the stranger behind and headed toward Liam. Love him? She had to prove to herself she didn't.

15

All evening, Kohl had tread carefully. Grace had been spooked by the sudden appearance of her ex—and maybe by his own instinctive urge to fight the guy—so he'd worked damn hard to reassure her at every turn.

The thing was, he didn't feel all that secure himself.

What did she think of *him*? He was a solidly built man, a former soldier, a farmer for all intents and purposes now. Did she find him too bulky? Maybe she didn't like his dark hair. The bruise that shadowed his jaw was already half disguised by his fast-growing whiskers. That could turn some women off.

And of course there was her physical vulnerability to worry about. Maybe the abuse she'd suffered made her wary of a man's touch. She'd held his hand, true, and there'd been that one kiss, but by touch he meant . . . *touch*.

He was afraid to look at her now, as they drove from the restaurant through the darkness, because looking at Grace made him want so much to touch. Throughout dessert, as their evening together was wearing down, he'd had to keep his attention on his double chocolate brownie because she was the sweet he really wanted to taste.

Now he cleared his throat. "Would you like to, uh, do something else now? We could find someplace to get a drink . . . maybe karaoke . . . ?"

"Not tonight, if that's okay? I'd much rather it just be the two of us."

Gulp. What did that mean exactly? Was she ready to be taken back to where she was living or did she mean she wanted the evening to extend a little longer? What would he *do* with her for a little longer? He'd just about tapped out his small talk and his veneer of social nicety was already strained thin.

"Take me to Tanti Baci," Grace said.

His stomach felt like it was grinding on a tray's worth of ice cubes. Tanti Baci? She wanted to go to his bungalow at the vineyard?

Throwing his mind back, he tried recalling in what state he'd left it. Fact was, the army had molded him into someone fairly tidy, but he'd been in a nervous rush. And what did he have to offer a woman in the refreshments department? He couldn't exactly pour her a tumbler of José Cuervo, and that might be all he had besides tap water.

And then . . .

"I don't make my bed," he confessed. Oh, God! Had he just let that pop out? His fingers tightened on the steering wheel. He didn't even know how to begin to take that comment back.

"You don't have to show me your bedroom," Grace said.

Okay, but . . . but then he thought of what they could do. The same thing that generations of Edenvillians had done before him. His jangling nerves stopped their rattling and clanging as he pulled onto the gravel drive that led to the winery. Then he steered onto the even narrower path that led to his modest two-bedroom home.

When they emerged from the car and into the dark, instead of leading the way to his front door, he turned in the opposite direction. "Let's take a walk."

Moonlight glinted palely against the copper in her hair when she turned her head to look at him. "A walk?"

Yes, a walk. Because he was out of words that would tell her more about himself. On his way to perform Edenville's customary mating ritual in the customary location, he could take her through the grounds of where he worked. It could explain more than he ever could about who he was. He'd started the job because he'd had to restart his civilian life somewhere, but the vineyard had become more than a reason to get up in the morning. It had brought him peace, he'd begun to realize, to shepherd life through its never-ending cycle. His first day on the job he'd arrived burned out and nearly hopeless. As the time of harvest neared, he saw that he was cultivating something new of his own. Inside him was growing . . . hope.

Finally, he was beginning to see a life beyond the autumn when they'd bring in the grapes. It was because of the vineyard . . . and it was because of Grace.

That symptom of his disorder—the "limited future" part—was diminishing every moment he spent with her. In September or October, depending upon the weather, they'd pick this year's crop. But that wouldn't be the end. He already had a long list of tasks that needed to be accomplished to ready the vines for next spring. The seasons of Tanti Baci stretched out before him. He saw them now, one after the other after the other. Unless . . .

A worry made him frown.

"Is something wrong?" Grace asked.

Now wasn't the time to talk about financial difficulties. But walking the vineyard brought them to mind, too. He worried what would happen if the winery didn't make it. Allie and Stevie were determined to save the family legacy, but he'd sensed a deeper disquiet within Giuliana recently. She'd been tidying offices and clearing files in a way that signaled she was preparing the place for some kind of upheaval.

"Kohl?" Grace brushed his forearm with her hand.

Sexual heat waved across his skin. Just a casual caress and he was forced to clench his hands to keep them at his sides. He didn't want the sisters to lose Tanti Baci any more than he wanted to lose the new connection he'd found with Grace. By wanting too much, too soon, he could frighten her away.

Control, Kohl! If the vineyard was the solid world that he needed in order to reconnect with being a flesh-and-blood person again, she was the beautiful dragonfly winging through it, the one who allowed him to believe that there were things in life beyond flesh and blood. That there were things that could soar above the ugliness of his wartime memories.

He so did not do whimsy, but she seemed to embody every intangible that gave life magic.

In a few minutes they were standing at the base of the wedding-cottage steps. The blooming white rosebush that had camouflaged the cornerstone had apparently been transplanted that day. The security lights illuminated the patch of turned-over earth and the snowfall of petals left behind. They perfumed the air with a cool and rich scent that paired well with the snap of cinnamon that was Grace's signature.

Taking in a breath, his head spun.

He must have stumbled a little, because Grace was touching him again, her hands gripping his forearms. "Steady," she said.

Steady was what she did to him. He closed his own fingers over her elbows, so they were connected like a plug and socket. Energy flared between them, flowing from his body to hers. She felt it, too, he knew it, because he heard her quick intake of surprise.

"Yeah," he whispered. It was sexual and magical. But as fantastical as it felt, it was undeniably real.

She shivered.

"Cold?" He glanced over his shoulder. "I thought we might take a tour of the cottage." The keys to the door were in his pocket. "It's as good as new, now."

She hesitated.

Kohl smiled. "You're not afraid of ghosts, are you? I think Anne and Alonzo are the friendly kind."

"You believe you'll see them?"

He hesitated. She was asking if he believed this feeling, this thrill of awareness that was humming between them, was something besides a sexual thrill. True love? They both knew the legend. He shrugged, unsure of himself again. Unwilling to commit either way.

"Daniel is superstitious," she said, turning her face from him. She broke free of Kohl and spun around. Her palms rubbed her upper arms. "He throws salt over his shoulder. He considers Friday the thirteenth an unlucky day. If he comes across a black cat, he kicks it."

Anger fired in Kohl's blood. Had he kicked *her*, this sweet bit of magic? When he'd beaten his wife, had his cowardly excuse been his fear of that gift that made her unordinary?

"Grace." He strode forward to put his hands on her shoulders. "You can trust me. I'm not him."

"I know."

But it wasn't enough. He needed to be certain that she saw him as different from that other man. He needed her to talk freely of herself and know that he accepted everything about her. "You're beautiful," he said, then hung his head. "I've said that too many times."

She stifled her laugh with a hand over her mouth.

The soft sound made him turn her toward him. "Honey. You know me." And she did, he thought. In the short space of time they'd been acquainted, he'd shown her every side of himself. He held out his arms. "I want to know you, too."

When she was silent, he brushed a hand over that sunset hair. "How do you do it?"

"I-I don't know."

He was gratified that she didn't pretend she didn't understand. Then she glanced up at him, glanced down again. "It's a tingle, I guess. It doesn't work every time. But often someone says they're looking for something and . . . it just occurs to me where it is. Nothing special."

Nothing special? That was the first thing that his Friday upbringing could help her with. Once you'd been named Kohlrabi, or Marigold, or Zinnia, you could never really see yourself as someone like everyone else. It gave a person a certain kind of resilience, and for the first time, he could see some real value in that.

"My mother's going to love you," he said, grinning.

"Kohl . . ."

He cupped her face in his hands and kissed those tender lips. She smiled through it and his heart jumped, then stabilized. There it was again. Even lip-to-lip, she steadied him.

Her head ducked again, breaking the kiss.

He pressed his lips to the smooth skin of her forehead. "You wanted to be a Flaky Friday . . . just think about it. With your special talent, you're well on your way."

"You really are okay . . . well, you don't think it's weird?"

"I don't understand it, but I don't need to." You couldn't explain love, either, could you?

Her gaze came up. A little dimple peeked at the corner of her mouth. He found it adorable. "Have you lost something?" she asked, her voice shy. "I'd like to find something for you."

He'd seen her do it before, but frankly, a part of him still had his doubts. "I saw your daddy witch a well once."

She stiffened a little. "I'm nothing like him."

"No." He touched her pretty hair again.

"So . . . what's missing?" she insisted. "What's missing in your life?"

He ran his finger down her nose. "Right now, not a thing."

Her dimple winked again. "That's it exactly, Kohl. A person or a thing."

She was serious. He looked around him, seeking inspiration. His gaze lit on the cottage, and what came to him was not even a serious thought. "The Bennett-Baci treasure," he said. "Where is it?"

He thought she'd laugh it off. Perhaps she didn't know enough about the uncertainty of its very existence, because her expression was solemn as she cocked her head and closed her eyes. She swayed a bit, and her hand reached out to touch the cottage wall.

At that, her eyes popped open. Her gaze on Kohl, she blinked. Then her head turned. She was staring at the cornerstone. "It's there," she said.

"What?"

"It's under that metal plaque."

He didn't believe it. But he couldn't exactly say so. With her gaze on him, he slowly reached into his pocket for his pocket knife. "Under the plaque?"

"It's a cornerstone, right? Often important things are buried behind or beneath them."

It took some poking and prying. But it wasn't that difficult to free a corner from the masonry. And then the entire plaque was loose. "I'm going to have to figure out a way to explain this tomorrow . . ." he started.

And then he saw it. The space. And in the space was a metal box, like the one that had housed Anne's diary. But inside this box wasn't a book. This something was oddly shaped and rolled in crumbling paper and dusty flannel. And inside the packing materials was—

"Bells," Grace said. "A pair of bells."

Kohl squinted. He supposed she was right. Each the size of a . . . kohlrabi, they were a dark-stained metal. Jewels encrusted the edges and they were set on a lacy stand of more metal, almost like a crown.

He shook his head. "Wow . . . just wow."

She smiled, and it was such a life-giving sight that his heart took flight—just like a dragonfly. Oh, he was so doing whimsy. Kohl caught Grace up in his arms. "You are amazing."

Their mouths met. Though his heart was still soaring, he felt steady, strong . . . himself. Finally, after all this time, himself.

"You found it," he said against her lips. But he didn't mean the treasure. She'd found something more valuable—inside Kohl she'd found the better man who'd been missing for so long.

~

Grace Hatch squeezed her eyes tight shut and hoped to goodness she wasn't dreaming. But she couldn't be, she couldn't, because she was in Kohl Friday's arms and pressed into her back was the metal edge of those bells. She'd found them . . .

. . . And he'd taken it in stride.

Taken her into his warm, sure embrace.

"Kohl," she said against his mouth.

He lifted his head to gaze on her with his dark eyes. For so long she used to watch him from afar. First those growing-up years and then later, when he'd returned to Edenville, she'd see him around town. One of the perks of her job at the winery was the secret thrill she got out of looking at him every day on the grounds of Tanti Baci. Just glimpsing him made her feel so safe.

Now, though, now he was looking at *her*. And she didn't feel quite so secure.

He touched his forehead to hers. "I hear wheels turning."

She voiced a niggling doubt. "Giuliana."

"Ah." He leaned over to deposit the bells on the bed of rose petals, then straightened to sweep his palms over her hair. "She was good to me and I'm grateful for that. I thought it meant something more . . . but now I realize . . . it's nothing compared to what I feel for you."

Grace's heart expanded in her chest. The pressure on her ribs was the best possible hurt. It healed so many of her lingering bruises and unseen scars. "I didn't know it could be like this."

He smiled at her. Then he straightened and took a step back. "But I have to be honest, honey. I'm not suddenly Mr. Sunshine. Though I've been improving lately, I still sometimes drink too much, I still sometimes have blackouts."

She reached out to place her fingertips on his chest, and his heart thudded against them. "You'll never scare me. Or scare me off."

He covered her fingers with his own and laughed. "I'm not trying to do that . . . believe me. But you have to know who I am and what kinds of things I've done. I was out of it the night the cottage was trashed. I lost time the evening of the fire at your apartment, too. I might even be smoking again—please, God, don't tell my mother—because I came to with matches in my pocket and—"

Kohl froze. His handsome face turned horrified. "Jesus. What kinds of things *have* I done?"

He stepped back again, leaving her hand clutching at air. "Kohl," she said. "You can't imagine—"

"I can't know." He put his hands to his head and took another step back. "I watch cop shows. I had means and opportunity."

"And motive?"

"I'm a bad-tempered son of a bitch. Maybe I was mad at Giuliana for going back to Liam. Maybe I wanted to hurt her."

"Don't be silly." Grace's own temper lit. She'd never realized she actually had one before this moment, but now she felt hot and fierce and ready to do battle. "She hadn't gone back to him the night of the fire. And you'd never hurt someone like that. Maybe you'd slug somebody, or punch a wall in frustration, but you wouldn't do anything sneaky and mean."

He yanked on the ends of his hair. "How do you know, Grace?"

Her heart was everywhere, throbbing in her fingertips, pulsing in her belly, making her toes tingle. Grace Hatch had been the "little rabbit" Kohl had called her for twenty-four years. She'd been the downtrodden daughter and the abused wife. What she'd never, ever been in her entire life was a woman. The situation called for that now. The situation called for her to be the fighter this time, and wage war to get through to her man.

She stepped up to him, toe-to-toe. Her fingers fisted in his shirt and she used them to draw him close. "Because I know sneaky and mean firsthand, Kohl," she said, her voice fierce. "I could never be in love with someone like that."

Breathing hard, he stared at her. Then he broke. He swept her up in his embrace, taking her feet straight off the ground. Her heart seemed to break, spilling a sweet, hot liquid that felt like joy. Dropping her head back, she laughed. And then harder, when he swung her in a wide circle.

In that movement, she was both the carefree child she'd never been and the cherished woman she longed to be. "Kohl." She was still laughing as he took her around and around. "I'm getting dizzy."

"Then we're even." But he stopped twirling and let her slide down his body. Her breath caught as her body skimmed along his hard muscles. Every one.

He groaned. "Grace . . ."

"Make love to me," she said, her voice husky.

"What?" He looked around. "Here?"

She laughed again. "No. In that unmade bed of yours."

"What the lady ordered." He swooped to retrieve the tarnished bells.

The action gave her second thoughts. "Oh. Should we make some calls to the Baci sisters tonight?"

"Nope. Tonight, all the treasures belong to me."

~

Vern and Rand Bristol were waiting for Giuliana outside the caves when she made it to the entrance a few minutes before seven o'clock. She quickly let them through and punched the security code, eager to not be seen with the brothers by anyone. They were her secret until after the Vow-Over Weekend.

The caves were their chilliest in the mornings, so she'd dressed in jeans and thick sweatshirt over a thinner tee. It should have been enough. But still, as the doors closed behind her, she shivered so hard her teeth nearly chattered.

She hadn't wanted to leave the soft sheets of Liam's bed. They'd gone out with her sisters and brothers-in-law the night before after all. The other two couples had laughed and teased throughout the meal, trading ridiculous ideas for baby names. Of the worst, one sounded like a Harry Potter incantation. The other was just plain silly.

Fabulosa Magnifica Parini.

Myauntiescool Andspoilsme Parini.

And she hadn't been able to do anything but move her food around her plate and remember that her husband had suggested to Jack that "Liam" might be a good name for the baby.

"You're not eating," he'd said then, leaning close and spearing a chunk of roasted zucchini from her plate. He'd held his fork to her mouth. "You need to keep up your strength."

She worried she'd never be strong enough to resist him.

"Giuliana?"

Shaking herself, she realized that Vern and Rand were staring at her. "I'm sorry . . . I missed what you said."

"We were saying we're happy to poke around by ourselves if you'd like. You seem a bit preoccupied."

"Oh." She shoved her hands in her pockets. "Fine. I'll tidy up the tasting area." Being alone was best right now. "I can let you have twenty minutes, okay?" Longer could risk discovery.

The men disappeared down a side passage. She aimed her feet straight ahead to where the carved bar stood. To one side was an old wooden wheelbarrow that displayed Tanti Baci T-shirts sized from small to XXL. Operating on automatic, she began checking the stacks to ensure they were arranged by size. It was one of the first jobs her mother had given her at the winery, besides watching over her little sisters.

Then, the tasting room had been part of what was now the administrative offices. In the early mornings, before visitors arrived, Stevie and Allie used to ride their tricycles on the sidewalk outside. She and her mother would work beside each other, one eye on the younger girls, as they moved around the retail area tidying merchandise.

Closing her eyes, Giuliana could remember her mother's smile as she watched the little Baci girls careen back and forth. The maternal content had been catching and she had shared smiles with her mom over their antics. Though they were only a few years younger, she'd enjoyed her status as the oldest. The happy mother's helper.

Big Girl. Remembering that funny nickname, she chuckled to herself. They'd had an idyllic childhood and she was glad they'd enjoyed it so fully, without an inkling of their troubled future ahead.

A loud clatter caused her eyes to pop open. Her heart jerked as the cave doors flung open and a passel of people rushed inside. Their footsteps echoed loudly. Allie, red-cheeked, followed by Penn, a bemused smile on his face. Kohl and Grace next, who looked extremely pleased with themselves . . . and each other? Jack and Stevie brought up the rear, walking at a more sedate pace.

Allie skidded to a halt, her face breaking into a grin. "Ask them, Jules! Ask them what they found last night!"

"Who?" She glanced around at the people circling her, pausing for a moment on her middle sister's face. "Steve, you feeling all right?"

The other woman waved the concern away. "Jack's already told me I have the pallor of death." Her fingers crept around to her lower back. "Have we got a surprise for you."

Giuliana swallowed and tried not to keep herself from looking in the direction of the secret visitors. "Why don't we go discuss this in my office? It's warmer there and I can make coffee."

"We need something stronger than that!" Allie crowed, pirouetting on one foot just like she did when she was five years old.

"Penn, she's going to hurt herself," Giuliana cautioned. "Can't you do something?"

Allie stopped midturn. "Stevie's right. Cluck, cluck. We don't need a mother hen . . . we need a bottle of something sparkly!"

Laughing, Penn shook his head. "Your mood is bubbly enough."

Giuliana slid a glance toward the last place she'd seen Vern and Rand. "In my office. I'm sure I have what everyone needs in there." Sweeping out her arms, she tried herding the group toward the doors.

Allie groaned. "Jules. Please. Ask Kohl and Grace what they found last night."

Okay, just get it over with. She turned to the vineyard manager and his companion. "What? What did you find?"

From behind his back, Kohl withdrew his hand. Cupped in his big palm was something tarnished. Something of metal and . . . diamonds?

"It's bells," he said. "We found it behind the cornerstone plaque. Another of Alonzo's hidey-holes, I guess."

Giuliana stared at it. "What kind of bells?"

"Wedding bells," Allie answered. "That's my guess. Silver and gold and diamonds. I've got to do some research. I'm not even cleaning it up until I find out more information."

"You're telling me . . ."

"It's the treasure," Liam finished.

Her head jerked up. She hadn't realized he'd arrived. He was staring at the item, a small smile on his face. Then his gaze lifted to hers. "What the hell, Jules. I think you coming back to Tanti Baci has brought the place good luck."

Oh, no. No, it hadn't. And as if to prove that, from the side passage her secret visitors made an appearance. "Hey, there." They looked uncomfortable, as well they should, Giuliana thought, because they knew their tentative deal was supposed to stay under wraps for another week.

With a high humming in her ears, Giuliana could only make a vague gesture at them. "Early, um, guests."

Liam had gone still. She read his silent comment: *Oh, God.* His head shaking, he looked at her again. She supposed he knew something.

"Vern and Rand Bristol," he said, proving he knew *them*, at least.

Allie picked up on the tension. "What's going on?" she demanded, all her exuberant bubbles popped. "Liam, you seem to understand."

"When it comes to your sister," he said, "I'm always at a loss."

Allie whirled toward her. "Jules?"

Really, could the morning get any more messed up?

"They're buyers," she said, weary of all the deception. "I've decided to sell them the Tanti Baci land."

There was a moment of charged silence. Everyone stared at her. Then Stevie suddenly moved, one hand grabbing Jack's arm, the other cupping her belly. "Something's wrong."

16

Liam ran to the farmhouse for Jack's car so the other man could drive Stevie to the ER. Nobody argued about that choice, nor about anything else. The fighting would come later, Liam figured, after the Baci sisters were assured that she was fine.

Surely Stevie was fine.

Once he returned to the winery, Liam did what Liam did best: he put on his stoic face. Others took their cue from him. The Bristol brothers had apparently made tracks while he was retrieving the sedan, so he only had to hold doors for Jack as he carried his wife out of the caves and gently deposited her into the car. Liam retained his impassive expression as they all gathered on the sidewalk.

"Call us as soon as you know something," he told Jack.

"Of course." The other man tucked a blanket he'd dragged from the backseat around his wife, then cupped her cheek in his hand.

Stevie closed her eyes and turned her face into it. A tear seeped from beneath her lashes.

Allie made a little sound and Penn pulled her into his arms. Liam glanced at Giuliana, but she was looking away, her expression remote. Stoic, like his.

"Let's all wait at the farmhouse," he said.

Kohl and Grace decided to go about their usual tasks. They handed Allie the treasure, wrapped in some kind of material, and she took it absentmindedly. Then she and Penn, Giuliana and Liam, trudged down the gravel drive to the Baci home.

In the kitchen, the sisters busied themselves making coffee. Even with this mundane task to distract them, the tension in the room seemed to have its own heartbeat. Two minutes living with it and Liam wanted to run as fast as he could in the other direction.

But calm and collected Liam couldn't do such a thing. Still, his gaze met his half brother's and the other man seemed to understand. "Hey," Penn said, "I have some items on the Honey-Do list you can help me with while we wait, Liam."

Liam knew Allie would hate the term "Honey-Do list." When she didn't react, Penn's eyes widened. "Alessandra . . ."

His wife shook herself, then turned toward her husband. "What?"

He stared at her a moment, then sighed. "You know I love you beyond bearing, right?"

"Yes." Her mouth curved in a small smile and Liam had to look away from the intimacy in her gaze.

He was damn happy to follow Penn outside to the close-cropped grass in the backyard. There, he managed to inhale a few deep breaths. While the palpable strain in the kitchen had been uncomfortable and Allie's clearly shaken reaction disturbing, Giuliana's lack of one had nearly rocked him off his feet. Running sounded so damn good again.

"You okay, bro?"

He turned to Penn. The other man had dragged a couple

of cardboard boxes from a nearby shed. "Of course I'm all right," he lied. He knew his expression appeared unruffled. He was good at looking that way. "I'm always all right."

"So you say now. Wait until you see what I have for you to do."

Bemused, Liam studied his half brother, who looked even more of a reflection of himself than usual. Apparently they'd reached for similar articles of clothing when they'd been yanked out of bed by the call from Kohl and Grace. Both of them wore jeans, plain white T-shirts, running shoes. "You actually have a chore for me to do? I thought we were just dodging all the anxiety percolating with the coffee in that kitchen."

"Of course I have a chore." And with that, Penn turned over one of the boxes. Tangled strings of outdoor lights landed in a heap on the grass.

"And FYI, I wasn't dodging my wife and her feelings." There was an edge of cool reproof to his half brother's usually genial demeanor. "I thought Jules needed a shoulder and it didn't look as if she'd open up with you around."

Hell. Was he that forbidding? He stared at Penn. "Thanks for making me feel like an asshole."

"Cold fish," Penn said, almost cheerful again. "That's why you get the crappy task."

"Was that supposed to be a pun?" Liam asked, annoyed. "Cold fish? 'Crappie'?"

"No. It really *is* crappy. You need to straighten out those strings of fairy lights and make sure they all work. Allie wants them decorating the farmhouse on Vow-Over Weekend."

Shit. Liam stared down at the jumble of wires and little bulbs. He remembered Giuliana talking a while back. *When we're done with the Vow-Over Weekend, there'll be freedom.* "Do you think . . ." He didn't even want to say it out loud.

Penn was rummaging through the other box. "I think

we should tackle one problem at a time. Right now I'm working on a flowerbed irrigation issue. You untangle the lights."

"Hollywood asshole," Liam muttered under his breath. "Should've known you'd go all Zen on me."

"I'm sorry, what was that?" Penn asked. "My mind was on my Emmy award and my favorite brand of green tea chai."

Liam rolled his eyes but took a seat on the grass and began unspooling the mess at his feet. Penn was quiet, too, and the only noise was the buzz of bees sniffing around the blossoms on the two citrus trees in the corner of the yard. His thoughts were as snarled as the lights, and even as he tried tugging one free—the discovery of the treasure, say, or the shocking announcement of the sale of the land—it was quickly subsumed again by the larger scramble.

The images were worse: the tear on Stevie's cheek, the distress on Allie's face, Giuliana's frozen expression.

Through an open window, he heard the sisters' voices. They'd moved from the kitchen, he decided, and were taking seats in the dining room. "Put some sugar in your mug," Allie directed.

"I don't like my coffee sweet."

"Use it anyway, you're looking shocky."

The telephone rang. He and Penn both froze. Footsteps clattered against the hardwood floor. Then returned to the dining room.

"Jules, it was nothing," Allie said, on a sigh. "A robo-call." There was a long pause. "Jules? *Jules?*"

Liam tensed to move. Then he remembered Penn's words. *I thought Jules needed a shoulder and it didn't look as if she'd open up with you around.*

Shooting a look at Penn, he shook his head at his brother. Okay. Give her the chance to share with her sister her concerns over Stevie.

"She can't lose the baby," Giuliana finally said, her

voice tight. He could imagine her fingers clenched in a white-knuckled igloo on the table.

“We can hope she won’t,” Allie replied. “But no matter what, Stevie will—”

“Don’t say she’ll be fine. Don’t say she’ll be fine like it won’t matter if there’s no Fabulosa Magnifica or My-auntiescool Andspoilsme.”

“Of course it would matter,” Allie said soothingly. “But it wouldn’t be the end—”

“It *would* be the end of the world!” Giuliana interrupted. “It would be the end of the world as she knows it.”

Liam went to stone. Only inside him was movement. His heart beating in a jagged rhythm. His blood lurching through his veins in hot, caustic bursts.

“Jules.” Chair legs scraped. “I was going to say it wouldn’t be the end of her hopes for a family with Jack.”

Penn’s gaze went from the open window to Liam. His Hollywood half brother’s face was guarded, a mirror image of what he suspected was his own expression. Liam had learned to be cautious, cagey even, when he was ten years old and started lying for his father. *Never give away the truth.*

Chair legs scraped again and he imagined Allie taking the seat beside her sister. Her voice softened. “What’s going on, Jules?”

“Stevie—”

“This isn’t about Stevie.” Allie was going into scary-Baci-girl mode—tenacious and demanding. “Don’t. Don’t turn away from me. Tell me what’s wrong.”

Don’t tell her. Liam’s heart rate spiked. *Don’t say it out loud. Please don’t make me hear it.* He could feel the weight of Penn’s gaze, and he wished it could cut a hole in the soft earth and then sink him.

Bury him before he had to hear his wife say—

“I lost my baby. Ten years ago I lost a baby.”

Allie gasped.

Liam's face remained the unperturbed mask he'd cultivated over the years. He could feel it settled into the calm lines of a mature man, visually unmoved by a long-ago disappointment.

"I was in Tuscany—" Giuliana's voice broke.

Her distress snapped his equanimity. He jumped to his feet. Disappointment? Who was he kidding? It had been a fucking catastrophe.

"What happened?" Allie said.

"We'd heard the baby's heart."

His own battered against his ribs, a desperate prisoner, rattling the bars of its cage. He remembered the moment, the nurse at the clinic pressing the wand on the golden skin of his wife's belly. Thanks to pregnancy tests, they'd known she was pregnant, but then, with that *whoosh-whoosh-whoosh* sounding in the room, he'd *known* it. He and Giuliana had made a baby. An odd euphoria had seemed to lift his feet from the ground. *No one and nothing can take her from me,* he remembered thinking. *This cements it.*

What a fool he'd been.

"It *was* a baby," Giuliana was saying. "Though they tried to tell me, after, that it was nothing. A positive test could be wrong, they said."

Oh, God. This was new. He didn't know they'd tried to take that away from her . . . Giuliana had needed to mourn and someone had tried to tell her she was grieving over a mistake.

"I heard the heartbeat, Allie. I heard it."

"Shh," her sister said. She must be touching her sister now—holding her hand or enfolding her in her arms. "I know you did, Jules. I know you did."

They'd heard the heartbeat. He'd taken both her hands in his, looked into her eyes, and as the nurse turned up the volume of that *whoosh-whoosh-whoosh*, he'd silently pledged himself to her again. *I'll never leave you . . .* Not two weeks later, he had.

Giuliana would have tears on her face now. She'd had tears on her face in Tuscany, when she'd miscarried the baby, he supposed, but he'd missed them on both occasions.

"I was so alone," he heard his wife whisper.

"Alone?" Allie's voice turned sharp. "Where was Liam?"

Ah, there it was.

But she didn't answer. Instead, she said, "I didn't worry at first. I hadn't had morning sickness. Maybe the cramps were my version. When it was more, I called the clinic.

"Don't worry, I was told. It's probably nothing. Put your feet up and the symptoms should stop."

"Oh, Jules." Allie sounded so sad. "They didn't stop."

"No. Soon . . . soon I knew there wasn't hope."

There was a beat of silence, then Allie repeated her question. "Jules, where was Liam during all this?"

He'd already been gone then. Answering the "emergency" call from his father, when his and Giuliana's own crisis was bearing down on them.

"A few days before, he'd flown back to California." There was a brittle quality to her voice. "I called him when it was over."

"Oh, Lord," Allie muttered. Then she raised her voice. "Given how you two have been at each other's throats this last year, that conversation didn't go as it should."

How would that be? If he was in the room with Allie right now, he'd demand she tell him. How the hell should he have dealt with it? Over six thousand miles away and the girl he loved called him, heartsick and hurting. The powerlessness had made him want to kill something.

But so much had already died.

"You're wrong, Allie," his wife said, her voice dull. "He handled it really well. He told me what happened was for the best."

The words slid between his ribs like a blade so sharp he didn't feel it at first. He could even look over at Penn, and it was only then the wound began to bleed. Because on that near-doppelganger's face, he saw the pain he'd never been able to express and that he'd pretended didn't exist for the last decade.

A whooshing sounded in his ears. Like that noise that had filled the tiny examining room at the clinic as the nurse discovered their child's heartbeat. In the distance, Liam heard the phone ring again.

But he couldn't stay. On stiff legs, he turned. At first he just managed to walk, and then he managed a jog, and finally he was able to run. He didn't stop, not even when he heard the woman he'd abandoned call his name.

~

"Wait!" This time it was Giuliana chasing Liam through the vineyard. She put on a burst of speed at the same time that he gave up the race. Her feet stuttered in the dirt as he halted, his back to her, his hands hanging loose at his sides.

Wary, she approached him slowly. When she'd gone outside to find the men following that second phone call, Penn had told her Liam had taken off . . . after he'd overheard her conversation with Allie.

"I'm sorry," she said, still four feet away.

He twitched. "Oh, shit." His right palm swiped over his face. "Stevie and Jack lost their baby?"

"No!" She swallowed the sudden lump in her throat. "No. Jack called. She and the baby are fine. They recommend a few days rest as insurance."

"All right." He nodded, his back still turned. "Okay."

She took another step closer, her gaze on his wide back and the masculine jut of his shoulder blades. Sometimes she forgot he was the companion of her childhood, the young boy who'd been the acknowledged leader of their little band. His style was never the ruthless dictator. Little Allie always got her turn. If there was some special treat to share, he'd established the rule that whoever divvied up the pieces had to take the final portion. You'd never seen such equal-sized slices.

Before he'd become the man whose bed she'd been sharing for the past weeks, he'd been the teenager who walked her across the chasm between girlhood and womanhood. Her passionate nature had advocated flinging herself across the breach, but Liam had kept a gentle hold on her. Never taking too much when she would have given him all much too soon.

For the first time she wondered, what had she ever given him in return?

"I'm sorry," she said again.

"For what?" He turned to face her.

"For telling Allie . . . for Penn overhearing . . . for sharing a secret that was private between us."

He was already shaking his head. "Don't apologize. I'm beginning to see that keeping secrets hasn't done either one of us any good."

The sale of the Tanti Baci land. In all the upheaval she'd forgotten that everyone knew about that now. *Oh, God.*

Liam lifted a hand, then. Good-bye? He turned away.

"Wait!" she called again.

His back stiffened. He glanced back. "Why?"

She remembered what he'd said after that other vineyard pursuit. "Because it's time." It was a repeat of his words. "Because we can't go on like this. You just said it, the secrets aren't doing either of us any good. Neither is not talking about . . . what we lost."

"It's too late, Jules." He sounded tired. "So many years have passed. You've made decisions, I made huge mistakes . . . what will dredging it up do?"

"I don't know what for you," she answered, honest. "For me . . . I think I'll get back something I'd let myself forget."

This is what she needed, she realized. Coming back to Edenville and Tanti Baci had reminded her of happy years that she'd banished from her memory in order to banish the pain of that one single summer. But there'd been so many good times and she figured if they could get past this that she'd be able to cherish that happiness once again.

Her hand lifted to touch him, but she let it drop. "You weren't just the man who left me in Tuscany. Until these last few weeks, I'd forgotten the boy who taught me to fly a kite. The one who was more patient than my dad and let me learn to drive a stick shift on his precious BMW Z3. You were protective and tender and careful with me, always."

To ensure she kept her hands to herself, she shoved them in her pockets. "What happened that summer, Liam? Where'd that person go?"

His head dropped. "When we were in Tuscany . . ."

"By the time we arrived, you were already turning inward. But after . . . after the miscarriage, you seemed almost uninterested in me. You let go of our marriage so easily."

He spun to face her. "It wasn't easy."

"What was it then?"

A muscle ticked in his jaw. "I made huge mistakes, I admit to that. Let it go." He turned and started striding off again.

But she'd made that mistake herself before, so, gritting her teeth, she caught up with him. When he glanced over, she avoided his eyes and took up the sunglasses she'd hooked over the neckline of her shirt. Slipping them on, she kept stride with him. Two people headed in the same direction.

On the path that they'd worn when she'd believed their lives were destined for the same road forever.

She scanned the vineyards surrounding them, the organized rows masking the capricious nature of creating wine. She'd not truly understood that, she supposed, until she went to Tuscany and experienced her own failed growing season.

"That girl loved you so much," she said. "I was devastated when I lost the baby."

"You think I don't know that? You think it didn't kill me that I wasn't there for you?"

Stretching out her right arm, she let her fingertips tickle the leaves as she passed along the vines. They were both the gatherers of light for the vine and the guardians of the fruit, acting as a natural canopy from the sun's heat. What fabulous romantic partners they were—being providers as well as protectors.

Liam had been those two things to her, and she'd thought, then, that she *did* know him. So what came after didn't add up. It never had.

"Were you ashamed of me?"

He stopped short. "What? No!"

"Then why did you want us to keep our marriage a secret? Because I was too young, you said." Which, in hindsight, didn't make a lot of sense. But she'd thrown herself forward without thinking too hard, being her impetuous Italian self.

"You *were* too young," he muttered, starting to walk again. "I should never have come up with that stupid idea to go to Reno."

"If I recall, it was my stupid idea." She felt her mouth curve into a smile. "Face it, Liam, we should have just had sex and not worried about a marriage certificate first."

"I was trying to do the right thing." He slid a look at her and it held a spark of amusement. "But you were hot-blooded. Insistent. Dissatisfied with anything but everything."

"You say it like it was a bad thing." She could be kind, she found, to her younger, ardent self. That girl had suffered the devastating loss of her mother and then found such joy again in life with the person she loved. "Did my passion embarrass you?"

He let out a wry laugh. "Clearly, you have never been a twenty-year-old man."

"And yet you didn't want anyone to know we'd eloped."

He hesitated.

"After everything, I think you owe me an explanation." She steeled herself, unsure what to expect.

His head ducked. "You'll think I'm a fool."

"It's better than me thinking you're snobby, arrogant, conceited, self-important, egotistical—"

"You can stop now."

"—condescending, bigheaded, overly proud—"

"I wanted to keep it safe."

"It?" She held her breath.

"Us." He hesitated. "If it was a secret, it belonged to us alone. No one could screw it up, no one could pass judgment—"

"Now you're thinking about your parents."

He retreated into silence for a moment, then spoke again. "I was afraid my father was going to fuck up my marriage, just like he'd done with his own." Liam's voice was bitter. "Looks like I was right."

Giuliana thought back to that summer in Italy. "You said your dad wanted you back in the States. Just a few days, you said." Now that she knew more about Liam's relationship with his father, she could guess why he'd returned. "He wanted you to—what? Cover for him again?"

"Something like that." They'd reached the side gate at his house, and Liam unfastened the latch and held it open for her. They crossed into the courtyard and the breeze moved the fountain's shower of water so that the veil of drops shifted right and then shifted back, like a swarm of bees operating in unison. Liam stared at the feature as if he'd never seen it before. "Dad's latest paramour was threatening to tell my mother about the affair. I was supposed to come home and soothe the waters."

Giuliana stilled. Something about what he'd said and the angry thread in his voice . . . She glanced at him, but, as usual, could read nothing in the carved mask that was his profile. "Soothe . . ." She felt a little sick as a thought invaded her mind. "Soothe *her* waters? The other woman's?"

"I told you!" he burst out. "I told you I worried he'd dirty what we had, somehow."

"Liam, you wouldn't—"

"I didn't." His hand slashed out and he moved away from her. When his calves hit the edge of one of the chaise lounges, he dropped onto the cushions and put his head in his hands.

"Liam . . ." She sat beside him. This wasn't her childhood friend or the love of her teenage years. This stranger was the man she'd never allowed herself to know. The hot-blooded, reckless young woman she'd been had hurt too much to stick around long enough to meet him. "You said that maybe losing the baby was for the best."

"I didn't mean it that way. That you thought so . . . that maybe I let you think so . . . that was just another of my mistakes."

She lifted a hand to touch him, then let it fall to her lap. "What *did* you mean, Liam?"

"That it was best we didn't stay together." He drew his fingers through his hair, then turned his head to look at her. Control was written in the stark lines of his face. His expression was composed, his blue eyes a cool glacial lake. They were fixed on her face. "That summer I came back early from Tuscany so he wouldn't hurt my mother—and what happened? I hurt you instead."

"Liam . . ." Her hand crept toward him.

He jerked away. "Don't. Don't touch me. I'll screw that up, too. Don't you see? I'm so much like him, hurting the people I care for, messing up my very own family."

Her mouth was dry. "Losing the baby wasn't your fault."

"Failing you was. I'm so like him. That's what I worried about and why I let you go. I'm so fucking like him!"

His eyes blazed blue and it took her a moment to realize there were tears in them.

And in that brightness she saw the stark emotion that he'd disguised for the last year. In them was raw pain, boundless disappointment, a river of regrets she supposed they both deemed impossible to ford.

She'd been angry at his icy control, but she'd give her soul to not see beyond it now. Liam's inner life sliced hers open. Love leaked out, and her head went dizzy with it.

I'm still in love with him, she thought, and the knowledge was like an old toothache returning. Familiar. Painful.

She loved him so much that it was a very good thing she'd taken such drastic steps to move out of his life. Leaving meant she couldn't put her already-damaged heart on the line again. Leaving meant that this time she'd be turning her back on Liam instead of the other way around. It was for the best, just as he'd said.

But her gaze didn't stray from his tense shoulders as he strode off. And she discovered she was still reckless enough to rise to her feet and follow him. Perhaps they both might feel better if she offered the comfort they could have used ten years before.

17

In the steamy shower stall, hot water cascaded over Liam's body. It rinsed the soap from his skin and suds circled the drain at his feet. He'd lathered up three times already and still didn't feel clean, but the unwanted emotion that had welled up in the courtyard had receded once more to its dark place. He could breathe again.

Once the valves were flipped off, he stepped out and grabbed two towels. One went around his waist, the other he ran over his chest and then through his hair. The bathroom door opened into his bedroom with a pop.

In her jeans and T-shirt, Giuliana was sitting cross-legged in the middle of the big unmade bed, her feet bare of anything but cherry pink toenail polish. He shifted back, then rethought his retreat. Taking another few steps forward into the room, he crossed his arms over his chest and trained his gaze on her face. "What are you doing in here?"

She lifted a delicate shoulder. "This is where I've been sleeping."

He assumed that was over. He wanted that to be over, didn't he? The closeness of sex and sleep was something he couldn't risk anymore, not when all that old pain was finding it so easy to slip its locks. "We'll move you back to the guest room."

"It won't change anything," she said.

He was afraid she was right, but he didn't want to go there with her. When he'd left the courtyard, he'd hoped to leave all the revelations of their conversation there, too. Revisiting it was just asking for trouble. So he played dumb. "Change what? I don't know what you're talking about."

Her eyebrows drew together and her nostrils flared in a dramatic fashion. It was one of those expressive, Baci faces that used to make him laugh. Giuliana could communicate whole stories with just a flutter of her extravagant eyelashes, and it had fascinated him, accustomed as he was to silent family meals where no one said really anything, even when their mouths were moving.

Clearly she was irritated with him and a little impatient. "Liam," she said. "You can put me out in a storage shed, but it won't change . . . Never mind. I just thought you could use a friend right now."

He didn't need anyone for anything. He'd made damn sure to become self-sufficient in the last ten years. "We're not friends, Jules."

"We used to be."

"We used to be a lot of things and 'used to be' is the operative phrase, isn't it?" He had the icy tone down pat.

But it didn't scare her off. She scooted on her cute little ass, bringing herself closer to the end of the bed. "Look. We have a history. Nobody could understand that history better than me. I thought if you needed to talk . . . I could listen. Maybe . . . maybe I could . . ."

She'd run out of fuel, probably due to his impersonal, implacable stare. Perfect. The quicker she gave up and got out, the quicker he could get on with his life. The more she was close to him, the more she rubbed against him, the more he discovered his personal demons were able to escape that place where he'd bottled them in the back of his mind.

"While I appreciate the offer, Jules," he said, walking toward the door that led into the hall, "no." With a flip of his wrist, he turned the knob and held it open. "If you'll excuse me . . ."

She climbed off the bed. "Fine," she said, visibly wounded by the rebuff.

He didn't want to feel regret about that, either. So he tamped it down, too, and watched her cross the carpet. For just a second, he allowed the image of her in his bedroom to imprint on his memory, like the indentation of her head on the pillow beside his. His lungs inhaled her scent as she passed. *Good-bye,* he whispered inside his mind, crowding close as she crossed the threshold so he could take in a final breath of her.

She whirled then, her dark hair winging outward. "You don't have to be this way—" she started, her voice hot. Her wild hand gesture caught on the towel around his waist.

It started to slip. Too late, he reached for it but missed the falling fabric.

Giuliana didn't seem to notice. "I only wanted to make you feel better . . ." Her voice trailed off as her gaze dropped, taking in his nudity. "Oh."

Her scent, her nearness, her entire pretty package had already acted upon him. His cock was rising as she watched and he was helpless to stop it. Damn! He wasn't supposed to be this vulnerable. So she had to go. Now.

With deliberation, he palmed the stiff jut of his flesh, knowing just how to get rid of her. "If you want to make me feel better," he said in a hard voice, "there's just one thing I need."

Her eyes still downcast and her attention on his moving hand, she flushed.

His voice hoarsened. "It's the only thing I want from you, sweetheart."

"Really?" She sounded wistful.

"Only." He had to be strong.

For another moment, she looked. Then her gaze rose. They stared at each other for a second, longer moment. He continued stroking his cock, doing what he must to drive her away.

Her tongue slipped out to moisten her lower lip. "It would be my pleasure," she whispered, moving his hand to replace it with hers.

He swallowed his groan. "Giuliana . . ."

"Shh." Her other palm pushed against his chest and he stepped backward. She kept the pressure on his breastbone and he continued moving, until the back of his legs hit the end of the bed. She pushed again, and he fell to the mattress, his erection sliding through the circle of her fingers.

Before he could take a breath, she was crawling over him. Her mouth fastened on his. Without thought, his hands found her waist, slid down to her hips, applied enough pressure to bring her flush against him. The denim of her jeans abraded the skin of his groin, a gentle but cruel pleasure.

He rolled, reversing their positions. Now he was between her parted thighs, his weight flush to her pelvis, his upper body propped on his elbows. "This is how we play this game," he said.

Her mouth trembled. "Oh, Liam. It's not a game. It's never really been a game."

Of course it was. It had to be.

He slid his hands under her shirt to cup her breasts. The lace of her bra tickled his palms and he quickly found the middle clasp. With a twist of his fingers, he had her silky skin in his possession. Her naked flesh was hot, her nipples budding as he brushed them with his thumbs.

She moaned. The sound galvanized him. He stripped

the shirt from her and untangled her arms from her bra straps. Then he mouthed her skin, tasting all the scented sweetness from her throat to her breasts. He ringed them with kisses and then sucked on her nipples, trying to ignore the way her twisting lower body enflamed him.

But he had to taste more of her. The flat of his tongue circled her areolas and then traced a path down the middle of her torso. Kneeling to the side, he laved her navel while he yanked open her jeans and slid them lower on her thighs along with her panties.

He moved to the end of the bed and slipped her clothing all the way off. Then he stroked her legs with the flat of his hands, starting at the top of her small feet, working past her ankles, and smoothing up her calves. He pushed gently on her knees and then her inner thighs, creating a place for himself on the mattress between them.

"Liam . . ." She moved restlessly.

He ignored her, still taking that slow journey over her skin, like a man learning her by touch alone. His fingertips found the hot creases at the juncture of her thighs and she jerked and moaned again. He notched his fingers and thumbs in those sweet crevices and pushed outward to open her more fully to his gaze.

The sound she made was anxious and he soothed her by running one thumb across her clitoris. "It's going to be so good," he promised her. "Better than ever." The last time ever.

She dug her heels into the bed and lifted herself into his teasing thumb. "Don't make me wait."

He leaned down to kiss that tender skin between her hipbone and mons. He tongued the heated warmth of it, then sucked there, lightly. She lifted into the stinging kiss and he sucked harder, knowing he'd leave a mark behind.

Wanting to mark her forever.

Forever his.

He kissed the little bruise, then shifted to the other hip. As he kissed her delicate skin, he let his finger slide through the folds of her sex. As he slowly penetrated her slick opening, he deepened the kiss. She lifted into his possession again, impaling herself deeper and pressing her skin into the hot suction of his mouth.

He laved the second mark, his heart pounding against his ribs. It thumped harder as he lifted his head and took her in: flushed face, tight nipples, splayed legs. His hand at her sex, his finger nestled inside her. He drew it out, mesmerized by each emerging wet inch, and then took her again, with two. Her dark curls were damp with her arousal and he ruffled the fingers of his free hand through them, delicately brushing the hard button of her clitoris with each stroke.

Her palms were pressed tight to the sheets at her side. She was trembling, her breasts quivering as desire took her higher. "Liam," she whispered again, a warning note in her voice.

She was close to climax.

"Not yet." He took his fingers from her body and brought them to his lips. Her brown eyes were fixed on him as he drew off their wetness into his mouth, tasting her. He savored the flavor and reached for more, curling his fingers as he breached her body again.

Giuliana moaned as he withdrew them and he paused with their glistening length poised over her belly. He could hear his own harsh voice on that day that she'd run from him in the vineyard. *I want to write my name on your belly with your come.*

He saw those possessive marks he'd made inside her hipbones. He saw her tousled hair, her swollen mouth, her breasts.

Her belly, where their child had, so briefly, slept.

Shaking his head, he tried putting that from his mind.

This was not a moment for reflection, but for sex. Her skin turned him on, her slender limbs, her taste . . . He put his fingers to his mouth again and sucked it off.

I want to write my name on your belly.

Ten years ago he'd made her pregnant. Now he'd marked her, those kisses flaming against her skin.

Her pretty skin, he reminded himself. Those rounded breasts. The triangle of curls that shielded her pussy.

His gaze traveled up to her liquid brown eyes and he couldn't separate her anymore into those sexy parts. She was Giuliana, the girl, the woman, the one he'd never been able to forget.

"Liam," she implored. "Come inside me. Come inside me now."

But he had one thing to do first. A final secret to tell. His fingers dipped inside her body again. She cried out, her inner muscles clamping down to hold him there. Recognizing that the crisis had arrived, he placed his other hand over the top of her sex, applying steady pressure to her pelvis even as he curled his thumb inside the open petals to stroke the sensitive center.

His breath soughing harshly in and out of his lungs, he watched her gather and make the final leap. Crying out, she tightened around his penetrating digits, bathing them with more fluid.

Her eyes closed as she calmed. He was gentle as he withdrew from her body, but she shuddered anyway and opened her eyes. "I don't want it to be over," she said, her voice hoarse.

"We're not over." Not yet. He would take her up again, this time with his cock inside that heated channel. But he had something to write first, and he started at that first red passion-bite on her hip, moving across with his forefinger toward the other. She watched through half-closed eyes, her gaze languid.

She didn't ask what he was doing. It only took a moment. Then he reached for a condom. With a little smile, Giuliana sat up and took it from him. He saw the liquid on her belly glisten as she rolled the rubber over his rock-solid shaft.

And then he was on top of her again, their bodies shifting against each other. She cried out as he entered her. He gathered her closer and buried his face in the shiny length of her hair.

That dark place in his mind opened. Each thrust seems to release another flow of pain from it to mingle with the consuming pleasure of this last episode of sex with his wife. A tender anguish clutched at his heart and that was hurting now, too, so much that he had to hide the dampness in his eyes against Giuliana's silky locks as he sealed his secret message with the weight of his body against hers.

She was already planning on leaving Edenville. He had no faith that he'd make a better husband now than he had ten years before. But neither fact changed what he'd written across her flat belly, in that place where there could only be honesty between them.

I'll love you always.

~

Giuliana's schedule for the rest of the day was too busy for her to spend much time thinking about what happened in Liam's bed that morning. As a matter of fact, she had a lot of things she didn't want to think about, so the small, midweek wedding taking place in the cottage during the late afternoon served as yet another welcome distraction. A little frisson rolled down her back when Allie asked her to do a ride-along as the younger woman chauffeured the bride and groom to a cozy B and B nearby. But it was a favor for Napa Princess Limousine—Stevie's business—so Giuliana didn't see how she could refuse.

Once they reached the inn's parking lot, her job was to ferry the fresh flowers into the bridal suite while Allie toted their overnight bags. She returned to the car, the sight of the groom carrying the giggling bride over the threshold burned into her mind. Her hands, clothes, and hair held on to the scent of sweet peas and roses.

Sliding into the passenger seat, she slid Allie a wary glance. Now was the natural time for her to bring up the sale of the Tanti Baci land. Would her youngest sister understand?

She needed both her sisters to understand.

But the traffic was heavy as twilight descended, and Allie seemed to be saving her focus for the cars around her. It was nearly dark by the time they reached the turnoff to the winery. The silence between them was only broken by the crunching sound of the tires across gravel. Then the car turned into the lane that led to the farmhouse and they both let out a little gasp.

Allie braked. “Oh. Pretty.”

The simple lines of the old farmhouse had been edged with white fairy lights. It appeared magical from this distance, or maybe that was just because Giuliana had so many enchanting memories of her childhood there. Perhaps the whole past year had been worth it—and maybe even the heartache after, because surely there would be heartache after—if she had been able to reclaim that time that had been lost to her.

The limo moved forward to halt in the parking area beside the house. Both sisters climbed out, then Giuliana hesitated. If she went inside to check on Stevie, she'd have to face both sisters at once. If she took the shortcut to Liam's house, she'd have to face *him*. They'd been silent after their lovemaking, getting up and dressing as if nothing had happened. As if she hadn't sensed the good-bye in every move, in every touch.

As if she hadn't asked for just that very good-bye by planning to sell the land.

Allie gestured with her hand. "Come inside. We'll open a bottle. Feel like chardonnay?"

She felt like screaming. Her sister's polite hospitality only scraped against her already raw nerves. "I don't know . . ."

"Liam waiting for you?"

The farmhouse was the rock, Liam the hard place, and Giuliana couldn't find breathing room between the two of them. "I . . . I guess I can have a glass while I see Steve."

But they found Jack in the kitchen, who said his wife was asleep. He put an arm around each of the sisters and hugged them close, his mouth brushing the top of Allie's head and then Giuliana's. "I love her so much," he murmured. "I was so damn scared."

Air couldn't get past her tight throat. Giuliana clasped Jack just as tight. "Everything's fine," she told him, rubbing his back. "Everything's going to be just fine."

And it struck her once more that no one had comforted Liam when he'd received her call from Tuscany. While she'd been by herself in Italy, he'd been just as alone in Edenville. In that tense house with his strained parental relations, very alone.

Jack bussed each of the sisters on the forehead and then moved away, a smile banishing the last shadow of worry in his eyes. "So, we celebrate now, yes? What can I make for my lovely sisters-in-law?"

She had to smile back. He could be such a gentleman, handed down from both his European and his Southern families. "Jack," she said, letting impulse guide her. "Stevie's such a lucky lady to have you."

He went serious again. "She's my light."

Giuliana might have lost it at that, but then the kitchen door opened. Penn walked in and was instantly leapt upon by Allie, who peppered him with kisses. He hitched up her butt with both hands, and she wrapped her legs around his waist. "Thank you for putting the lights on the farmhouse," she said, and gave him a few more juicy smacks.

"I helped," another voice said. "What do I get?"

Liam. His gaze settled on Giuliana as he walked into the kitchen and she felt her cheeks go warm.

Allie threw a smile in his direction. "A glass of wine with the rest of us. Jack's opening chardonnay."

Jack obliged, though Liam opted for beer. Somehow Giuliana was swept outside with the group, settling on a picnic table placed on the close-cropped grass. Hands occupied, her youngest sister left the house last. Allie set a plate of cheese and crackers beside a battery-operated lantern.

Finally, she took a seat across the table from Giuliana and placed in front of her the item that Kohl and Grace had found.

About the size of two teacups, the fairy lights and lantern illuminated the metal that shined dully beneath its tarnish. The decorative gemstones were dirty, too, but managed a muted wink or two from beneath the dust. Giuliana slid along the bench, edging away from it. Perhaps it wasn't the legendary treasure, but it appeared to be silver and gold and there were "sparklies," as little-girl Allie called any kind of jewel. What else could it be?

"I made a call to a friend who runs an antiques store in Napa," Allie said. "We think it's a wedding cake topper."

Giuliana jerked her gaze to her sister's face. "Anne and Alonzo's?"

"Maybe. We should page through her diary again, see if there's a mention of it. But it makes sense. My friend tells me toppers came into vogue in the 1890s and were customary by the 1920s. The tradition is said to have been launched by Queen Victoria in 1840. She had an ice sculpture on top of the cake served after her wedding to Prince Albert."

Giuliana studied the piece. The filigree base and delicate fluted shapes with their gemstone edges wouldn't look out of place gracing a tiered confection. She could see it now, Anne in white lace, her veil thrown back, Alonzo's handsomeness matched by his dark suit, the both of them arm in arm beside baked layers swathed in ivory icing and crowned with—

"We can sell it," Allie said, her voice brisk.

Giuliana gaped at her. "Sell it? Why would we sell it?"

"I could ask you that very same question, about the Tanti Baci land."

Oh, had she walked into that one. "Maybe you think I should have discussed my plans with you—"

"'Maybe'?" Allie leaned forward. "Of course I think you should have discussed your plans. With all of us."

Giuliana swallowed. "We should wait until I can talk to Stevie, too."

"I'll give her the highlights," her sister said through her teeth.

Penn ran a hand down the long length of his wife's hair. "Take it easy, sweetheart."

Her gaze didn't waver from Giuliana's face. "I'm afraid to take it easy, Penn. If I take it easy, the next thing I know we'll all be out on the street, our belongings piled around us."

Giuliana winced. She knew exactly how that felt, since that had been her on the night of the fire. "The farmhouse isn't part of the deal."

"Why *is* there a deal?" Allie asked, throwing up her hands. "I don't get that."

Fear that her sisters wouldn't had been the very reason Giuliana hadn't shared her plans with anyone else. Though she wanted Allie and Stevie to see it her way, she'd known she was risking her relationship with them by going through with the sale. So she'd put off revealing it as long as possible.

"You know it's dragging us all down," she said, looking at each of the people around the table. Liam hadn't joined them, but was instead standing off to the side, half in shadow. "Not so much the Bennetts, but their stake is much smaller than ours. For the rest . . ."

"We're not drowning." Allie shook her head. "Since the first wedding last summer, we've been coming up for air more and more often."

"But for how long can we sustain all the swimming?" Giuliana countered. "You and Penn have to fit in your duties here and the lives you have going in Southern California. Stevie and Jack have other projects besides their obligation to Tanti Baci. The limo business for Steve and then Jack's My Aching Back vineyard."

Allie opened her mouth, closed it. Giuliana breathed a sigh of relief. Maybe she'd made sense to her sister. "You see—" she started.

"What I see is what you don't," Allie interrupted, her voice hot. She rose to her feet. " 'Duty.' 'Obligation.' Maybe that's how you feel about what we have here, but Stevie and I, and Penn and Jack, we see . . . we see . . ." Her sister blinked rapidly, then she cut her gaze to Penn. "I'm not crying."

"Your tears don't bother me," he said, sliding his arm around her hips and pulling her back down to the bench. Then he looked at Giuliana. "Neither am I bothered by juggling the winery and what's going on down south. Family's become pretty important to me."

"And, obviously, to me, too," Jack added. "I think I can speak for my wife and say—"

"Nobody gets to say but me!" Giuliana didn't want to hear another word. "That's the point. I'm the one who has the opportunity to make the hard decision, and I'm making it for all of us."

"Jules." Allie scrubbed her face with her hands. "Look,

I know it was looking bleak a year ago. And it hasn't been easy since, either. But come on, give us a chance—"

"I don't believe in second chances."

Allie jerked back. "What? Of course you do. You agreed to give it a year . . ."

Her sister went silent. "Oh, *Jules* . . ."

Giuliana looked away. "Oh, Jules, what?"

There was another tense silence, then Allie spoke again, her voice hushed. "You never actually thought it would work, did you? Edenville didn't want to see us give up. And your sisters were pressuring you. So you granted us these months in order to appease me and Stevie, or your conscience, or the community at large—probably all three."

So her sister *did* finally understand.

But from the look on Allie's face, not in a way that led to forgiveness. The night took on a chill that Giuliana felt as she slid off the bench. Standing beside the table, she tried thinking of a way to end the conversation. "I . . ." She rubbed her forearms with her opposite hands, attempting to bring warmth to her flesh. Right hand at her left wrist, she stiffened.

Liam stepped out of the shadows. "Giuliana?"

She hadn't looked at him since taking her seat at the picnic table. Now wasn't the time to meet his eyes, and she didn't, instead moving her gaze around the grass. She bent to look under their seats.

Jack stood up. "Jules? Looking for something?"

"My bracelet." She ringed her fingers around her wrist, trying to remember when last she'd been aware of wearing it. "It's not here."

Penn clambered from his seat. "Maybe I can help—"

"No, no. Never mind." She couldn't take their assistance after the argument. "It doesn't matter. It wasn't worth anything."

At that, Liam receded into the shadows again. Giuliana took it as her signal to head away. Another night on her office love seat wouldn't kill her.

"Jules," Allie called.

She kept on walking. "What now?"

"Just a little advice is all." Her sister paused, then spoke again. "You can't find what you don't go looking for."

18

"We could have gotten drunk in the wine cellar at your house," Penn complained, looking with distaste at the sticky surface of the bar in front of him.

"I shouldn't have listened to Allie and instead stayed at the farmhouse and watched over my wife," Jack said, then glanced at his brother-in-law. "Fine, fine. Allie was right. My hovering was making Stevie crazy."

Liam paid scant attention to them. He was lining up his second round of double shots in alphabetical order: gin, scotch, tequila, vodka, whiskey. Jack winced. "You know that isn't a good idea, buddy, right?"

"Very good idea," Liam replied. "Love this place. Came with Seth on his twenty-first birthday."

Jack looked around. "Was it this seedy then? And if so, why are we here now?"

Liam grinned at him. "I'm in a seedy sort of mood."

"He's halfway to shit-faced," Penn declared.

Liam shoved at his half brother's shoulder. "Take that back."

Penn looked around Liam and spoke to Jack. "Have you ever seen him like this before?"

"No."

"That's because I suppress"—Liam said the word slowly and it came out two perfect, crisp syllables—"my appetites. Not like dear old dad."

"Shh," Penn cautioned.

"Why? For God's sake, everyone's aware he catted around, Penn." Liam added a throaty growl to his voice. "You know, rowr, rowr."

His brother grinned. "Okay, just for that I'm glad I came, though I wish I had my video camera on me."

"You." Liam pushed his brother's shoulder again as the other man kept on grinning. "Why do you have to be the smiling one? People say we look enough alike to be twins, but I'm not laughing all the time like you are."

He caught Jack rolling his eyes and swung on his stool to confront the other man. "Zis true. Oops." He turned to face his brother again, his head revolving faster than his body. "*It's* true."

"Uh . . ."

His finger poked Penn in the chest. "Explain."

"I'm happy?"

Liam shook his head, suddenly morose. "I think you're right. I could hate that about you."

"And you'll hate me even more if I let you go through with this," Penn murmured. He started sliding shot glasses out of Liam's reach.

Sighing, he watched them go. "I wish Seth was here. Seth would let me get drunk in peace. 'Stead I'm drinking with Penn, the Nosy Parker brother."

"Yeah, that's me," the other man agreed, "whoever the hell Nosy Parker is. But even when you hate me, you still love me."

Liam grabbed the glass of whiskey before it went the

way of the gin, scotch, tequila, and vodka. He curled it protectively against his chest. "I really do, you know."

Over his head, Penn exchanged glances with their other companion. Liam called over his shoulder, "I love you too, Jack."

The prince of Ardenia laughed. "You're just full of that feeling tonight."

"I know," Liam said, nodding. "'Swhy I'm gonna dance with every single woman here. I'm gonna spread my love around."

Jack cast a look about the room. "I think you're out of luck, my friend. They're clearing the floor for a karaoke competition."

"Karaoke. Hell." He hung his head, and then a brilliant idea occurred to him. "Let's go to another bar."

"I think we'll just sit tight in this one for a while." Penn signaled the bartender and a second later there was a big mug of black coffee in front of Liam. "Give you a chance to sober up before we climb back into the limo. I believe I'm really glad I brought the big car now. It has the smoothest ride."

Liam took a sip from the double whiskey he'd been hoarding. "I want to be drunk the rest of my life."

"Yeah? Why's that?"

Penn thought he was kidding. "'Cause walking the straight 'n' narrow hasn't gotten me shit," Liam explained. "Best times I ever had was when I was acting out of character."

Jack nudged the coffee closer.

"You don't believe me?" he said. "I made out with the girl and then I married the girl, all the while arguing 'gainst my better self. Greatest days of my life."

Yeah, it was starting to make sense to him. The solution was clear. "If I stay drunk, see, I won't remember how that was and I'll be happy being lonely."

Penn put the coffee in his hand. "Your logic is a little waterlogged, bro."

It was true he couldn't keep his mind going in one direction. It wanted to go backward. It wanted to see Giuliana in his bed that morning, her beautiful golden skin, her tender mouth. Then it rushed off to remember her as she'd been in the farmhouse yard, coming clean about the sale, looking agonized as Allie made the connection that her big sister had never truly believed in saving Tanti Baci.

I don't believe in second chances. She'd said that.

The bartender passed by, a paunchy guy with a crew cut and a colorful tattoo. "Maybe that's what I need," he told his friends, pointing. "What is that? The Tasmanian Devil?"

Then something flashed in the light and his gaze shifted, catching on the wrist of a second person behind the bar. It was a woman and she wore a bracelet, a gaudy thing that almost hurt his eyes to look at. No. What hurt was . . .

The reminder of Giuliana's missing bracelet. No, what hurt was . . .

He'd bought her that bracelet.

Whether it was some male gene that caused him to overlook detail or some self-protective instinct that had resulted in selective blindness, he'd not paid attention to what she'd regularly worn around her wrist for . . . the last year? Had it been that long, or just a number of months? Whatever the answer was, there was a clear recollection now in his head.

A holiday street fair. *Ferragosto*—the Feast of Assumption. They'd wandered around, hand in hand, happy. Oh, God, so happy.

She'd stopped at a jewelry booth and put out a gentle finger toward bright and shiny things hanging on a stand. He'd watched her stroke a pretty bauble—made by mouth-blown glass beads they'd been told by the artisan. The ones that attracted Giuliana were the smallest of the gleaming objects, the size of BBs. Especially hard to make, the old Venetian said, but more valuable because of it.

She liked the bracelet that was strung of beads of blue—like Liam's eyes, she declared. He'd bought her a different bracelet though, one that used those same small bits of glass, but between each minute sphere stood a lustrous bead of gold. The added element to remind them, he'd thought then, that they'd someday celebrate their golden anniversary.

God, what a foolish romantic he'd been.

So out of character. So not like the cold fish he'd become in order to prove himself a better man than his tomcat father. His head went woozy again at the conflicting animal metaphors. Or maybe it was because of the whiskey he drained.

The empty glass clinked on the bar top. The second bartender swiped it up and again his gaze caught on her bracelet. Giuliana had given up on hers, despite what Allie had said. *You can't find what you don't go looking for.*

A thought struck. Lurching to his feet, he headed for the exit. In the entryway, Penn and Jack caught up with him. "Hey, where you going?" his half brother asked.

Liam thrust out his palm. "I need the keys. I need the keys to the limo."

"Uh, I don't think so." Penn shoved his hand in his pocket.

"Just give me the damn keys!" Liam yanked on his brother's arm, hard enough that his hand came free, the keys dangling from his fingers. He lunged for them, just as Penn tossed them to Jack. With a grunt of frustration, Liam changed direction.

"Jack—"

"Is there a problem here?" Kohl Friday asked as he came through the door. Grace Hatch was hovering a few steps behind him.

"No problem at all," Jack said, just as he pitched the ring to Kohl, "as long as you hang on to these."

Aggravation had Liam seeing red and his head was swimming with booze, but he could clearly make out Kohl's gleeful expression. "Well, well, well," the other man said, twirling the key ring on his forefinger. "Who would believe golden boy Liam Bennett drunk off his ass?"

"I'm going to knock *you* off *your* ass," Liam promised, and gathered himself to charge. Just as he was about to spring, Kohl tossed the keys back to Jack. Liam followed the arc, swinging around, his movement deflecting the force of Kohl's big fist against his jaw. Still, it was enough to destroy his balance.

"I owed you that," he heard the other man say as he fell. Then his head hit the ground, hard, and the dim foyer went black.

Someone was trickling water over his face. He sat up, sputtering. "Jesus. Now you're gonna drown me?" The small circle around him—Penn, Jack, Kohl, and Grace—looked relieved. "What the hell is wrong with you people?"

"It was the most effective way to keep you here. You've been drinking."

"So you should commit murder?" There was a lump on the back of his head, but the blow had sobered him more than he liked. "I just wanted to look for the bracelet in the limo." But hell, why was he going to do that when Giuliana wasn't interested in doing it herself? *It's not worth anything,* she'd said.

"Oh." Jack winced. "We thought you were going to get behind the wheel."

The paunchy bartender arrived on scene with a double shot of whiskey. "On the house."

Grace made a little sound. "Should he have that, what with the head injury?"

Liam grabbed the glass and downed it, the burn at his throat overriding the ache in his head. "I have a lot more hurting me than that," he told the woman. Then he clambered to his feet, swaying a little. Penn grabbed his arm and Liam eyed his brother, albeit a little blearily. "I really, really want to get drunk."

This time nobody tried to stop him as they gathered around the bar again. He wondered if they were maybe paying the place to water down his drinks, though, because his buzz was only at the half-numbing state when a pair of karaoke candidates took to the small raised stage. Shocked, Liam glanced into his glass, then back up at the would-be singers. Maybe he was drunker than he thought, because it looked to him as if Kohl and Grace were taking up microphones.

The most silent man in Edenville, the one who went to bars on his way to yet another drunk and disorderly, was opening his mouth to . . . sing. Jesus. It was the song, "Cruisin'" that Huey Lewis and Gwyneth Paltrow had sung as a duet in a nineties movie. Liam didn't have an opinion on the professionals' performance. But these amateurs . . . they stank.

When they finished up to applause and returned to the bar, Grace flushed, Kohl with a proprietary hand on her shoulder, Liam could only stare at the former soldier. "Shut the fuck up, Liam," the other man said, even though not a word had passed between his lips.

"But—"

"When you love a woman, maybe you forget your freakin' image for a second. Maybe you take that big stick out of your ass and take a chance on something even bigger."

Liam's hand tightened on his latest whiskey. What was this fixation everyone had with the stick up his ass? Annoyance rose, and then . . . hey. Was Kohl maybe a closet genius? Hadn't Liam expressed that very sentiment earlier in the evening? "Walking the straight 'n' narrow hasn't gotten me shit," he murmured, repeating himself. Maybe he needed to forget his image. Maybe he needed to . . .

Take a chance.

Take a chance that you can convince her to stay.

That was it! Liam decided he couldn't let Kohl Friday prove to be a bigger fool than he. His thought process hiccupped. Something was wrong with that last statement, he knew it, but he didn't have time to puzzle out the answer. Instead, he jumped to his feet, staggered a little, then steadied himself by putting his hand in someone's platter of nachos.

"Christ, Liam," Jack complained.

He ignored him to find his half brother Penn's face in the slowly revolving room. "Get Giuliana here," he ordered. "I gotta song to sing."

~

Liam didn't know what Penn said to get Giuliana to the bar. He didn't know how many mugs of coffee he downed waiting for her. He did know it was a hundred bucks he handed over to the karaoke emcee to give him a turn the second she showed up.

It could have been fifteen minutes, it could have been an hour, before a prickling sensation ghosted over his skin. His head turned, and there she was, her hair waving around her face, her color high. She wore a button-down shirt he thought might be his, along with jeans and those dimestore flip-flops he should have chopped into rubber confetti.

He slid off his barstool and made his way toward the stage, his gaze remaining steady on her wary face. For the first time since that morning when she'd announced her sale of the land, he felt in control. Yeah. He felt better for the first time in ten effing *years* because he was doing something instead of standing by while his world fell to shit around him.

The emcee thrust a wireless microphone in his hand as he stepped onto the platform. Then the man gestured toward a binder, thick with plastic-sleeved pages of songs. A loud voice called out, "Go, Liam!"

It pierced his boozy haze. He blinked, his focus zooming outward. What the hell? There were a hundred people in the place, all looking at him. The emcee was pointing at the binder again. "What song?" the man asked.

Jesus Christ. A . . . song? Putting his hand to his suddenly clearing head, he clunked his skull with the microphone. He jerked it down. Had he really committed himself to some melodic confession? How much had he had to drink?

Liam put the mike down, backed away . . .

And saw Giuliana mirroring his move, her feet in retreat, heading for the exit.

"Wait!" he yelled, grabbing the microphone again. The emcee brandished the song binder once more, but he pushed it away. A song was for cowards—or people who could actually sing.

But speaking truth in front of an audience . . . Jesus, he was going to feel like an ass. He was going to have to let go of his dignity and lay himself bare in front of his brother, some biker types, and a bunch of people who found it entertaining to spend their evenings squalling out rock anthems and show tunes.

In one corner was a woman in a rhinestone halter top who looked like the hygienist at his dentist's office. In another, a big man in a black ball cap stood with his arms folded over his chest, his avid gaze taking in the scene. Liam couldn't swear to it, but it looked like his fourth-grade teacher had just bellied up to the bar.

The thought of an audience made him a little ill.

But remember? He was taking a chance. *Doing something.*

So instead of paying attention to the roomful of distractions, he spoke to the only one who mattered. "Giuliana."

His mouth was dry. Apparently his hundred bucks afforded him a beverage, too, because the emcee pressed on him a cold glass of water.

His hand trembled as he brought it to his mouth. He would have liked to think it was a result of the booze, but now he felt sober as a judge . . . and his wife was looking at him with the gaze of a very skeptical juror.

"Giuliana . . ." He closed his eyes, unspooling the reel of his memory. This morning, the last year, the golden summer in Tuscany, the kisses, the childhood games. For as long as he could remember, she'd been his co-conspirator, his co-leader, his cohort. No wonder that for the last decade he'd been walking around like a man with a missing limb.

Opening his eyes, he looked into hers. "You were created for me," he said. "I called what we have together a curse, but I was wrong. So stupidly wrong. You were created for me just as I was created for you. I think we're a promise one hundred years in the making."

She was breathing fast, her chest rising and falling with each quick breath. He leapt off the stage and walked toward her, winding his way through the crowd. Her eyes widened as he approached. A foot from her, he halted.

"Don't go, Jules. Don't leave me again."

And then she did just that, spinning on the rubber soles of her thongs and rushing for the door.

Astonishment froze him for a moment and then he dropped the microphone. He'd really expected this to work. After another moment he took off after her, pushing past anyone who got between him and the door. Outside, he whirled around, trying to locate her in the parking lot.

Headlights flashed on and he raced toward them, only to find her tight-lipped behind the wheel of her newly repaired car, her expression impossible to read in the greenish glow of the dashboard. He banged on her window.

She rolled down the glass and then she was hissing at him like a cat, her voice furious. “So this is what a head injury looks like!”

“Huh?”

“Penn said you'd hit your head. That you had a possible concussion.”

He rubbed the back of his hair. “Kohl sucker punched me.”

“Good. Because that means I'm not the only sucker around here.”

“That's Penn's doing.” But he could tell she wasn't the least bit moved by logic or what he'd said in the bar in front of the whole fucking world. It infuriated him, but he kept his voice cool. “I just made a fool of myself for you.”

Her eyes rolled. She dismissed his risk with a wave of her hand. “You arrogant ass. It was just your way of assuming control again. For some reason you don't like the idea of losing even your little piece of Tanti Baci, so you resorted to emotional blackmail and tried manipulating me in front of our family, our town.”

Liam froze, feeling sick again. Emotional blackmail. It was a Calvin Bennett trait, one of those faults he'd always feared might be handed down from father to son.

“Jules, no. I'm sorry. But I—” He couldn't tell her that he loved her, though. She would only see that as more manipulation. Sick again, now with frustration, he rubbed his hands over his face.

“Good-bye, Liam. I'll be spending the night at the farmhouse.”

And like that she was gone, leaving him to stare at her red taillights as she shot out of the parking lot. They reminded him of those red rosebushes at the end of the rows of grapes in the Bennett vineyards. How had the old man lived with that reminder of love lost?

Once Giuliana left Edenville, he was going to remove

them one by one with his very own hands, just as she'd ripped out his heart.

~

After leaving the bar, Giuliana drove around the dark streets of Edenville as if they were a maze and she was seeking the way out. But she wasn't lost—except, in a sense, to herself. The fact was, after a day of so much emotional turmoil, all feeling had fled. Suddenly, she was numb.

Where was the passionate, impetuous Giuliana Baci who hadn't thought twice about eloping with the love of her life when she was eighteen? Where was the woman who'd translated the loss of her baby and her anger at the young man who'd betrayed her into a living, breathing grudge that had sustained her for a decade?

Her passion, her grief, her temper, they were mere shells now. As vacant as her heart.

It was much later that she found herself at the farmhouse. She tiptoed up the steps, figuring she'd wrap herself in a quilt and sleep on the couch. It would be a relief to escape the emptiness inside her.

A light in the kitchen blazed. She considered leaving it burning, but she'd left the porch fixture on in case Penn and Jack were still out. With the rest of the house quiet and dark behind her, she pushed open the swinging door.

Stevie sat at the table, a carton of ice cream in front of her. She held a spoon and wore a pretty, lacy peach robe and a guilty expression. It almost immediately eased. "Thank God, it's you."

Giuliana discovered she could still experience relief, despite the dullness of the rest of her feelings. Her sister was feeling better if she was digging into rocky road. And if her sister was nudging the chair beside her with her foot, extending a silent invitation for her to sit, then she wasn't completely despised.

On her way across the scarred linoleum, she grabbed

her own spoon. Then she slipped onto the wooden seat, cocking her head to study her sister, who looked both feminine and fertile. Her skin glowed. Apparently the day's rest had done her good. "I take it Jack wouldn't approve of late-night snacking?" Giuliana asked.

"Not so much what I eat, but that I ventured down the stairs by myself to do it. He's threatening to carry me everywhere." She grinned, looking again like the softball-playing tomboy who'd always sported scraped knees and splinters. "Though it's kind of nice being treated like a princess, I admit."

"You *are* a princess."

Stevie's grin widened. "Still amazes the hell out of me."

Giuliana dipped her spoon in the chocolate ice cream. "You were the one who loved your fairy tales."

"Yeah. We always thought of Allie as the big romantic, but it turns out I'm the real daydream believer."

"Any doubts that our little sister had about happy endings have been put to rest by Penn."

Stevie nodded, then the curve of her mouth flattened, and she reached for Giuliana's free hand, clasping it with her slender fingers. "She told me. She told me about your baby. I'm so sorry."

Had she admitted that to Alessandra only this morning? "It was Liam's, too," she murmured, remembering that anguish she'd seen in Jack when he thought about losing the child he'd made with Stevie. She returned her sister's grip. "But that was a long time ago and your doctor said you're fine. Your pregnancy isn't in any danger."

"No." She placed her hand over her belly. There was just the slightest of curves. With her height, Stevie was going to be one of those enviable women who looked the same from the back for nine months and only showed a cute bump from the front. "But, Jules . . . no matter what happened . . . it's Jack who makes me feel safe."

Giuliana slipped her hand from her sister's. "That's

nice." Her glance wandered away, and caught on the leather-bound book also on the table. She reached for it, then snatched her hand away. "You have Anne's diary?"

"Don't think I don't know you slipped it back into Allie's tote bag the other day." Stevie dropped her spoon in the ice cream carton, then snagged the book and drew it close to her. With a gentle finger, she flipped it open and started turning pages with a delicate movement. The handwriting was heavily slanted and faded in some places. They'd raced through it on the first reading, sometimes being forced to give up on the meaning of a passage, the ink was so washed-out. They'd been so eager, if not exactly hopeful, to find a clue to the treasure.

And if they'd now discovered it . . . "Selling the wedding bells won't change things," she warned her sister.

Stevie looked up.

Giuliana appreciated her dead insides now. If her decision about the land was upsetting her sister, Giuliana found she couldn't feel it. And she had the advantage of logic on her side! "No matter how much we could get for the topper, if that's indeed what it is, we'd eventually run through that money, too, to keep the winery going."

"We could still turn it all around," Stevie said, her voice mild. "Did Allie tell you? We've sold out the Vow-Over Weekend."

Giuliana shook her head. "Why would you want to prolong this? We've lost so much already . . ." She focused on Stevie's finger, leafing through the book page by page. "We lost Mom and Papa." She'd lost her baby and Liam and she might lose her sisters if she didn't convince them that her approach was best.

She grabbed her sister's moving hand and held tight. "We can cut those losses if we get out from under Tanti Baci now. It will make it easier to walk away."

"You ran away before, Jules. How did that work out for you?"

Her sister's comment couldn't pierce the anesthetized casing around Giuliana's heart. It only frustrated her and she sat back in her chair, Stevie's hand sliding from hers.

The younger woman tapped the old diary. "Anne faced a similar problem to you, when you think about it," she said. "Her family was against her choice, making her decision that much more difficult."

She glanced up at Stevie. "Yeah. And she ignored their wishes to turn her back on Liam."

Her sister's mouth quirked. "We don't have to repeat the past quite so literally, do we? The point I'm trying to make is that if you love something—or someone—you don't just give up on it. Remember what Anne wrote? The lesson that ended all her indecision and heartache? She had to learn to live without fear."

Giuliana sighed. Living wasn't a problem. But with her dead heart and her weary soul, she figured she'd lost her capacity to love . . . and she didn't really regret it.

19

They closed the winery to tours and tastings on Thursday before the Vow-Over Weekend so they could prepare for the event. Still, Tanti Baci was swarming with people: those setting up the large tents they'd rented, others delivering chairs and tables, the caterer and her assistant doing a walk-through to determine the final placement of the planned food and beverage stations. The *Wedding Fever* TV production crew had been in and out.

Giuliana had her own long list of tasks to accomplish, as did her sisters, their husbands, and even Liam. They moved around each other like watch parts, ignoring the underlying tension.

Allie, with Stevie and the men behind her, had cornered Giuliana first thing in the morning, right after the impromptu meeting they'd held in the small conference room to hash out some last-minute details. "You'll do your part this weekend, right?"

"What?" she'd said. "Of course I will."

"Just checking." Her little sister's dark eyes were flinty.

"I wasn't sure, since you're selling the place and on your way out of town again . . ."

"I'll put in one hundred percent," Giuliana declared. She'd felt herself bristling at the questioning, but then she'd forced herself to let her insult go. Her family was upset by her decision, she got that. The only way she could hope to salvage a relationship with them was to do everything she could during Vow-Over and believe that there'd be some resultant, healing goodwill.

"You'll see," she'd promised them all. "Whatever needs doing, I'll be doing it."

With that, they'd called a tacit truce that she hoped would last until the last guest on Sunday left the property. And it didn't seem there'd be time to do battle anyway. Workers needed direction, vendors had questions, the phones were ringing off the hook.

The high point of her morning: she opened a supply closet and found Kohl and Grace in a clinch. The couple had sprung apart, but the younger woman had turned a pretty shade of pink while Kohl just looked pleased with himself. "I misplaced my tool belt," Kohl said. "Grace knew right where I'd left it." She didn't point out that it was at the couple's feet, as if it had just been unfastened.

The low point came when she faced off with Liam in the winery caves. She was pushing a dolly loaded with cases of the wedding *blanc de blancs* on their way to Anne and Alonzo's cottage. They would be serving the wedding wine there to couples and their guests following the renewal of their vows.

He was frowning down at his cell phone as he strode forward and she had to stop or mow him down with the dolly. Since it wasn't easy to maneuver, he nearly walked right into it. At the last second, his feet halted and he looked up.

It was the first time they'd been alone together since their confrontation in the parking lot at the bar. She'd felt dead inside then, and now wasn't different. Though she was aware of her thumping heart, her emotions were still flatlining. She realized, suddenly, that the detachment she'd always cursed in Liam was hers.

It was a mode of self-protection, of course. A withdrawal from pain. The aloofness wasn't arrogance at all.

"Sorry," she said.

He shoved his phone in the pocket of his jeans. With them, he wore a ratty T-shirt that had a rip in the sleeve. It was a very un-Liam-like look. After the bar night, he'd likely had a hangover, but a few days of recuperation didn't appear to have done much good. "Sorry for what?" he asked, his voice tired.

It wasn't the time to share insights. She was tired, too. "I'm in your way." It was the first thing that came into her head and she gestured to the dolly.

His half smile was wry. "Yeah. I'm kinda used to that, though."

"Only for a little while longer."

"I remember." He nodded. "We've almost finished up with your four weeks to freedom."

She'd said those words. Talk about arrogance. Though she didn't feel much besides a dull twinge, she could admit now that escape from the past and from the ties of Tanti Baci wasn't an option. No matter where she went, she'd carry them with her.

She pushed the handcart forward, and Liam stepped to the side to allow her to pass. As she made her way toward the doors, she could feel his gaze on her back.

"Your things are still at my house," he called. "If you drop by anytime before seven o'clock tonight, you'll have the place to yourself."

If she was careful, she wouldn't even have to face him alone again.

"Perfect," she called back. "I'll leave my key behind."

The next hours flew by as she continued knocking items off her to-do list. Of course, others were added to the bottom, and she was interrupted often to give an opinion, hold the end of a tape measure, or plug in an extension cord. After a quick lunch break, it continued in the same vein. When she realized how thirsty she was, she loaded a wheelbarrow with ice and drinks, and rolled it around, offering beverages to all and sundry.

Passing the wedding cottage, she heard murmuring voices. With a quartet of cold water bottles in her hands, she mounted the steps and peeked inside. The florist and her assistants were tying flower holders and ribbons to the ends of each of the boxed benches. On the weekend, they'd fill them with blooms.

"Water anyone?" Giuliana called out to the women. "Or anything else you need, since I'm free at the moment." It took a second for her to absorb their suddenly alarmed expressions. It took just another before a loud sound started emanating from a far corner. A third passed before she identified the noise.

A baby was crying.

Delle Michaels, the fifty-something florist, grimaced and put down her tools. "She's awake." With quick strides, she made her way to a infant carrier and pulled a wiggling bundle in pink free. The child quieted. "My four-month-old granddaughter," she explained to Giuliana. "I love her to pieces, but when she's awake, she's a snuggler, which is not conducive to work that requires wire and pliers."

"Maybe if we put her closer to us," one of her assistants suggested. "If she sees us moving around she'll be content in the carrier."

"Maybe," Delle said, and put the baby down.

The crying started again.

"We won't get everything done on time," a second assistant cautioned, "unless we're all working."

With a sigh, Delle retrieved the baby and kissed her on her chubby cheeks when the child instantly stopped the waterworks. "I know, I know." She sent an apologetic glance at Giuliana. "My son and daughter-in-law had an emergency babysitting need."

"Sure," Giuliana said, backing toward the door. "I understand."

"Terrific!" Delle smiled in relief. "So you won't mind holding her for an hour, will you, Giuliana? Or until she falls asleep, whichever comes first."

"*Me?*" Giuliana took another step in retreat. "I mean, I, uh . . ."

"You said you were free," Delle reminded her, bustling forward. "And you like babies, right?"

"Well, uh . . ." And before she could come up with another excuse, Delle placed the pink bundle in her arms.

She tucked a thin flannel blanket around the baby. "See? She's quiet again already. Her name is Molly." Delle patted Giuliana's arm. "Take her for a walk. If she doesn't see Grammy, she's probably even less likely to fuss."

Giuliana swallowed. "I . . ." Then her own words came back to her. *Whatever needs doing, I'll be doing it.* "We'll be just fine, Delle."

She'd go find one of her sisters and pass the infant off. "You understand," she said to the baby as she descended the cottage's porch steps, her gaze already roaming for a familiar face. "It's nothing personal."

The baby wiggled in her arms, and Giuliana hitched her closer. "Nothing personal," she repeated, glancing down at the round cheeks, the baby mouth with its pronounced upper lip, the big blue eyes.

Molly's eyes.

Giuliana stared down at her. "It's no Fabulosa Magnifica or Myauntiescool Andspoilsme," she murmured.

The child responded with a squirm and wrinkles developed on her tiny forehead. She appeared annoyed.

"But it's not a bad name," Giuliana hastened to say. "Molly has a very nice ring to it."

The lines smoothed out, as if she was appeased by the

compliment. So Giuliana kept talking as she walked, and Molly's eyes fastened onto her face as if the conversation was riveting. What was riveting, Giuliana thought, was the feel of the infant against her. Though she was light, Molly was surprisingly . . . solid. And warm. She didn't remember a baby being so warm.

Giuliana wasn't sure she'd ever actually held one in her arms. Like every other teenage girl, she'd babysat on many occasions, but her charges had been toddler-sized. The kind you ran after or rolled a ball to, not the kind you held close to your chest. Heart to heart.

Instead of heading to the administrative offices, where she'd most likely discover a sister, Giuliana found herself turning into the vineyard. "Have you seen grapes growing before, Molly?" she asked, turning in a slow circle in the red dirt. Silt coated the bottom of her thongs and crept onto the bare parts of her feet.

Good Baci dirt.

"Aren't the grapes pretty?" She tilted her arms so that the baby could see a pale green cluster.

Healthy Baci grapes.

"We'll make wine with them next fall."

Traditional Tanti Baci wine.

"When you grow up, Molly, maybe at your wedding you'll serve the *blanc de blancs* that's from the grapes grown at this very vineyard."

If the Bristol brothers decided to continue making it.

If they didn't decide to scrap one hundred years of Baci history. Once the land was sold to them, they could yank out the vines and plant plums or pears or any number of things, just like growers had done during Prohibition. Or they could let her family's land go fallow. Unused. Lifeless.

What Giuliana had been feeling inside.

The baby made a little noise, and Giuliana looked into those serious blue eyes. Her gaze was strangely wise, she thought, and then the rosebud mouth moved. Curved.

Giuliana froze, the smile piercing her breast with a smooth stroke. It found her heart, and the bittersweet pain jolted it awake.

"Oh, Molly," she whispered. "Oh, no."

The baby wiggled against her and Giuliana shifted her closer, cuddling that warm, pliable weight against her. Her skin smelled of soap, her downy hair was soft against Giuliana's lips. Molly didn't seem the least bit bothered by the rain of Giuliana's tears on the crown of her head.

She was feeling again. *Oh, God.* Feeling everything.

From her connection to the land at her feet to the ache of love in her chest.

Just as Molly was no inanimate doll, neither was Giuliana—though perhaps she'd been living like that for the last year. Going through the motions of being a Baci and a sister without taking a real breath as either one. She'd railed at Liam's closed-off emotions, but she'd been no better, using that as an excuse to keep away from him and everyone else in Edenville for the last ten years.

He'd hidden his emotions away.

She'd hidden from everyone who might cause her to have any beyond the most superficial.

She said she didn't believe in second chances, when it was really that she didn't want to risk trying again. Losing her mother and then losing the baby and then losing Liam had left her so bereft.

"Oh, Molly," she whispered. She tried brushing away the flow of tears with the back of her hand, but they continued to fall. "Allie was right. If we don't look for what we've lost, then we lose everything."

She spun again in the dirt, more slowly this time, to absorb the beauty of her surroundings. Stark blue sky, fertile earth, lush vines.

Growing grapes.

It was all so beautiful it made her eyes sting all over again.

"Let me tell you how it works, Molly," she said, rubbing her wet cheek against the baby's head. "When you harvest the grapes, you have to deal with the bees. I always get a sting or two when we're picking. But that's part of the process. You have to take the pain here and there if you want to hold that sweet, warm fruit in the palm of your hand."

She took another breath of the baby's delicate scent and then held her away to look into her serene gaze. "I'd forgotten that."

A breeze caught her hair. It stirred the leaves on the vines and felt like a chilled breath against her skin. Prickles stung the back of her neck and instinct took over, causing her arms to draw Molly close again and her shoulders to round, creating a haven of her body for the child.

"Jules!"

Liam. Relief coursed through her and she turned toward his voice. He stood at the end of the row, staring at her. She saw herself as he would: dusty feet, tear-wet cheeks, baby. Her heart lurched in her chest, remembering what he'd said to her in the bar.

Don't go, Jules. Don't leave me again.

She saw this clearly, too, now: she'd been the one to run. He'd left Tuscany before she did, but he'd been at home all this time.

He paced toward her, his gaze never moving off her and Molly. "What's wrong? You're crying."

It was so hard to breathe, let alone swallow, as she absorbed his familiar face. It took two tries, then she licked her lips. "I am crying," she whispered. Then she took another breath and smiled. "And so are you."

His hand jerked up. He wiped the moisture away with the heel of his hand, clearly embarrassed. "I . . . seeing you with a baby . . ."

"Liam!" Penn was at the end of the row now, driving one of the Bennett ATVs. "Coming?"

He glanced back, then looked at Giuliana again. Another tear trickled down his lean cheek.

"Liam!" Penn yelled. "Get your ass in gear!"

When Liam flipped his brother off, she could almost laugh. "I . . . I don't know what to say . . ." he started, his voice hoarse.

You have to learn to live without fear. "Maybe . . . maybe I do."

He scrubbed the heel of his hand against his face, his gaze suddenly hard on hers. "Jules?"

"Go with Penn," she urged. "I'll be at your house tonight. At eight." Though they had so much to accomplish, the sisters had sworn to each other they'd clear out before then. She and Allie had agreed on one thing. They had to ensure Stevie got plenty of rest.

Now Giuliana hoped her message was clear. He'd told her she'd have the place to herself if she came before seven. She would arrive later, when the two of them could be alone. Together.

~

Her message must not have been clear, Giuliana thought. It was closing on eight P.M., and Liam hadn't arrived back at his house. Or maybe . . .

He wasn't interested in what she had to say.

That could be likely, given that he hadn't responded to her call to his cell phone or her text. He'd not tagged her on her phone, either.

Alone in Liam's house, she decided waiting wasn't an option any longer. It was nearing full dark as she set off, taking the shortcut. It vee'd at one point, one leg going toward the winery. She took the other that led to the farmhouse.

Approaching the back door that opened into the kitchen, she heard laughter. Through the windows, she saw Penn and Jack moving back and forth. The husbands were cooking and the group looked relaxed and happy.

She hesitated. It wasn't so much about being the fifth wheel. They wouldn't close her out of their circle because she wasn't paired up. But there was the Tanti Baci land—and her part in the threat to it.

Still, she steeled herself to join them. The laughter stopped when she pushed open the door. Jack smiled, though, and Penn, the most easygoing of the bunch, came forward to pull her inside. Her other brother-in-law poured her a glass of the cab they were apparently drinking with burgers and fries.

Her sisters didn't give away their thoughts, so she surveyed the platter of red meat and the steaming batch of crispy fries on the counter. Fine, it looked great, but her maternal instincts reared their head.

"I hope you're planning a salad to go along with that."

Without a word, Stevie turned around to grab a bowl of watermelon slices she put on the table. Allie placed a bowl of greens, tomatoes, and avocado beside it.

She could feel the weight of her sisters' gazes. It was nothing compared to the weight of responsibility she'd felt since she was sixteen . . . no, before that. Could they understand? "She always told me to look after you. When she knew she was dying of cancer, she said it was my job. That I would be a good mother to the two of you."

"Oh, Jules," Allie said.

Giuliana covered her eyes with her hand. "I was so sad when she died."

It was Stevie who touched her. She put her arm around her shoulders. "You were the one closest to her."

"She loved all of us equally," she replied, hearing the fierce tone of her voice.

"Of course," Stevie said. "I get that. But I also get that you being the oldest put a heavier burden on you."

"When things changed with Liam . . ."

"You mean when you started kissing Liam," Allie put in, a bubble of laugh in her voice.

That lightness lifted her heart a tiny bit. "I found new happiness. It wasn't so dark everywhere."

"Oh, Jules." Allie again.

"But I left you guys. I wasn't supposed to."

"Giuliana." Stevie spoke with the confidence of a woman who had figured out things about her own life and love. "You didn't abandon us. We were constantly talking. You monitored closely—very closely at times, I'll say—what we were doing."

"I should have stopped Allie deciding to marry Tommy when she was barely out of high school," Giuliana confessed.

"Pfft," Allie responded, waving a hand. "I couldn't be swayed and I see now why you didn't say I was too young—hello, pot, kettle—but that's not about you."

Penn moved close to his wife. His hand smoothed the back of her long hair. "Okay?"

She sent him a smile and then went on tiptoe to kiss his mouth. "Okay. But man, are these oldest siblings annoyingly over-responsible."

Giuliana's mind instantly turned to the man who wasn't home. "Liam . . ."

"Also annoyingly over-responsible," Penn confirmed.

"Do you know where he is?"

His half brother shook his head. "Is something wrong?"

"No." She didn't want to admit he'd stood her up.

"Will you eat with us?" Stevie asked. "Allie's getting fat. We can halve her portion."

The youngest Baci gasped. "I am *not* getting fat."

"That's not what you said when you tried on my blue butterfly top."

"Wait." Giuliana felt compelled to jump in. "Wasn't that *my* blue butterfly top?"

Stevie grimaced. "That's right. I borrowed it a while back. Before the fire."

"Doesn't matter. It never looked good on me."

"The butterfly top doesn't look good on anybody," Allie declared. "Can the three of us at least agree on that?"

Giuliana found herself smiling at them. This is what she'd missed and what she wanted again. Borrowing clothes, exchanging frank opinions, being sisters again. Being sisters always. "The Three Mouseketeers," she murmured.

"Ladies," Jack interrupted, "I'll burn that blue top if we could all just sit down and eat. I'm starving and Stephania has Fabulosa to consider."

Giuliana was too restless for a meal. "I'm on my way."

Allie caught her hand. "Really, Jules. Stay."

"No, not for dinner." She squeezed her sister's fingers. "But about the other . . . yes." Whatever happened with Liam, she belonged in Edenville, with her sisters and working to keep the Tanti Baci legacy alive.

Her sisters exchanged glances. "Yes?" they said together.

She nodded. "Yes. The contract with the Bristols was just in the exploration stage and I'm not selling a square foot of family land unless we all agree. I say we carry on with the Vow-Over Weekend and then we carry on making wine for the next one hundred years just as we have for the last."

~

She made it out without a meal but could live for a long time on the hugs and happiness that had filled the kitchen. Penn had wanted to drive her back to the Bennett house, but she'd insisted he sit down to dinner. The walk would do her good. If Liam was still AWOL by the time she returned, she'd pack up her grocery bags and head back to her sisters.

They'd likely torture the truth out of her, but a pity party might be just what she needed. Getting over him wasn't an option, but she'd have to find a way to deal. Running away had never worked and she refused to try it a second time.

The sound of tires on the gravel drive had her heart

leaping. Liam? But it wasn't his Mercedes. Instead, it was Kohl's dusty Jeep. He braked beside her and rolled down his window. "Can we give you a lift somewhere?"

Giuliana waved at Grace, then shook her head. "I'm fine."

"We're going out to dinner. Want to come?"

"No, thanks." She hesitated. "But, uh, have you seen Liam?"

Kohl glanced over at Grace. "No. Not since we buttoned up for the night. Do you need something?"

"No. I just sort of . . . lost him."

The vineyard manager looked at Grace again. There was a moment of silence, then the other woman piped up. "I think he's at the wedding cottage."

"What?"

"Anne and Alonzo's cottage," Grace said.

Why would he be there? Had they gotten their signals crossed? "Did you see him, Grace?"

"I, um, think I did." It was difficult to read the other woman's expression in the darkness, with only the dashboard glow to see by. "Shall we go with you to check it out?"

"No." Still puzzling over it, Giuliana waved them on their way. "Go on and have your dinner."

She watched them continue toward the road, then hurried in the opposite direction. It seemed all was in order as she approached the winery buildings. The newly erected tents stood undisturbed. The caves and administrative offices were quiet, the security lights creating small puddles of brightness in the dark. Beyond them was Anne and Alonzo's cottage. Her heart started pumping. Besides the security lights there, she could see another light glowing inside.

Liam. She paused a moment to gather her thoughts, then started forward again.

She had to look for what she'd lost.

As she mounted the steps to the porch, she could see that one of the double front doors was ajar. Her rubber thongs rendered her steps silent and she paused again before crossing the threshold. Risk never came easy.

On a deep breath, she pushed open the door. It let out a little squeal.

A man turned.

It wasn't her husband.

This dark-haired person stood beside the table set with bottles of *blanc de blancs* and glassware. A coil of rope sat beside them. The lacy tablecloth was askew and one of the wine bottles had fallen to the floor.

It rested against Liam, who was lying there, too, his body still, his eyes closed, a trickle of blood on his forehead.

20

Giuliana's heart slammed against her ribs and she took a step forward just as the thinking part of her brain kicked in. *Run!* it said. *Get help!*

But the stranger beside Liam spoke, too, in an accent she found vaguely familiar. "Come on inside, ma'am." There was a gun in his hand, pointed at her. She might have still chanced flight, except then he pointed it at the unconscious Liam. "You try to leave, I'll shoot him."

She didn't move a muscle in either direction. "What do you want?"

He shook his head, ignoring her question. "You're early. Who told you we'd be here?"

"Grace—" she began, and at the word she knew his identity. Not a stranger. Grace's ex-husband. He'd approached her at Vincenzo's when she was there with Liam. And then again, on the Edenville street. He'd been wearing a ball cap that day and talked to her about his voodoo aunt and his superstitions. *This guy had been watching her.*

"Ah, Grace." He gestured her inside with his free hand.

The hand with the gun continued aiming downward, at Liam. "As soon as I take care of you, the two of us will be back together."

Giuliana came farther into the room, her steps slow.

"Sit down, sugar. I need to deal with your husband before I get to you."

Get to me how? *Deal with him how?* her brain screamed. But she tried appearing calm as she slid onto the last bench at the rear of the room. Twisting in her seat, she could see both him and Liam. "What's, uh, what's your name?"

"Daniel." He leaned down and fished under Liam's inert body. When he straightened, he had a cell phone in his hand. "He whipped this out pretty fast. I don't think he managed to call, though." His thumb moved and she guessed he was checking the log.

"What, uh, do you want, Daniel? I don't have my purse with me, or even my keys to the winery offices, but I could get them. We have a little bit of cash there."

He glanced at her, his expression scornful.

"Or wine! We have wine!" She gestured to the bottles on the table beside Liam. On the opposite wall was another table with even more *blanc de blancs*. "That's a sparkling white, but we make a chardonnay and a very nice cab, too."

"I don't want your money or your liquor, sugar." He pocketed Liam's cell phone. Then he strode toward her.

She slid down the bench. "What *do* you want?"

He held out his palm. "Your phone."

Stalling seemed like a good idea. "Why would you want that?"

Annoyance crossed his face. "Sugar—"

"I don't know why you're here. I don't know why you'd want anything to do with me and Liam."

He glanced over his shoulder. The body on the floor was so still.

How bad was Liam hurt? "Let me go to him," she pleaded. "I know first aid."

"He'll be fine," Daniel said. "I just coldcocked him with my gun. The fire will do the rest."

Her blood didn't run cold. It just stopped running altogether. And her mind went very, very quiet. "Fire?"

"I wasn't trying to hurt anybody with that arson at the apartment. I just wanted Grace out of there. I thought if she didn't have a place to stay, that she'd come back to me."

Giuliana swallowed. "It was you who started that."

"Mmm." He shook his head. "I didn't think she'd really go through with it . . . leaving me. Sure, I knocked her around a few times, but that's the only way to get through to her. Her dad told me that."

Giuliana's fingers curled into fists. She wasn't stupid enough to take a swing at him herself, but she wanted to knock *him* around, she did. After she'd been mugged, she had revenge fantasies for months. They were all coming back to her.

From the corner of her eye, she saw Liam twitch. Her belly tightened. *Don't call attention to yourself,* she thought, sending him the silent message. *Don't give him another excuse to hurt you.*

"I remember our conversation on Market Night," she said, babbling whatever came into her head so Daniel would keep focused on her. "I remember you have an aunt who practices voodoo."

"Yeah." He frowned at her. "Now hand me your phone."

She slowly stood. "I don't have one on me," she said. *Damn.* It was a fact. She must have left it at the farmhouse. Wearing only her jeans and a Tanti Baci T-shirt, it was easy to prove the truth of her statement. "See?" She patted her front pockets, then twisted to show there was no telltale bulge in the back ones, either. Remembering something Grace had once said to her, she tried looking apologetic. "I'm forgetful. My papa said all three of us girls put together were hardly as useful as half a son would be."

Daniel's mouth quirked. "Grace was like that. Always

forgettin' stuff. I like raspberry jam on Saturdays, not strawberry. I decided I like my shirts washed inside out, but could she remember that?"

Petty bully, she thought to herself. Who knew you could be scared spitless and incensed at the same time? She bet if Grace remembered raspberry was his Saturday favorite then the next weekend he'd change it back to strawberry. Instead of showing her disgust, she sighed. "I have a memory like a sieve."

Still searching for another delay tactic, she darted her gaze around the room. It snagged on the framed photograph on the fireplace mantel with some other vintage Tanti Baci memorabilia. The items used to sit in the display case damaged during the vandalism. Hah. She could guess the culprit of that crime now.

Her eyes focused on the picture of Anne and Alonzo, arm in arm between flourishing vines. "Uh, what was it you said about evil spirits, that day we met up?"

"You don't want to wake 'em." His brows came together and he cocked his head. "What made you mention that?"

"It's just that we're here in the wedding cottage." Behind Daniel's back, Liam's legs moved again. Then she saw him wince and his eyes half opened. She raised her voice, hoping to help orient him. "We're here in the cottage of the couple who founded the winery, Daniel. My great-great-grandparents. They're supposed to haunt the place."

The man twitched. "Nah."

"Oh, yeah. When you were married, didn't Grace ever tell you that? It's common knowledge in Edenville."

"She's a quiet thing," he said. "When I get rid of this place, then she's going to see that she needs to come back to me. Without a job, she'll have to."

Panic tightened her throat. *Get rid of this place?* "Tanti Baci has been in my family for a hundred years."

"Yeah? Grace was my wife for three. She'd still be my wife if you hadn't given her a job."

"I'll fire her. Right now. Give me Liam's cell phone, and I'll call her this instant and tell her not to come to work tomorrow." She'd call 911 first. Or after. She just needed to get her hands on that phone!

Daniel sighed. "My wife is stubborn when she gets a mind to be. You could fire her and she'd still be back here tomorrow. I think it's best if I stick to the plan. Burn the place down, with your meddling self and your husband inside the cottage. I'll get the offices next. That farmhouse while I'm at it."

"Oh, Anne and Alonzo will be very unhappy if any of that happens." Giuliana didn't have to fake her shudder.

"How quickly does a vineyard burn?" Daniel asked, as if it was a perfectly natural question.

Perfectly natural to discuss the destruction of her heritage. Her family. Not only was he talking about harming her and Liam, but Allie, Penn, Stevie, and Jack were at the farmhouse. And Myauntiescool Andspoilsme.

Her blood *was* running cold now, but a fiery resolve was kindling in her belly. "Anne and Alonzo would really hate for something to happen to the vines," she asserted. "People have seen them, you know. Their ghosts. We had a man make off with some of our root stock once. Not half a mile away, he ran into a ditch and was thrown through his windshield. As he lay dying, bleeding from a wound that sliced his scalp from his skull, he whispered to the emergency workers he saw Alonzo Baci standing in the middle of the road, a pitchfork in his hand."

There was a sheen of sweat on Daniel's upper lip and a little tic was fluttering the corner of his right eye. Over his shoulder, she saw that Liam was on the move, crawling toward their captor, the wine bottle that had been beside him in his hand. Her heart started beating in double time, but she didn't let her focus stray.

"Then there was what we call the Dick and Balls incident."

Daniel swallowed. "What was that?"

"Some young buck was riding his motorcycle through the rows, trying to impress my baby sister. He lost control and plowed through several vines. The motorcycle went down and he slid along the dirt, only stopping once his—well—private parts were speared by a stake his wild riding had dislodged. He begged the two people that appeared beside him for help, but they just laughed at his predicament. Later he identified them as my great-great-grandparents.

"We call *him* . . ." Noting the creeped-out look on their captor's face, she paused for effect.

Daniel licked his lips. "You call him—"

Pop!

The sound cracked like a gun shot. Daniel jumped, whirled, his arm lifting.

From the opposite direction: *Pop! Pop!*

When he spun the other way, Giuliana shoved at him with all her might. He stumbled into Liam, crouched at his feet, who took advantage of the other man's imbalance and yanked him down, his hands going for the wrist of the arm with the gun. Giuliana leapt onto the villain's chest, then gripped his hair in her hand and lifted his head, only to slam it into the ground.

Adrenaline pouring through her like rocket fuel, she slammed it again. Then again. Nobody threatened her land or her family. Nobody hurt her man. She slammed it again.

"Jules." She heard her name from a thousand miles away. "Jules, he's out."

Her fingers still cramped in Daniel's hair, she looked over. Liam had the gun and he was rising to a stand. "I'll get the rope."

She was breathing hard and her hand was locked in a claw she couldn't straighten. When Liam returned with the coil, he gently pulled her free. As he began unraveling the rope, she crawled toward the fallen cell phone. She wasn't convinced her knees would bear her weight.

"Clever you," she said, her voice a croak as she bypassed the puddle of wine spilling from the abandoned bottle. "Popping the cork. It sounded like a gunshot and startled him."

Liam grunted as he rolled Daniel over so he could tie his hands behind his back.

"But you just had the one bottle," she said, frowning. "How'd you make those other two blow?"

Liam slid her an enigmatic look. "I didn't."

~

Less than twelve hours after the police carted off Daniel Mowdray, Liam let himself back into the wedding cottage. His belly jumped as his gaze found a figure silhouetted by the window.

His pulse didn't stop its chatter when he saw that it was Giuliana. "You should be back at the farmhouse," he said. He'd made sure she was safely there, surrounded by her sisters and their husbands, before he'd headed for his own home in the early-morning hours. "You've got to be exhausted."

She drifted toward him, looking anything but tired in a pair of faded sweatpants and her "You Had Me at Merlot" T-shirt. Her expression was relaxed and there was a pretty flush on her cheeks and a sparkle in her tip-tilted eyes.

"I feel pretty great," she said.

"You look pretty great," he murmured. *Beautiful.* "But what are you doing?"

"Reclaiming the cottage. I'm not letting that sleaze contaminate one of Tanti Baci's treasures."

He nodded, proud of her. Not just for that, but because he'd found out last night that she was giving second chances a shot and had decided against selling the land. It made the success of the Vow-Over Weekend just that much more important. "I talked to the police. I think we can keep the incident quiet, at least until Sunday when the celebration is over."

"Last night you told them the Vow-Over Weekend was why you were here. Someone called who said he was from the tent rental company?"

"Yeah, and there was a problem I needed to address immediately. When I got here, I saw the light on in the cottage."

"He hit you over the head when you came inside?" she asked.

"Apparently his plan was to get me to lure you here with a call when I came to. Then he'd tie you up, too, and start a fire." Thinking about it, Liam wished he'd been rougher when wrestling the gun away. And that he'd gotten in a few head drops himself, after he'd put a stop to Giuliana. "Crazy son of a bitch."

"*Superstitious*, crazy son of a bitch."

"Smart woman, to keep his attention like that—the Dick and Balls incident?"

A small smile curved her lips. "It bought us some time."

Neither one of them mentioned those mysterious and well-timed popping corks.

She cocked her head, studying him. "But what brought you here?"

Stalling, he slid his hands into his pockets and worried the item he'd tucked into the right one. "Uh . . ." A good excuse didn't immediately occur to him.

Giuliana ran her hand along the back of one of the benches, then slid onto the seat, in the exact place she'd been the night before when he'd come around. Finding her there, at the mercy of the man who'd just knocked him out, had taken him from quasi-conscious to fully awake in a split second.

"How's your head?" she asked, as if she could read his mind.

He struggled to keep his composure, still plagued by that memory of her confronting the man with the gun. "This past week has been a revelation, in more ways than one. Turns out my head's damn hard."

She smiled. "No surprise to me."

"We're both stubborn." He hesitated. "I guess that's why neither one of us filed for divorce."

"You'd guess wrong."

"Yeah." He blew out a breath. "That wasn't it."

And then all his cool fled. One second he was standing by the door, and the next he was at her feet, his head in her lap, his arms around her waist. "Jules," he said. "Jules, I love you."

To hell with Calvin Bennett and whatever legacy he'd left behind. Liam would love this woman generously or die trying—he wasn't giving her up this time without a fight. "I love you so much."

She curled over him, her hands in his hair. "I've never been so happy to hear anything in my whole life."

He looked up, into her beautiful face, his heart feeling too big for his chest. "You're crying." His thumbs brushed at her tears.

And just like the day before, she smiled through them. "And so are you."

He thought he owed them to her. "God, Jules. I didn't have the words to tell you how sorry I was about our baby."

"I understand that now." She stroked his hair back from his forehead. "I shouldn't have run away. I should have run *to* you and then maybe we could have figured out the words together."

"I don't know. I was pretty messed up."

"Then let's talk about the present. Now, I think we can make this work. Stevie told me something about Jack. She said he makes her feel safe and that's what you do for me, too. Take last night—I knew that together we'd be all right."

"I hope to God that's the last time we're put to the test."

"Oh, I suppose we'll be tested again, don't you? We probably know better than most people that it takes more than . . ."

"Love," he said, adamant. "Passion."

She nodded. "That it takes more than love and passion to make a relationship work."

"I need to realize I can't—and shouldn't—smother my feelings."

"I need to be willing to risk loss." She lifted an eyebrow at him. "Are we up to it?"

"Damn straight." His hands cupping her face, he brought her mouth to his for a sweet, sealing kiss.

When she broke away, they were both already breathing hard. "I'm still not clear on why you came to the cottage this morning."

His gaze slid away from hers. "Do you have to know?"

"Now that you asked that?" In her gaze, he glimpsed the often pesky girl of his childhood. "Of course."

He put his hand in his right pocket. "You'll laugh."

"Only better and better." And she did laugh when he shot her a disgruntled look. "Okay, I won't." Despite her primmed mouth, her eyes danced.

"The cottage seemed like a good place to think." Though he'd made up his mind the day before, when he'd spotted her in the vines. When he'd seen her with a baby in her arms and realized that he couldn't protect her or himself from hurt and loss. It had been absolutely clear at that moment that he wanted to face life and death with Giuliana, not without her. "An experience like we had last night . . . it can clarify things."

The person who knew him best in the world shoved at his shoulder. "You are so full of it. That's not why you came."

It felt good to laugh himself. "Fine. I'm a sentimental fool. I was looking for their blessing. And for a little good luck. I'm here to get Anne and Alonzo's ghostly okay on this." Withdrawing his hand from his pocket, he presented her with the glass bead bracelet that he'd found beneath the pillows of his bed. "We'll get a ring, too, but . . ."

Her expression went serious, and her eyes filled, again, with tears. He thought it was a good sign. "Liam Bennett, you *are* a sentimental fool," she whispered.

"I already said that." He was still kneeling at her feet, so he had to duck his head to catch her gaze with his. "Giuliana, will you marry me?"

"Yes, I'll marry you." She launched herself forward, and he caught her in his arms. "I already said that, too."

His heart beat hard against hers. "It bears repeating."

~

It wasn't their only do-over. They spoke their vows again, in front of family and friends at the fiftieth celebration of the wedding wine. Liam watched his wife walk down the aisle in Anne and Alonzo's cottage, feeling just like Penn. He barely suppressed beating his chest as she drew nearer.

She carried pink and purple orchids and had a few tucked in the upsweep of her hair. Her dress hugged her small waist and then belled in unadorned layers of some frothy fabric. Ed and Jed from the hardware store claimed she looked just like Audrey Hepburn. Stevie had whispered that a nearby bridal shop and the local alterations expert had colluded to get it ready in record time.

He had a fondness for her "You Had Me at Merlot" T-shirt and would have requested that if asked. But this was better.

"You take my breath," he whispered, when she put her hand in his.

She squeezed his fingers. "It's happy-ever-after this time."

They pursued that on a return trip to Tuscany. As she'd reclaimed the cottage, they both wanted to reclaim the joy of that long-ago summer. In bed, as the sun rose on their first honeymoon morning, she rolled her head on her pillow to look at him. "I've forgotten all my Italian."

He laughed, because it was yet another replay. "You know the most important word," he murmured to her, as he had ten years before. "*Baciami*, Giuliana. *Baciami*."

Kiss me.

Liam kept only one secret from his bride—that of his father's feelings for her mother and the real meaning behind the red rosebushes at the end of the rows in the Bennett vineyards. He went back and forth with what to do with them. It wasn't until they were nearing the end of their three weeks in Tuscany that the right answer occurred to him and he called Penn for assistance.

When they arrived back in Edenville, the traditional bushes were still in place in the vineyards. Instead of pulling them out, he'd had another planted near the front door of the Bennett house. It flowered there, a hybrid that bloomed with both red *and* white roses—a symbol of their united families and a gift to welcome his Baci girl home.

Epilogue

Molly Michaels was getting married in the morning. Not really. She was only thirteen years old and a mere junior bridesmaid (though so much better than being a babyish flower girl like her younger cousin!) and it was fun to pretend it was her wedding scheduled for Saturday morning in the Tanti Baci cottage.

She played make-believe during the entire rehearsal, then was cut loose while the photographer took even more pictures of her big sister and the college guy who was her fiancé. Her dad thought they weren't old enough for marriage, but her mom reminded him they'd been the exact same age when they'd said "I do." Her Grandma Delle had rolled her eyes and said, "*Young love.*" Like it was a disease. (Molly thought it sounded interesting, now that she was thirteen.)

Outside the cottage, she ran into one of her best friends, Fab Parini, whose family part-owned the winery. At school, the students thought Fab was short for

Fabiana, but at their last sleepover, Molly had crossed her heart and hoped to die before finding out that Fab's real name was Monique and Fab was short for Fabulosa, something silly her relatives had taken to calling her before she was born. Molly loved that story and wasn't surprised because the Parinis all had exotic names. There was Fab's little sister, Suzette, as well as her eight-year-old twin brothers Mario and Alonzo (who were pretty adorable when they weren't sticking grapes up their noses and telling fart jokes).

Fab's brothers and sister were hanging around the grapes, clamoring for a game of hide-and-seek in the vines. Fab said they had to wait until their cousins finished up the homework they were doing in their mom, Alessandra Bennett's, office. They were seven and five, so it didn't take very long before Elena and Sam were milling about, too.

Molly was torn about participating. While she was bored with standing around, she didn't know if she wanted to chance getting dirty when she had on a very pretty pink dress with puff sleeves and her mom had let her wear a tiny dab of mascara and a swipe of lip gloss (well, her mom hadn't noticed that Molly had dabbed the mascara and swiped on the lip gloss—weddings were all consuming for mothers of the bride, she'd discovered). She was still undecided when Fab's other girl cousin, nine-year-old Devon Bennett, arrived. But then Devon's brother appeared on-scene and Molly's interest piqued. Liam Bennett (but everybody called him Lee, on account of his dad having the same first name) was a grade younger than Molly. But he was already a head taller, with blond hair, blue eyes, and square shoulders that looked as if they belonged on a high-schooler.

Molly heard he played basketball, baseball, *and* piano. He glanced at her as he joined his passel of young relatives, all of them talking at once, arguing about the rules of the game. “Wanna play?” he asked.

A little tingle warmed the pit of her stomach. She looked down at her pretty pink dress and then up at the very, very cute boy. “Sure,” she said. Young love. (If it was a disease, how come she felt so happy catching it?)

AUTHOR'S NOTE

As has been mentioned in the other Three Kisses books, *Crush on You* and *Then He Kissed Me*, the Napa Valley is designated as an agricultural preserve, which restricts the kinds of events that can be hosted at the area wineries. Over the years, the rules have been challenged and revised. For my fictional purposes, the "I-dos" will go forward at Tanti Baci forever.

I would like to acknowledge my early-morning walking buddies, Lisa and Micki, who are kind enough to listen to me hash out my stories as we stride along. Their interested ears are on either side of their smart and busy brains, and they've helped me unknot a plot tangle more than once. Thank you so much!